The Best of Crimes

K.C. MAHER

RedDoor

Published by RedDoor
www.reddoorpublishing.com

ISBN 978-1-910453-71-1

A CIP catalogue record for this book is available
from the British Library

Cover design: Clare Connie Shepherd
www.clareconnieshepherd.com

Typesetting: Tutis Innovative E-Solutions Pte. Ltd

Printed and bound in Denmark by Nørhaven

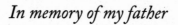

In memory of my father

1. FAST FORWARD

One

May–August 2015

On the plane home, I tried to tell Amanda what I had already said as well as what we had agreed not to say. But before I could speak a syllable, she draped an arm around my neck and reached over with her other hand to press her index finger against my lips. Later, driving north on I-95, I said, 'You're worth—' and she slapped my leg while putting a finger to her own lips. We had agreed not to talk. She had told me it had been perfect. Making any comment now would only detract from that. Also, she refused to entertain in any way the concept of 'Goodbye.' Because it wouldn't change anything.

Too soon, we were there. I stopped the car in front of the village library. Amanda opened the passenger door and I rested my hand momentarily on her shoulder. She scarcely nodded, straightened her spine, and slid out of the car, gently closing the door behind her. And without a word, without glancing back, Amanda skipped away and up the library's concrete steps. The huge, heavy wooden door opened to a narrow strip of darkness, into which she disappeared.

Resolute, I drove a few feet farther, coming even with the police station's Main Street entrance. Turning right onto Ferris Court, I parked on a street dappled by leafy shadows and checked that my backpack held the used boarding passes and hotel receipts. Quickly, I stepped onto the sidewalk and opened the police station's side door.

Chief Carl Peterson was standing, arms crossed over his chest, just outside his small office. 'Go home, Walter. Your wife, the middle-school social worker, the principal, and I all agree. We're in complete agreement.'

'I've committed a serious crime.'

'As far as I and everyone who lives in this village are concerned, you have not.'

'In New York, second-degree kidnapping is a class B felony. I knew that when I abducted thirteen-year-old Amanda Jonette for thirty-one hours.'

'I have no doubt,' Carl said, 'that she was delighted to be wherever you went.'

'May I sit down?'

'Go home, Walter.'

'Not before I write a full confession.'

'You know, part of my job is preventing suicide.'

I shook my head. It was important to own up to my guilt. We argued our opposing points of view until Carl, losing patience, stormed out and went home.

Alone in the station, I sat at his desk and carefully recorded my crime in a notebook, which I had bought at the Orlando airport. The chief's stapler was in his top drawer and I used it to attach receipts and tickets to the notebook's cover. While I was contemplating my semi-legible handwriting, Detective Jim Buckley appeared.

He knocked on the doorframe. 'Hey, Walter. Where's the chief?'

'Not here.' I stood up and handed him the notebook. Buckley refused it. He didn't even open it, but perhaps had noticed the stapled receipts. If he refused to respond, I told him he must put me in a squad car and drive me to the county facility. Buckley protested, but seeing that I was determined, did it anyway.

At the jail in Valhalla, the sheriff and guards treated me like any thirty-four-year-old man who had kidnapped a thirteen-year-old girl. Wearing an orange jumpsuit, I spent the night handcuffed to a metal pole.

The next morning, my wife, Sterling, arrived screaming at me and at the authorities, who mostly ignored her. When she stopped yelling and wept, I asked her to ring my former boss at Bank of America, because I was supposed to meet him for lunch tomorrow.

Hearing this, she began keening.

'Sterling, please. You've helped a lot but I'm counting on you to see me through this.'

Furious as she was, she would manage far better than I ever expected.

Following a cursory investigation by the FBI, the magistrate broke standard procedure and allowed character testimonies. These took nearly three months, but saved me from going on trial. And not being tried by a jury, my attorney said, was critical. 'Because the more you tell them there was no sexual misconduct despite appearances, the worse it can get. Like if you say, "Don't even think about it," the more they're gonna think about it. Basic human nature.'

Lucky me, getting away with thought crimes. Nevertheless, a class B felony in New York means five years mandatory. So last week, I began my incarceration at the Federal Correctional Institution in Otisville.

2. TIME LIKE WATER

Two

1999

Walking to Lehman Brothers that first day, I felt as if I finally belonged to the whole of spiraling existence. Along the Hudson River, I strolled the esplanade beneath an early summer morning sky so blue that the clouds appeared to swirl upward. And everywhere I looked, life beat in time with my heart. Plants reached for the sun. Giant allium flowers, heads like pink globes, waved on tall stalks.

Two girls jumped inside double-Dutch ropes turned by two other girls. The quick and nimble pair inside the ropes called out back-and-forth rhymes, spinning one direction and then the other. They clapped hands, in time.

At the South Cove Park, a tall young Asian man rollerbladed in precise opposing arcs around miniature orange cones set in a line. Thin and graceful, he moved fluidly, his ponytail swinging past his waist.

I was eighteen years old, a privileged math prodigy with two graduate degrees. Having leapfrogged my adolescence, I imagined life ahead as an undulating Fibonacci sequence, in ever expanding perfect proportion. My stride, in new black oxfords, matched the subliminal, subterranean rhythm.

I wore a business suit tailored by a Parisian man on Greenwich Street, a white dress shirt, and a green and blue silk tie of interlocking ellipses. Lena, one of my mentors and lovers at Harvard, had given me the tie. Martha, who didn't know about Lena, had given me the silver cuff links shaped like infinity symbols.

Near the marina, the shifting tide seemed to reflect the newness of the day. My life felt almost equal in promise to the enormous Twin Towers that loomed over everything.

Inside the World Financial Center's mahogany vestibules, brass elevators transported people to and from the global institutions upstairs. On the eighteenth floor, I reached the Lehman sanctuary, another towering circular space.

A sharp-featured woman in a pastel-green suit and muted pink lipstick stood from behind a curved desk. Her knuckles pressed into the top as she squinted at me.

'Don't tell me,' she said. 'You're the wunderkind. Sit there. I'll let him know hope has arrived.'

She sat in her swivel seat and crossed her legs inside tailored pants, a pose that revealed matching pastel-green four-inch-high platform pumps. She pushed a button and spoke in a noticeably softer, sweeter voice. 'Mr. Ferraro? Your boy wonder is here.'

An opening appeared in the seemingly seamless curved wooden wall several feet behind her. Vince Ferraro emerged, shook my hand, and said, 'No doubt Sterling gave you trouble.'

'Hardly,' she sniffed.

'My pleasure, Sterling.' I winked at her. She turned her head in a way that hinted at a repressed smile.

Inside his office, Vince declared the mortgage-backed portfolio I had developed for my thesis was outperforming most of the others at Lehman.

'Good for it.'

'Better than good, Walter. Because now that you're on board, the day will come when I'll need to use the tortoise and hare analogy.'

He referred to an approach that was hard-wired in me, of limiting risk first and seeking profit second—reversing the Lehman Brothers paradigm. I opened my brand-new briefcase and handed him the spreadsheets I had created since our last meeting.

Vince's expression grew sly as he perused the structure I had built using actual Lehman holdings. He seemed pleased and I wondered yet again how he had managed to persuade his superiors that I should be given the job—inexperienced, underage, and at a starting salary I had been told was exceptionally high.

My only recommendation had come from my Ph.D. advisor, who happened to be Vince Ferraro's cousin. Professor Pierson, who had advised me since I arrived at Harvard, was adamant that I live 'outside' a while before entering law school.

In any case, Vince coveted my risk-averse, apparently profitable structures and approved of my person. I impressed him further (or more likely amused him), by saying flat-out that I couldn't formulate these things any other way. No business culture would make me flip.

He said I was exactly what he wanted and must answer only to him.

Sterling escorted me down a wide, carpeted hallway to my office. Her large breasts and platform pumps complemented her impressive bearing. When she noticed, however, that her very high heels still left her several inches shorter than me, she hurried ahead—no doubt unaware of how appealing I found this perspective. The deep center vent in her jacket flared apart and flapped shut with every step.

My guess was that she was thirty, maybe a little more. That's what I hoped. All through graduate school, my romantic partners had been women in their early thirties.

Inside my new office, sunlight poured through huge windows.

Sterling asked, 'Do you want to face the Statue of Liberty or the trading floor?'

Before I could say, 'Give me the statue,' she said, 'The floor.'

*

I arrived before 7:30 the next day because I needed to be there for the morning call—the daily routine in which Lehman's trading desks around the world shared news and outlook. Before long, Sterling filled my doorway, holding a jumbo-sized cup of hazelnut coffee. 'Cat got your tongue?'

The next morning, same thing. 'Cat got your tongue?'

An image loomed of an enormous feline piercing the tip of my defenseless tongue. I said, 'As it happens, today I've got the cat's tongue. Want a peek?'

She made a face. 'You're awfully young. What if HR learned you were offering me "a peek at your tongue"? It's called a double entendre, Walter.'

'And is the name for your greeting called a trap?'

'Be nice or I'll write you up.'

'I'm always nice, Sterling. In fact, I'm sorry. Let me buy you a drink after work.'

'I don't think so.'

'One drink, one time.'

'You're not even old enough to drink.'

'I won't tell if you don't.'

She shifted her weight, and the effect of her arms folded beneath her breasts stirred me so that I had to look away. When I glanced up, I focused on her face, keeping mine straight.

'Perhaps,' she said, 'we should meet after work and review the rules.'

She proposed the bar downstairs, P. J. Clarke's, at seven. We sat under an awning with a view of the marina. She ordered a cosmopolitan, and although I had no clue what that was—and was not carrying a fake ID—I said, 'Make that two.'

The waiter brought dark-pink icy drinks and asked Sterling, 'Does your handsome friend belong to you, or did you bring him for me?'

'Can't you tell?'

'I will soon.'

The cosmopolitan tasted like a cranberry-flavored headache. I ordered a Heineken.

'Does this answer my question?' the waiter asked.

I confirmed that I was with Sterling but thanked him for his interest.

He liked that. 'For once you've picked a good one, Sterling.'

She laughed, slightly embarrassed, and said she would drink my slushy cocktail.

I asked about her family. Her father, she said, had been a veterinarian in Maine. Her mother was his assistant until he died last year—heart failure. 'Now my mom saves the whales.'

'I'm sorry.'

'No, my father was insanely happy his whole life and not afraid of dying.'

'Brave.'

'Well, he wasn't religious. But he lived a good life, which he said wasn't as easy as it looked. The idea of nonexistence comforted him.'

'Wise and brave.' Why did my words sound so awful? I meant them, but they rang all wrong. Sterling didn't flinch but stopped talking and leaned back, studying me. The waiter arrived with a third cosmopolitan, saving me from her gaze.

'Three,' he said, 'and no more unless your friend is escorting you home.'

Sterling waved him away, as in not to worry.

'What were you like growing up?' I asked her.

Well. Her parents had named her Susan, a boring, moth-eaten name she changed upon entering college. 'At eighteen. Not fourteen like you.'

I felt her remove her high heels and took it as a signal to make the first move—something I had never had to do before—my female professors had always taken care of that. I would need to persuade Sterling with charm and style I didn't possess.

However, having already factored in the seriousness of an office romance, I was extremely serious. Halfway through her third drink, her complexion glowed evenly and her hair begged to be mussed.

'What else?' I asked.

She sighed, sipped, and reported: fat girl throughout childhood; college, no longer fat; first boyfriend; first heartbreak; revenge; a fiancé who ran away and good riddance.

'Tit for tat,' she said. 'What's your story?'

I'd tell her anything and everything, but would she like to walk? Twilight was falling soft and slow. She arched her back and nodded. I paid and tipped the waiter well. Glad he knew

Sterling, glad he liked me, glad he hadn't carded me—and most important, glad he had brought that third drink when he did.

Walking together under the esplanade's shade trees, I said I loved the hour before the skyscrapers lit up.

'None of that, Walter. You said you'd tell me everything.'

All right: my parents were scientists working to cure AIDS. Since I was eleven, they had been traveling the world, designing and refining antiretroviral drugs, leading conferences, conducting studies. And—paying Exeter to educate and care for me, even during holidays and through the summers.

My parents sounded great, battling the plague—whereas my new job made the rich richer. (I did not say that my family was inordinately rich, although my parents had always pretended otherwise.)

Almost invisible, the new moon hovered behind the Twin Towers, which were starting to glow. A single sailboat floated in the distance. And then, I heard myself say the one thing I had least intended to share. 'When I was eleven, my sister died suddenly. She was seventeen.' I cringed, hearing my words hang in the air. 'She wasn't like a mother to me,' I added. (Perhaps the worst thing I could say.) I cleared my throat, glanced at Sterling, and grimaced apologetically.

'Emily acted up in public once too often and was picked up by the police. Before my parents sent her away, we acknowledged we would probably not see each other again.'

Sterling wanted more.

So I told her. When Emily died, I was at prep school. My parents were away on their lifesaving mission. 'They wrote a note to me. Tragedies happen. They were bereft but couldn't interrupt their work. I should keep studying.'

Had all that really just spewed from my mouth?

Skyscrapers blinked on. Sterling rested her fingertips on my wrist. 'Your sister died and your parents wrote a note that didn't explain why or how?'

I stepped back and stared at my feet. 'Told you I'd tell you everything.' A sigh and shuffle because I didn't dare to look at her. 'I've never gone into this with anyone before. The headmaster tried talking to me. But when I was eleven, all I wanted, because it looked like the only way to go, was to push straight up and out as fast as possible. My parents didn't contact me, but they paid my way—summer school, tutors, the works. Exceptions were made for me, so I could test out of my age group. And then, out of high school and into Harvard. Where I was, just like you said, "a boy wonder." After Ph.D.'s in economics and applied mathematics, my mentoring professor said it was time I tried a real job.'

Catching a sense of compassion in her eyes, I looked directly at Sterling and smiled. I didn't raise a finger, except possibly in spirit, and offered this silly line, which I had polished in my dreams. 'If your parents are esteemed by every dean in the land and you study like a madman howling at the moon, one day you, too, might wake up and find you've been transformed into a teenage mathematician.'

Sterling giggled, saying, '*O-o-o*-kay.'

After a pause, I invited her to dinner, swearing that I was an excellent cook.

'Walter, I'm too old for you.'

'No, you aren't.'

'If nothing else,' she said, 'consider the gap in experience.'

'You don't know how experienced I am. Anyway, we're here.' We came to a stop outside my building, a Battery Park City condo I'd been living in for two weeks. Vince found it for me.

Nice, new, on the fourteenth floor, with a living room balcony facing the river.

I played Miles Davis for her, *Seven Steps to Heaven*. She watched the sunset from the balcony while I made my specialty—pasta primavera.

An enjoyable night, followed by an enjoyable month and, then, by an entire, enjoyable season.

*

In August, I moved in with Sterling. Vince silently approved—or, at least, didn't say anything. We worked long hours, I especially, but that didn't detract from the sex. At eighteen, I wanted it every waking hour.

When we'd been living together for several weeks, Sterling said, 'Isn't dating the worst?'

'Are we dating? Because if so, I like it.'

'I was warming up to discussing our future.'

'Let's not discuss it,' I said. 'Let's do it.'

'Do you mean that?'

'Of course.'

'Nobody's a wunderkind for long, Walter. The clock is ticking.'

I laughed. Why not? Racing through life was how I had always lived. 'Marry me, Sterling.'

She flew to my side, said, 'Yes, absolutely,' and whipped out a magazine with an ad for Cartier's matching wedding and engagement rings.

*

Too young to buy a beer, I had money, interesting work at which I excelled, and a big, sharp, sexy woman.

Of course, I had only skimmed life's surface and didn't have a clue how to find the depths. My hope was that being Sterling's husband would speed up the process.

Sterling, admirer of boasters and showboaters, wanted to marry me, who would never be either, although I would definitely be able to provide her with 'an enviable lifestyle.' I hadn't told her about my trust fund, because it embarrassed me.

She knew I hated it when people with money acted as if their plain good luck made them superior and flaunted their advantages in everyone's faces. I preached too often and too stridently about it. But if I would shut up about that, she bargained, she wouldn't brag about her possessions—even if, she said, that was half the fun.

We made several agreements like that, ones that are impossible to keep. I gave her the Cartier engagement ring on her thirty-second birthday. She shrieked with glee, phoned her mother, and talked for half an hour. Then she waltzed about, admiring the ring on her hand before cuddling up beside me and saying, 'You know what else?'

I didn't.

She stood and paced nervously, which puzzled me. Sterling didn't get nervous. Still, I let her talk around the point, a process she sometimes described as 'easing into it.'

Finally, I asked, 'What else? What is it?'

She was pregnant, due in seven months.

I jumped up, hands overhead, and yelled for the ultimate home team: 'A baby—*our* baby!'

She laughed with relief at my unexpected elation, and said she had been worried I might feel trapped.

'No, I feel—redeemed!' I picked her up and kissed her face until she ordered me to put her down. Higher than high, I wanted to tell the world. Sterling wanted to keep it quiet— until I reminded her that we didn't have much time to arrange a wedding unless she wanted to get married next week at City Hall, or walk down the aisle in a maternity wedding dress. 'The other option,' I said, 'is to wait until afterward.'

'No' to all.

So we visited her mother, Kaye, in Bar Harbor, Maine to deliver the good news. Kaye took to me immediately and whispered she hoped I wasn't the type to go along with the dreadful name Susie had taken after leaving home.

'Worse. I call your daughter by a pet name I can't say in front of you.'

Kaye laughed. 'So, Susie, you landed a good one.'

'Shut up, Mother.'

*

We set the date for November 5. Sterling ripped through the rigmarole. My parents, somewhere in Eastern Europe, sent word that, regretfully, they couldn't get away, but they mailed us a fat check so we could take a honeymoon. Instead, we deposited the funds in our new joint account and Sterling gave her notice at Lehman.

2000

April 30, Olivia was born. Never before had I held a newborn baby. Cradling her, I felt that, after a lifetime of midnights, here, at last, was the light. An hour old, Olivia's tiny arm and tinier hand seemed to reach for me.

Within a few hours of her birth, I found myself in a taxicab on the West Side highway, en route to work. I hated missing a minute with her, so I convinced Sterling that, as a new mother, she needed a full night's sleep. 'Leave the night feedings to me.'

'You mean it?'

I did. At one in the morning and then again at four, I would wake in rapturous wonder and cradle my infant daughter in my arms while she sucked a latex nipple.

*

When Olivia was three months old, Sterling convinced me that the suburbs would be better for raising a child, and we promptly moved to a river town in Westchester County. Our house perched on top of a steep landscaped hill that a developer had named Oak Grove Point. We had a big backyard and a double garage. Natural woods surrounded us, creating an illusion of solitude, although eighteen new homes stood along the spiraling lane to the hilltop, and a smaller house was going up across the narrow turn-around where we lived.

*

It was during our first week of residing in Westchester that I met Jimmy Quinn while waiting for the train. A broker with Cantor Fitzgerald, he, his wife, and their five-year-old son lived in a great landmarked home next to the ancient stone aqueduct that carried water from an upstate reservoir to New York City. In the mornings, Jimmy dozed until the Metro-North pulled into Grand Central. Then he would wake, stretch, and, grabbing his stuff, clap my back, suddenly talkative. All through the station and inside the subway car downtown he told stories in which he played the fool or trickster. He told jokes I had heard a hundred times. His patter was rhythmic and his expressions hilarious. His sideways grin alone cracked me up. Friday morning, when we'd ridden the train together since Monday, he said, 'Tonight at nine, poker at my house. Saturday morning, basketball at the river park. You, me, three local guys, and a case of cold beer.'

'Great. Poker and basketball are the two games I know. I'm not good at them. But I know the rules.'

'You do? Nobody else does. We think we do, but we don't. Know what I'm saying?'

For the first time in my life, I felt like I had a real friend. When I was a kid, I had spent time with roommates or teammates and been friendly with guys who were friendly to me. But the friendliness had always required effort, a meeting of more than halfway. Jimmy and I understood each other without trying—even though in most ways we were opposites. The other poker players, three volunteer firemen—Wayne, Pete, and Dennis—would shake their heads. 'Jimmy Quinn and Walter Mitchell—guess that figures.'

Jimmy tried to explain that I was no Wall Street wheeler, dealer, or cheater. And they said, 'We know, 'cause he's your opposite.'

Every morning, Jimmy bought Lotto tickets—one for himself and one for me, because I didn't buy into that scam.

'What do you mean "scam," Walter? You work for Lehman Brothers. You've gotta love scams.' A ticket in each hand, he'd say, 'Pick one.'

And before we parted, off to our respective skyscrapers on either side of West Street, he would laugh about how I'd dance when my winnings came raining down on me.

Jimmy would say, 'Luck is luck.'

And without missing a beat, I'd say, 'Fuck luck.'

Three

September 11, 2001

People say I carried a pregnant woman down fifteen flights of stairs. No recollection of it, at all. Endless memory, though, of choking on ash—and of the procession of people trudging alongside the river. I don't recall, either, a group of stunned survivors peeling off and flowing into a side street. But, evidently they did, and I followed. This I know because I *do* remember the mob of bodies, caked with blood and debris, inside a bar where a giant TV blared. I drank alcohol from a fire brigade of open bottles. Layers of death motes clotted my insides; they still do. Splintered window shards poked through my shirt, but didn't hurt. At some point, I mindlessly phoned Sterling, who screamed with relief. Wayne, the volunteer fireman, said I called him, asking, did he think it was possible that Jimmy had taken the elevator from Tower One's 105th floor to the lobby and slipped away just in time? Could he have had a premonition? Because certainly, if Jimmy had stood still among the rushing throng that morning, he would have decided—not me, not today.

*

The way I remember it, that whole September, the sky was painfully blue. The grass and trees were a dazzling array of green. The sweet, natural scents in the air were staggering.

Everyone mourned Jimmy Quinn. It seemed the whole town crowded into his stately old home. I met his parents, who stood in confusion, unsure where to look.

Three of his four brothers were drinking and fixing drinks for the guests. Every few minutes, they delivered fresh cocktails in desperate high spirits. They each at different times identified me as Jimmy's new friend.

Jimmy's oldest brother, Jack, who had his grin and wiry build, shook my hand. He winked and said, 'Just a second. I'll tell him you're here.' And then, 'Christ, will you listen to me? I can't believe it.'

The youngest, best-looking brother, Timothy, who had moved to Vermont in July, introduced me to his spouse, a big, bearded man named Bernard.

Timothy said, 'Jimmy always had hundreds of friends. But he said you were the one who really knew him. Like you had always known him.'

I nodded, glad to hear this, and tried to smile. 'We only met about a year ago. But Jimmy was the best friend I ever had.'

People came and went. They laughed, cried, and drank too much. Bernard took charge of calling taxis.

I wanted to say something to Bridget, Jimmy's wife, and to Colin, their six-year-old son, but whenever I strung together some earnest if banal words, I lost my nerve.

The view from Jimmy's backyard deck remains one of the most inspiring sights I've ever seen. Rolling mounds of native grasses and wild flowers sloped downhill for hundreds of feet to a shaded area. There, between two huge beech trees, a mesmerizing glassy light appeared somehow both distant and near. In fact, it was the Hudson River, which glistened day and night, due to some confluence of graduated heights and overall pitch, combined with the arc of the sky.

2002

I, along with everyone else at Lehman Brothers, worked out of other companies' spare offices. For months, I kept waiting for a new reality to reveal itself. Not as if this were a nightmare, or as if I might find protection by solving a metaphorical puzzle. I wasn't waiting for a spiritual awakening I didn't believe in. And yet—I would catch myself praying, desperately, for something to give me hope.

Often, while watching Olivia playing, I'd panic that, in another second, she would vanish forever. Then, I'd run to her and hold her until she wriggled free or pushed me away.

Sometimes, I woke up in a state of bliss, momentarily oblivious to what had happened. In an instant, though, the truth would take hold, followed by a slap of guilt for having forgotten.

More often, I woke with an overwhelming urge to quit my job and never return to the city again. Why wasn't I a painter, sculptor, or an inventor? Why wasn't I creating a testament to life and death? Wall Street was supposed to have been a mere stint—a transitional phase before law school. But I hadn't been married when I agreed to that plan. The instinct to flee was overwhelming. But because it sprang entirely from fear and grief, I stifled it. If I succumbed, fear and grief would rule me forever.

So, after witnessing everyday life explode into fiery pieces, I followed the same routine as before. Except now, whenever I entered Manhattan, I dreaded that at any moment my surroundings would crumble.

2003

As ever, the markets fell and rose. They rose and fell. Lehman bought Morgan Stanley's building in midtown; Morgan Stanley, a more cautious institution, was moving its people to New Jersey.

We pushed on. Some pushed harder, fearing the next cataclysm. Others denied trepidation. To me, the city smelled like death.

Wayne asked if I wanted to join the firehouse. He said that they always needed strong, agile guys who kept their weight down. Fat guys like him weren't good at scaling the rooftops of burning buildings. Wayne and I talked it over, drinking Stellas in the bar behind the Post Office, although we both knew I worked too many office hours to help out.

Wayne, Pete, and Dennis still tap their horns when they see me about town. We raise our hands and say, 'Hey!' But we no longer play cards or basketball.

I took up running. A short jog down the steep hill of Oak Grove Point led to a tree-lined path along the old aqueduct. From there I could run north to Rockefeller State Park, which was laced with undulating trails. On weekends, I ran faster and farther. At home, I lifted weights.

But no matter how hard I tried to fill my time, still I slogged through more empty hours than I previously had known existed. The bank promoted me into a new products group, which presented just enough challenge to keep me content. I no longer reported to Vince, although he continued to look after me.

Occasionally, I felt an inkling of newfound hope. I loved Olivia more than I'd ever loved anyone. With blue eyes and wild black curls like mine when I was her age, she was a happy, goofy child. At three, she was always laughing, and when she laughed it was straight from the belly. I lived for that laugh. I lived for Olivia.

Four

2004

During our fourth spring at Oak Grove Point, a single mother and her daughter, who appeared about a year younger than Olivia, moved into the little townhouse facing ours. One unusually warm Sunday, I opened the door, and standing below me was a delicate child whose skin glowed with burnished purity.

'Hello, honey,' I said, motioning for her to come inside. My intention was to invite her to play with Olivia, but her eyes filled with terror and she hurried back down the steps. Olivia pushed past me, yelling, 'Hiya!'

I watched the tiny child give Olivia a finger puppet, which my daughter stuffed onto her thumb before taking her new friend's hand, saying, 'Don't be scared. He's my daddy.'

From then on, Olivia and her adorable friend Amanda played together almost every day.

We still hadn't met Amanda's mother, but while I was at work, Sterling got to know the nanny, whose name was Jade. She was twenty-five, near my age. Her father had worked at the General Motors plant in Tarrytown, as had her grandfather and great-grandfather. Since the plant's closing in 1998, Jade's father sold aluminum siding. Her mother worked as a secretary at the high school.

For Olivia's fourth birthday, with Jade's permission, I took the girls to the Big Apple Circus. In the parking lot, Olivia insisted that her friend hold onto my thumb. 'Without it, you'll get run over.' Amanda wrapped her little fingers tight and I wiggled my thumb, hoping she'd smile. She looked up at me, not quite smiling, but no longer terrified.

At home, Sterling waited with cake and ice cream. Amanda had a present for Olivia in a paper bag. Putting it on the table, she whispered in Olivia's ear. And Olivia said, 'Daddy, can you wait in the kitchen?'

I wanted Amanda to see that I was glad to oblige. Perhaps men were unfamiliar to her. Or maybe she had never been around anyone as tall as me.

Eavesdropping from the kitchen, I learned that the birthday present had belonged to Amanda's nanny when she was little. Jade had brought it from her house, but there was no wrapping paper or Scotch tape at Amanda's.

Sterling said, 'See what's inside,' and Olivia ripped the bag apart. Ten metal rings fell on the floor. Olivia picked them up and handed them to Sterling, who asked me to come back into the dining room. Did I know what these were?

As it happened, I had enjoyed this toy when I was young. 'They're magic. Give me a second and I'll show you how they work.'

Stepping back into the kitchen, I ran my fingers around the rings and found the hidden seams. I practiced the trick twice without fumbling. But when I reentered the dining room, the children were gone. Sterling licked a glob of pink frosting off a spoon before waving it at me. 'Don't even think of sawing me in half!'

Ha! I kissed her neck.

The little girls were in the TV room. 'Abracadabra,' I said. 'Are you ready?' They sat together on the couch and giggled. I handed them each a ring, telling them to look for moving parts. 'The metal is solid, as you can see.' They giggled more.

'Watch.' Balancing five rings in the crooks of my two index fingers, I flipped them into my palms, hand over hand, 'Presto, change-o.' I spread open a shining chain of ten small circles linked together. 'Ta-da!'

That night, I read Olivia her ritual bedtime story. When it ended, she asked where the magic rings were. I fetched the toy from a shelf and offered to show her how to do it.

'No,' she said. 'You do it. If I do it, it won't be magic to me.'

*

Late one Sunday afternoon, when Sterling was playing golf at the country club, Olivia tromped into the kitchen with Amanda hiding behind her, asking for tea. 'The dolls are having a tea party.' I looked out the window at the slate patio. Three dolls were propped on small chairs around Olivia's toy table.

'Do you mean tea that's hot and watery or something more like tiny cups of chocolate milk, and perhaps a little plate of ginger snaps?'

'Chocolate milk! I mean that!'

My snacks for the dolls' tea party pleased Olivia so much that she invited me to join them. Beside Olivia's favorite doll, I sat on the slate, my legs folded. Amanda's doll was Olivia's cast-off— the one whose hair she pulled out.

*

In August, we noticed that three townhouses in Oak Grove Point were for sale. Within days, they sold. But before anyone moved in, another realtor put For Sale signs in the ground. The houses sold quickly again, though still nobody moved in.

Sterling said the time was right: We should sell this place, take the profit, and find a big, beautiful house we would enjoy all our lives.

I dreaded Sterling's idea of 'a big, beautiful house,' and told her we had all the space we needed.

'But we can afford a mansion.'

I laughed. 'Yes, but why?'

'Do you have any idea what Jimmy Quinn's house sold for?' His wife and son had only recently moved to Rochester.

'Sterling, don't.'

'All right. I'm sorry.' She kissed me. 'I can wait.' And she kissed me again. I liked this so much I asked if she wanted another child.

She didn't. 'Olivia's more than enough. Besides, I loved being an only child.'

I held her close. 'All right. But I'll love it if you change your mind.'

That same afternoon, I sat at the kitchen table, watching Olivia and Amanda through the big bay window. They were wearing bright bathing suits and alternating between skipping through a sprinkler in our yard and leaping hand in hand over to Amanda's yard, where they twirled through a sprinkler Jade had set up.

Sterling opened a light beer and sat beside me. She wondered aloud if my interest in the girls stemmed from having missed the second half of my own childhood.

'Why would you say that?'

'Because if I were you, this is just about the time I'd start wondering if an unstructured childhood was a beautiful, irreplaceable time which I'd thrown away because I hadn't known better.'

'Few boys where I grew up acted out fairytales on their parents' lawns.'

'You don't know that.'

'True, I can't prove it.' I took a sip of her Amstel. 'When did you get so whimsical?'

'I'm not whimsical. But I did my fair share of running through sprinklers as a kid, so I suppose it doesn't hold the same fascination for me.'

Usually, Sterling appreciated my interest in the girls, because it meant I was willing to babysit while she played with her adult friends. Tomorrow she was going to a party at the country club. If I wanted to join her, she said, she would hire a babysitter.

'Do you need me there? Because otherwise, I'd rather babysit.'

She tore at the beer bottle's label and said her friends envied her freedom within a secure and happy marriage.

Secure and happy—my feelings exactly—provided I was equally free to do what I wanted, which in this case was to stay home while Sterling swam among a morass of friends that weren't friends at all, but a self-centered group that traded supposedly funny insults.

2005

Lehman Brothers divvied up the year-end bonuses in February and that year the windfalls were larger than many expected. Even more unexpected to me was Vince Ferraro's retirement. He had bought a ranch in Montana, a lifelong dream. Out of protectiveness, which would prove more or less prescient, Vince set me up with his friend at Bank of America.

I was offered an attractive role, as a director in risk management. Before accepting the position, however, Sterling and I quarreled about my preference for law school. Finally, I rooted out the problem—me being a law student would embarrass her. How could Sterling explain that her hotshot Wall Street husband had jumped ship to become a graduate student? Yale full-time or Fordham's night program would inflict equal shame upon her. This, despite every assurance that we possessed ample resources for her to continue buying whatever she wanted, within the bounds of decency.

That made her laugh; what I considered decent. Most of her friends lived in grand estates and belonged to an unjustly exclusive country club, but that was another argument.

Overall, I was not unhappy with my work or my marriage. And while my plan had always been—someday—law school, I still had no idea what kind of law I wanted to practice.

*

To celebrate my promotion, Sterling suggested we take a vacation.

'Great. Choose a place,' I said. 'Invite your mother.'

Immediately, Sterling and Kaye decided on Hawaii, specifically a spectacular resort in Honolulu. So I reserved adjoining suites with ocean views at the pink, palatial Royal Hawaiian Resort in Waikiki. Sterling and Kaye, with Olivia in tow, would luxuriate on the beach, at the spa, and indulge in shopping expeditions. I claimed time for separate adventures, which suited Sterling just fine.

Our hotel had brochures for all sorts of aquatic experiences, but the pictures of hang gliding captivated me. In school,

I had studied Leonardo da Vinci, and the hang gliders in the brochure were strikingly reminiscent of his drawings for gliding machines. My guidebook rated a hang-gliding school on Maui as best, so several mornings I took a puddle jumper there.

I learned to work the emergency parachute and flew with an instructor strapped beside me. Gliding in the boundless, silent sky above lush tropical valleys and turquoise water, my imagination soared as if freed from its cage. Initially, the pilot operated the machine, but when he let me take the controls, the truth of Leonardo's work struck a chord in my mind and, it seemed, tugged at a deep internal cord in my being. His principle that all knowledge refers to nature seemed to spread through me.

In Waikiki I bought an edition of Leonardo's *Notebooks,* in which he declared: 'Let no man who is not a Mathematician read the elements of my work.' And, I thought, let no mathematician formulate unnatural theorems.

Most of my life I had excelled at work based not on nature, but on abstraction. For my Ph.D., I had derived proofs that were conceptually 'groundbreaking' but could not be tested in the natural world. Not surprisingly, within five years my proofs were replaced by others inferred from real occurrences at the edges of the universe. Since then, that field of inquiry had fallen by the wayside. Styles come and go in mathematics just as in fashion or finance.

The days I didn't go hang gliding, I took Olivia to the aquarium and the zoo, and we hiked to various nearby waterfalls in preparation for the thirty-five-minute hike at Diamond Head. I found the perfect walking stick for Olivia's hiking costume. To avoid the crowds and heat, we woke early, ate cereal, and slathered on sunscreen, arriving at 7:15. My backpack contained water bottles and my camera. Olivia, in pink shorts and pink-and-white checked shirt, posed for photos within the volcanic crater's cavernous spiral. After the hike, Olivia and I ate the same neon-green snow cones we had at the zoo.

Throughout these excursions—in fact, constantly at the back of my mind—I mulled over how removed Wall Street's derivatives and financial structures had become from reality. Inevitably, they would soon dissolve. Whether as an analyst at Lehman or a director at Bank of America, my job was nothing more than creating elaborate structures comprised of thousands of empty bits. Hollow structures bound to collapse. Unlikely but perhaps possibly, as an overseer of risk management I might slow the inevitable—by days or weeks. But no one could stop the industry's foolishness and greed, which was already spiraling out of control.

*

Bank of America felt different from Lehman Brothers. It was bigger and the trading desks didn't dominate its culture, which helped repress my twinges of foreboding. My new boss, Glen Engle, shaved what little hair still grew on his round head. Muscular and approximately six feet tall (compared to me at six-five), his focus and intensity made him appear giant-like. He appreciated my unobtrusive demeanor and in meetings often asked my opinion. Apparently, my reputation as a former wunderkind remained advantageous.

Within several weeks, I felt at home there. My new job, the same as the previous one, absorbed sixty hours a week, occasionally more. But I thrived on intense mental challenges. And not only was I was paid vast sums, I enjoyed the congenial atmosphere— even if it left me lonelier than ever for Jimmy Quinn.

*

Sterling escalated her ongoing campaign for us to join the country club. I was resolute, however, refusing on principle.

To me, belonging to a club established to exclude anyone of a different race, background, or religion was wrong.

Well into our usual argument, Sterling said, 'You know, the country club runs a great summer day camp for kids, swimming lessons included. Don't you want Olivia to learn to swim?'

'I'll take her to the Y.'

'Really. Just so nobody will think you're a snob.'

'Or a bigot.'

'But you don't mind living here.'

'I appreciate this town but it's as select as I'm gonna get.'

'Like Exeter's not select. Like Harvard's not.'

'Maybe they're the reason I can't understand adults spending their leisure time playing who's in and who's out.'

She pouted, which was nothing new. But a shadow fell, or the light changed, and I gleaned the extent to which Sterling participated in the country club activities: how often she played tennis and golf there; how routinely she enjoyed ladies' luncheons there…all those weekend theme parties held in the club's hilltop pavilions she attended while I stayed home and babysat.

From across the kitchen table, I said, 'Why not have dinner parties here, at our home, for your friends? Feel free to go all out: cocktails, fun, and games.'

'You make it sound stupid, but it isn't.'

'It's a compromise, Sterling. Have parties here once a month. Spend whatever feels right to you.'

'I don't know.'

'I'll help you.'

'How, Walter?'

'You tell me. First of all, I'll attend them.'

'Thank you.' She stood up, sat in my lap, and kissed me the way she did when preparing to ask for something more. I was assuming a bigger house, but instead she merely described how sleek and inviting all her friends' homes were.

'So hire a decorator and get creative.'

Within weeks, the local interior decorator became Sterling's new best friend. Nina Malloy wasn't eligible for the country club because she was a single woman. Nevertheless, she was friends with Sterling's friends, having attuned their feng shui.

Before long, our house at the top of Oak Grove Point had metallic-hued draperies, sliding glass doors, and an elaborate lighting system, among other things. The effect, I told her, was very nice.

'You mean elegant.'

'Yes.'

Sterling invited about twenty people, most of whom brought flowers or wine. Nina Malloy brought a jazz playlist and wanted everyone to stop talking and listen to Nina Simone singing *I Put A Spell On You*. Sterling tapped a glass for everyone's attention, but to no avail.

I should have known better than to invite Wayne, Pete, and Dennis, with their wives. I sat with the men in the kitchen, drinking whiskey and laughing at things Jimmy Quinn said or did years ago. But when I approached their sober, unpretentious wives, they sank deeper into the low bright-orange couch in the hallway. When I carefully poured more Bordeaux into their glasses, I felt the waves of their misgivings.

Thereafter, I left Sterling's guest lists alone. Every six weeks, I fixed drinks and listened to people's selfish opinions as if intrigued.

Before long, the parties morphed into occasions for flirting with other people's spouses. Sterling snuggled up to a lawyer named Harvey, assuring me it was all in fun.

These dalliances (pretend or not) were not my idea of fun. Middle-aged women in dresses cut so low I could count their stretch marks clung to me, asking how tall I was. Did it occur to them that I was twenty-seven years old? Of course not. I spent my life in disguise.

And yet, what had happened to me? I used to *love* older women. What was this?

All right, the older women I loved had been smart and determined. The women at our parties were sloppy and aggressive. I might have pitied them if they weren't always spilling their drinks on me. To compensate for being so judgmental, I behaved with extra attentiveness.

Until Nina Malloy pressed me into a corner, whining, 'Why don't you like me?'

'I like you fine.'

Why this angered her, I don't know. But Sterling arrived in an instant, set down a tray of drinks, and said, 'Don't waste your breath. Walter's a paragon of rectitude.'

But for two things I would have despaired: Olivia had a laugh to stop prayers, and her friend Amanda, a smile to stop time.

2006

Again, the rhododendrons bloomed. And every Saturday, while Sterling and her realtors scoured the school district for dream houses, I drove Olivia, Amanda, and Jade to the YMCA for swimming lessons.

Jade took the girls through the locker rooms, helping them get undressed, showered, and into their suits. When the lesson ended, she met the girls in the showers and helped again, even combing the tangles from Olivia's wild black curls.

From a glassed-in area, with the other parents and nannies, Jade and I watched twelve little kids splash and kick across the pool.

Jade told me that Cheryl Jonette, Amanda's mother, sold sports equipment throughout New York State. She was only home for a few days a month. Where Amanda's father was, or even who he was, Jade had no idea. When I wanted to know more, Jade cupped her hands like a megaphone and called, 'Amanda, kick! Kick, girl, kick!'

Of course, Amanda couldn't hear her, but we all did that.

The following week, Jade said Amanda was better off when her mother stayed away. Those monthly visits were brutal.

'Or no,' she corrected herself. 'They're not brutal. Just unpleasant.'

*

In early September—my most difficult time of year—Jade, Sterling, and I waited at the bottom of the spiraling hill as the girls danced around a birch tree, waiting for the school bus on their first day of kindergarten. I asked Jade if Amanda was enrolling a year early.

'No, she'll be five in November. The cut-off is December.'

The bus driver let us take photographs. Olivia draped an arm around her friend and stuck out her tongue. Amanda covered her eyes and smiled.

Climbing the hill home, we learned that Jade would be caring for Amanda only when needed, now that school had started.

'She's not even five years old,' Sterling said. 'When aren't you needed?'

Jade wasn't sure. 'I'll be around, just not as much.' At the front door, she waved.

*

The housing bubble was close to bursting, but Sterling said that if she found the right house, we were buying it. She couldn't wait. Except the more she searched, the less she saw.

Sterling's dream house had expanded during this searching phase. 'I know you won't buy anything grand. But I want a home of beautiful proportions, large enough so my mother can live with us.'

'Fine by me. I love Kaye. But you don't get along with her.'

'My mother and I express love by opposing each other. Unlike your fawning obsession over Olivia.'

'How—' I could not speak. How could she drag our innocent daughter into her greedy search for an ever-larger house?

'That's right!' Sterling said. 'It's creepy the way you fixate on her every development.'

'Creepy? I'm her parent; parents *should* pay attention to their children's development. You're the one, Sterling, with the abnormal fixation, obsessing over a dream house instead of your daughter.'

'My desire for a beautiful home is normal. Not like your bizarre desire to keep Olivia and Amanda just as they are, sweet little girls who will love you forever.'

I stepped back and checked my impulse to smash something. Then I walked outside and down the hill. About halfway down, behind four deserted townhouses, I noticed a basketball hoop. The half-court lines had faded. A basketball lay by the fence.

I shot around the key. Loving Olivia, cherishing my time with her, was a blessing. I dribbled, spun the ball, and tossed in a swish. Sterling got greedier by the day. She talked about perfect houses but was rarely, if ever, seized by the beauty of life. The girls would be grown up before we knew it. I dribbled and weaved and dunked. Their long-running fantasies, playing make-believe heroines in magical lands, were the ideal of childhood. I spun fast, jumped, and sank one, nothing but net. Let Sterling play her ridiculous grown-up games; I was going to enjoy the girls' childhood. I hit another from far away and jumped up from behind the pole to let the ball roll in off my finger. The air dimmed and I bounced an overhead off the backboard. Suddenly (it seemed), Jimmy Quinn tried to snatch the rebound. Running ahead of me but backwards, he was saying, *Give it up, Walter. Come on, it's mine.* I dribbled fast, imagining him trying to swipe it away while delivering his mischievous rap. As the sky darkened, he grew more distant yet still encouraging. *Nice one. Nice again.* From that day forward, Jimmy Quinn was always with me—just out of range, but cheering me onward.

2007

Initially, Bank of America had touted me as their risk-management genius, but as the housing bubble inflated and Wall Street's money machine whirled night and day, Glen Engel's bosses began insisting that my inputs were unnecessary. Soon I realized that the less work I did, the happier they were.

So, I saw a doctor for my first physical since college. I paid a long-delayed visit to the dentist, which revealed an immediate need for several more visits. On lunch breaks, I indulged in my love of Renaissance art by visiting the Morgan Library. One afternoon, I walked in the rain through Central Park and then went home.

Sterling wasn't there, but I heard the girls. Following Amanda's voice, I found them in the basement. They had been playing spies until Olivia became stuck between two slats of the open basement stairs. The top half of her body fit through, but her feet were planted on the other side because her bottom wouldn't fit. Amanda was poised on the floor, her legs tucked beneath her, reading Roald Dahl's *Matilda* out loud. Olivia was saying, 'Don't make me laugh.'

When she saw me, she said, 'Daddy, don't laugh at me.'

'This is easy to fix,' I reassured her. With a screwdriver and a flashlight, I removed the upper slat, careful not to step on her feet. During the process, we both asked Amanda to continue reading. I for one enjoyed hearing about the extraordinary, clever little girl and her dull and tasteless parents. Olivia was fine, but maintained that the squeeze had exhausted her and she needed to rest upstairs. 'Come with me, Amanda, and read some more.'

But Amanda waited. With her finger in the book, she stood in front of me, staring at the floor, and then glanced up, ashamed.

'Don't be like that!' Olivia said. 'I told you Daddy doesn't care.'

'About what?'

'I broke some flower pots,' Olivia said.

'No she didn't,' Amanda said. 'I did. I'm sorry.'

'Apology accepted. And good for both of you—Olivia for stepping up to take the blame and Amanda for honestly admitting a mistake. On Saturday, why don't the two of you come with me to the garden store? We'll get new pots and you can each get bulbs for indoor planting.'

The weekend was windy and rainy, so they were eager to visit the plant nursery. Amanda chose red tulips and Olivia black irises, despite being warned that they were unreliable indoors. I bought extras to compensate, as well as twelve of the recommended yellow iris bulbs. In the car, we agreed that mixing black and yellow would be interesting.

At home, the girls wrapped their bulbs in aluminum foil and stored them inside paper bags in the refrigerator. 'A few weeks of artificial winter,' I told them, 'and when we pot them, the sunlight from the bay window will hit like early spring.'

After potting the bulbs, Olivia lost interest. But ten days later, Amanda came running from her house as I eased the Mazda into our garage. Sterling and Olivia had already seen, but she had been waiting to show me the first tip of green pushing through the soil. In her excitement, Amanda's whole body hummed. I let her take my hand as she led me to the pots. We leaned over them, our chins in our hands, staring at the spot of green.

'Pretty soon there will be lots of nubs, which will grow taller and greener every day.'

'I know.' She smiled, waved, and ran home. The next week she drew a sketch of the shoots with green pencil, and left it for me to see. Olivia said, 'I gave her advice. At first, she made them too fat. And then too thin.'

'You're an excellent friend. What's happening with your flowers?'

Olivia's irises hadn't broken through the soil. 'I don't care either way.'

Sterling bought sketchbooks and two sets of colored pencils for the girls. On weekends, Amanda would knock on the door and proceed to spend hours drawing the stems, then leaves, and finally the green sheaths over the buds that curled away, revealing streaky green and red petals that turned a complete and vivid red.

When the buds were big and beginning to open, Olivia helped Amanda carry her pots home. She hadn't tended to her own flowers, and although Sterling had taken over watering them, they ended up limp and pale brown.

Olivia returned almost immediately from Amanda's. 'Her house is freezing. Her flowers will die overnight.'

'No, they won't. Tulips do well in the cold.'

Olivia scrunched her face in disgust. 'You wouldn't believe her life, Daddy. On weekends, Amanda does everything at her house that Judy does at ours.'

'Her mother must have forgotten what it's like to be six years old.'

'Amanda's smaller and younger than me but tons stronger. I tried mopping her kitchen floor. She said it's easier than the bathroom. But before I was halfway through, I had to come home and lie down. I was so tired, I watched TV all day.'

Later, Sterling told me what she thought. 'Amanda's a remarkable little girl and I'm very glad she and Olivia are friends. Any other kid, certainly one her age, wouldn't notice the house getting dirty.'

'Maybe her mother has a list of chores.'

'Most kids would ignore that, if nobody was around for weeks at a time.'

'What can we do?' I asked. 'Her mother doesn't even leave her enough money.'

'We can't do anything unless you want her to end up in foster care. Whatever you do, Walter, do *not* try to help. You'll only make things worse for Amanda.'

43

'That little girl has to fix all her own meals and eat alone. I was eleven when I felt abandoned at a fancy prep school, where I ate three meals a day at a table with six other kids.'

'Now you can eat anything, anywhere you choose. And Amanda doesn't eat *every* meal alone. During the week, she eats breakfast and lunch at school. On weekends, you always invite her to eat here.'

'Do I?'

'At least for dinner,' Sterling said. 'You need to be careful, because Amanda's super-smart and living with more responsibilities than many adults. If you don't hide your sympathy, she'll sense it and feel ashamed.'

'Ashamed—with me? I doubt it.'

'You aren't in a position to change things, Walter. If she knows you feel sorry for her, she'll stay away.'

'It's not just feeling sorry for her, Sterling. I feel responsible. She's Olivia's best friend.'

'Don't go overboard just because you didn't have any fun as a kid.'

I nodded but left the room before giving in to a fierce impulse to tell her she knew nothing about that.

Five

2008–2011

Wall Street shuddered, and in the third quarter, it collapsed.

On September 15, Lehman Brothers filed for bankruptcy, and dozens of my former co-workers phoned in distress. I wasn't worried about them. Those who had caused the crash would rebound. If they felt a pinch, they might lay off their children's music teachers and/or take less extravagant vacations.

It was Lehman's support workers—the secretaries, mailroom people, and the dining room staff—who were in trouble. They had listened to the bankers who advocated keeping the entirety of their retirement savings in Lehman Brothers stock.

Ultimately, the banking crisis' worst casualties were those on New York City's streets: the homeless men and women I hurried past or, I'm ashamed to say, even stepped over, early each morning and again each evening, the ones so poor they appeared to have nothing to lose. What they lost was the ghost of a chance, the possibility of employment—crumbs from the table. Their opportunities were gone. No crumbs would fall, because I had spent years gluing them together until they were appetizing enough to sell as a meal for bankers.

Suddenly, my risk management skills were in greater demand than ever. I worked nearly nonstop restructuring the bank's hollow products. I salvaged everything possible for Merrill Lynch, which Bank of America had absorbed. I was so valuable that, at the end of the year, the bank gave me a big fat special bonus.

This bonanza, huge as it was, didn't reassure Sterling. Her panic about money puzzled me, considering how astute she'd been as Vince Ferraro's gatekeeper.

Our personal losses were minor. We still had far more money than we needed. When Sterling remained sad and skeptical, I said, 'Now's the time to grab what you've always wanted. Million-dollar mansions must be standing abandoned all over the place.'

Surprisingly, she didn't relish snatching up an empty dream house. Many of her high-living country club friends, having splurged every credit offered them, were now moving to Iowa or Nebraska—wherever the cost of living wasn't preposterous.

Sterling stopped going to open houses and looked instead to a local contractor named Kevin Dalton. He was popular for building brand-new homes to replace old ones, called 'tear-downs' by the wealthy families who hired him. When she wasn't drinking daiquiris with Nina Malloy, Sterling began spending her time at estate sales with Kevin.

*

For the next three years, I woke before dawn, ran five miles, and caught the 6:35 train. I rarely returned home before 9:15 at night. Minimizing the damage done by defaulted debt, shoot-the-moon derivatives, and extend-and-pretend loans was a herculean job. Fortunately, I took satisfaction in salvaging possibilities from the wreckage.

We visited Kaye in Bar Harbor, or she visited us, regularly. The bond between Sterling's mother and Olivia was almost palpable—strong and unique. To protect Sterling from feeling jealous on these occasions, I did my best to lavish my wife with attention. Sometimes this pleased her. More often, my attempted intimacies only reminded her that her mother and daughter understood and appreciated each other—without her. To Sterling's credit, she accepted this fact.

Each year, I received larger bonuses and more vacation time. One year, instead of going to Bar Harbor, we rented a house on St. John in the Virgin Islands. Busy with her sailing club, Kaye was unable to join us.

Without Kaye there, Sterling and Olivia bickered.

Despite the beaches and terrific snorkeling, Olivia was bored and, somewhat to my dismay, spent every spare moment watching television.

When I worried about her boredom, Sterling said, 'Entire childhoods used to be nonstop boredom. Until, eventually, your imagination kicked in. Before we leave, Olivia will have learned to follow her thoughts.'

I liked this idea and took my pampered wife to bed.

We were away seven days. The flight home was exhausting. When Olivia had finally gone to sleep, Sterling nudged a bag of art books I had bought in the airport bookstore. 'Guess you've got quite the hobby.'

Why the word 'hobby' set me off, I can't say. 'Your hobby, Sterling, is drinking daiquiris with Nina Malloy.'

She laughed at that. 'Did I make calm, collected Walter mad?'

Indeed. So mad that I smashed a wooden chair on the kitchen's hand-glazed tiles. The next morning, I put the splintered wood into two garbage bags and carried them outside.

*

The next summer, while researching vacation spots, I found a lakefront house in the Adirondacks that I thought we should buy. Curiously, Sterling, who spent her life house-hunting, disagreed.

'I don't need two homes. Just let me have one beautiful residence in Olivia's school district.'

Fine by me. 'But what about a time-share? Olivia could invite Amanda to come up there with us.'

'First, we would have to find Amanda's mother to make the invitation,' Sterling said. 'And Cheryl Jonette is missing in action. Or has that escaped you?'

It had not escaped me. 'All the more reason for us to invite her on vacation.'

Sterling waved her finger at me. 'Do not make Amanda a charity case.'

'Inviting her to the Adirondacks is not making her a *charity case*. Don't act like I'm abnormal.'

'It's Cheryl Jonette who's abnormal. The way she leaves her daughter alone for weeks on end is criminal. But the legal system—really any intervention—would only make Amanda's life worse. And contrary to what you might think, she'll need more attention during middle school, not less.'

Six

Summer 2012

By the time the financial crisis subsided, I had acquired enough status at the bank to leave early on Fridays—just like the managing directors with houses in the Hamptons.

One Friday in June, I arrived home while the light was still bright and took Olivia by surprise. The guilty look on her face prompted me to ask, 'What are you up to, young lady?'

'Nothing, Daddy.'

I followed her upstairs and noticed Amanda in Olivia's bedroom, putting down a cell phone. Seeing me, she waved.

'I know what you're doing,' I laughed. 'You're calling boys.'

Olivia hopped in the air. 'Daddy, it's *so* fun!'

'I thought kids didn't use phones except to take photos and text.'

'That's what makes it so fun!'

In their last few weeks as fifth-graders, Olivia and Amanda invented their own language. Olivia showed me a note Amanda gave her in class. I didn't mean to decipher their code, but I couldn't help myself. I saw diphthongs in place of prevalent consonants. They reversed vowels and used 'y' for short sounds and 'e' for long ones. I assumed the scatterings of 'l,' 'm,' 'n,' and 'r' were phonetic, because when they spoke their private language, it flowed fast and comical.

When I told Sterling this, she said, 'Get real.'

But I loved listening to their coded speech—it was exactly like them to have created it. To my mind, Olivia and Amanda were the most brilliant kids who ever lived.

*

After being out with Kevin Dalton one Saturday, Sterling came home with a major announcement—she'd found her dream house! Or rather, she'd found the property for her dream house.

'We'll demolish the split-level eyesore and build new,' she said. 'Three tall stories and soaring windows throughout. We'll be able to see the river!'

'Did you bid on it?' I asked.

'Yes, and they accepted like *that*.' She snapped her fingers, happier than she had been in a long time. (And I was happy, too, because if she demolished one house and then built another, we wouldn't be moving for a while.) She wanted to show me the property right away and waited while I changed my clothes.

By the time we left, the bright daylight was dissolving into the first tiny grains that would soon become a soft, calm dusk. Olivia appeared, dancing in the road, showing off an old skateboard that her 'boyfriend' Simon had given her.

'Amanda has better balance, but I'm more daring. And don't tell us to wear helmets, Daddy.'

'Then don't ride it.'

Sterling dropped her voice. 'Come with me and leave them alone for twenty minutes.'

In the Volvo, she assured me that the girls couldn't ride the skateboard. They stood on it and tipped side to side, at best. 'Wait till you see the property.' She drove through the woods, along a winding road, and parked by a well-designed landscape. Goose bumps lifted the fine hairs on her pink arms. The split-level house at the opposite end, I agreed, looked out of place.

'Overall, it's beautiful, Sterling.'

She pointed to a distant spot between tree branches.

'Ah, the river,' I said, but my voice lacked enthusiasm.

'You can't see it, can you?'

'Yes, I can. It's right…right there.'

'We'll see it clearly from our bedroom window.'

'It's wonderful, Sterling. And if you're happy, I'm happy.'

'Really?'

'Of course.' She wished for me to be thrilled, but showing an elation I didn't feel would have been worse.

She knew that and patted my shoulder. 'Well, good.'

'No,' I drew her toward me. 'It's much better than good. Really, much better.' I kissed her, which felt so liberating in the open terrain and accumulating twilight that I leaned in and kissed her again for a long time.

Later in the evening, I mentioned to her that, before we knocked down the split-level house, we needed to have it certified as worthless and petition the zoning board.

'I never said it was *worthless*.'

'If you don't, the ruling will go against us.'

'Know-it-all.'

Sterling and Kevin Dalton met often, supposedly to discuss the demolition. The only crew Kevin trusted couldn't begin until next year. So, obviously, they talked about other things.

Autumn 2012

Another September, and Olivia and Amanda were in middle school. Like most sixth-grade girls, they preferred the mall to the daylong hikes that I proposed. Against expectations, I liked the mall's first floor. Around two huge escalators, the first level contained bright, comfortable chairs and a few long benches arranged near a wall of bronze, down which unending sheets of water flowed.

Darkness fell earlier every week, and that autumn—more so than in any other before it—I felt sad, almost sick, dropping off Amanda in her dark driveway leading to her even darker, empty house. One night, when Olivia was going to bed, I asked if the light in the second-floor window across the street, the light that was always on, shone from Amanda's bedroom. It did.

Spring 2013

Olivia decided at the end of sixth grade that she wanted to attend the year's last school dance. Held in the gym from 9:30 pm to almost midnight, the monthly dances hadn't interested the girls before. Amanda agreed to go with her and knocked on our door fifteen minutes early.

Sterling ushered both girls into the TV room. I was in the living room, poring over a book about the golden ratio in classical architecture, and couldn't help overhearing the conversation. In order to see them, I moved from the couch to a small chair. Olivia was wearing new clothes, sleek black pants and a silky blue sleeveless top that matched her eyes. Amanda was wearing an oversized YMCA T-shirt and a denim skirt Olivia had outgrown. Sterling didn't like the way the belted skirt bunched beneath Amanda's T-shirt.

'Wait here,' Sterling said. And then, 'I got this for you when I was buying Olivia some things.'

'Oh, my gosh, thank you! I love stencil tees.' After changing in the bathroom, Amanda said, 'I love it!'

'Why can't I have a shorty T-shirt?' Olivia said. 'Or one with palm trees on it?'

'You have so many clothes, you'll outgrow them before you can wear half of them,' Sterling said.

'I'm a spoiled brat, is what you're saying. Daddy, are you ready? In another minute, we're gonna get the anti-smoking speech.'

'Olivia, don't be rude. Apologize to your mother.'

She did so, barely.

When I returned from dropping off the girls, I coaxed Sterling into taking a walk. We strolled along the aqueduct, dark but for the light of nearby houses. She let me take her hand and we walked in silence for a few steps. I led my wife to a pair of boulders where we watched eighth graders smoking behind an ivy-covered fence. The smoke in the early June night smelled like marijuana. The teenagers' hushed voices occasionally burst into a few emphatic curses followed by laughter.

Sterling wouldn't sit on a boulder. She didn't wear jeans. That evening her tailored slacks were a luxurious beige material.

I suggested we go inside the church. She wasn't convinced, but I opened the door anyway. A white-haired choir practiced by the altar, but nobody stopped us from climbing the stairs to a room with a bench facing a pair of open windows. It overlooked the smoking eighth graders, a group that slowly grew. The light in the room wasn't strong, but when I draped an arm around Sterling and she brushed the hair away from her face, I noticed new lines on her freckled, reddish neck. She wore make-up applied so carefully you wouldn't notice it unless you looked closely. But I was entitled to look as closely as I wished. It saddened me to see small pouches under her eyes and the indentations running from the sides of her nose to the corners of her mouth. She was forty-four years old and had grown up by the ocean. Her hair felt dry and stiff. Once a month she went into the city and had several hues of brown applied at an expensive salon.

Sterling had a theory about the apex of girlhood, which she shared with me now. She'd seen her friends' daughters undergo an astonishing transformation during preadolescence. Before puberty, she said, some girls, not all, suddenly possess a striking, evanescent beauty, although for a lucky few, it can last most of their lives. At their peak, many girls also discover an intellectual acuity, with accelerating thought patterns. The apex of girlhood, she said, gives them tremendous physical allure and mental agility—right before the arduous trek of adolescence. Their hair sweeps over their guileless faces with a foreshadowing of womanhood. Their eyes burn vividly as their curiosity (if nothing else) becomes aroused. Their gestures and motions become distinctly feminine. Their gorgeous complexions (not a spot of acne yet) and confidence are compelling.

I pulled her closer to me and positioned her head against my chest. 'Why haven't I ever heard about the apex of girlhood?'

Possibly, she said, because nobody else talked about it. When she did, people sometimes looked at her as if she'd brought up an ugly taboo. 'But it's nothing like that.'

Sterling pulled away to look at me. She saw this metamorphosis occurring in both Olivia and Amanda.

'Was it like that for you?'

She kissed the palm of my hand and gazed down. 'It didn't happen like that for me. Remember? Fat girl.'

'So you became beautiful later.'

'We're not talking about me.'

Sterling wanted us to be alert to Olivia and Amanda's transformation. Because, she said, if *she* noticed this burst of feminine prowess—imagine how men would react.

A figure appeared in the doorway. 'You're not allowed in there. Come with me.'

We stood and saw that it was Allison Wright, the organ player. 'Walter, Sterling?' she said. 'I thought you were kids sneaking up here.'

'Were we noisy?'

'Enough so that I knew you were here. But you're right. Kids would have banged the bench.'

We hurried home. Inside, Sterling said she was tired and poured herself a goblet of wine, while I started the car to fetch the girls.

Summer 2013

When the days grew longer and warmer, I registered the next progressive loosening of the once tightly wound coil that held Sterling and me together: I overheard Nina Malloy ask her if she thought Kevin was attractive.

'Don't you?' Sterling asked.

In and of itself, this wasn't surprising. Kevin Dalton was attractive. Sturdy and ruddy, he had an outgoing, friendly personality that must have seemed fun compared to mine. I didn't blame Sterling. Our relationship wasn't built for sweeping passion. As long as she was in our bed at night and responsive to me, I wasn't going to overreact to a temporary flirtation.

One night in August, right before the girls started seventh grade, I got off the 9:40 Hudson Line and saw Amanda across the street, her long legs straddling her rusty second-hand bicycle. Under the streetlamp, she waved at me. I crossed the street.

'Hi Amanda, what you are doing?'

'This summer? I'm helping out at the Y.'

'No, I mean now.'

'Olivia and I were riding bikes but then she got invited to hang out with a bunch of eighth graders.'

'Didn't you feel like going?'

'I wasn't invited, but I wouldn't have wanted to go anyway.'

'Would you like a ride home?' She nodded, and I said, 'Here, let me put your bike in the trunk.'

'Did you see the ring around the moon?' she asked.

'Not yet.'

'It's huge in circumference but skinny and red.'

'Ice or dust refraction,' I said, closing the Mazda's trunk. 'Will you show me?'

'What?'

'The moon, when we get home.'

She nodded.

Driving up Main Street, we saw Sterling and Kevin drinking outside the Italian restaurant. I beeped the horn and Amanda waved.

Christmas 2013

Sterling and I had both noticed that Amanda's mother was showing up for fewer visits than usual. By Sterling's count she had been present with her daughter for fewer than ten days all year. So when Amanda told us that her mother had set aside extra time to spend with her during the winter break, Sterling decided to invite them to Christmas dinner.

'The girls aren't close at the moment,' she told me later, 'but really that's even more reason for me to have a word with Amanda's mother.'

At first, I wasn't sure what Sterling meant by 'the girls aren't close.' But on second thought, I realized that Olivia hadn't mentioned her friend for a while. In any case, I was relieved that Sterling intended to speak with Cheryl Jonette. For as often as I cringed at Sterling's suburban persona, she continued to speak her mind.

We listened for the Jeep Wrangler starting up the hill and when it eased into the driveway, Sterling stood waiting in front of the garage, her hands on her hips. Cheryl emerged, looking unkempt. I watched them talking and, when Sterling returned, asked what happened.

'I invited her to four o'clock dinner along with Amanda. But the woman swore her schedule made any get-together impossible. I said, "Name the day and time. Breakfast, lunch, a nice glass of water if that's the best you can do. Five minutes to celebrate the season with our daughters." But she claimed it wasn't doable. She's home for the morning to celebrate Christmas with Amanda, the morning being the important part. When they open presents. Then she's meeting her boss, who is also apparently her unofficial fiancé, whom she's decided Amanda shouldn't meet until he makes it official.'

Sterling had been leading me upstairs as she recounted all this. Her voice low, she said, 'I came *this* close to telling that bitch that it takes more than occasional visits to be a mother!'

Between our room and Olivia's, I kissed Sterling seriously. 'I loved your no-nonsense attitude from the moment I met you.'

*

At four, Amanda arrived bearing gifts. For Sterling, a set of gold beaded napkin rings, which she had made at school.

'They're perfect,' Sterling said, leading her into the dining room. 'Look how well they go with the china.'

And for Olivia, a big dark-red velvet bow. 'Headband or a neck tie,' Amanda said. 'Your choice.'

'Yeah? Cheryl just gave this to you, didn't she? It's your Christmas present.'

Amanda dipped her head. Her hair had become tawny that year, rich and lustrous, every strand a different shade of rose gold.

'I didn't think you'd mind me re-gifting it,' she said, 'because it will look so much better on you.'

'You got that right.' Olivia wrapped it around her black curls—and Sterling grabbed her elbow and hauled her from the room.

Amanda handed me a small gift-wrapped box. Inside was a three-inch-long Swiss Army knife, two blades.

I laughed, I was so pleased. 'Every man should have one of these.'

Sterling returned and said, 'Please excuse Olivia. She's staying in her room until dinner. And if she's rude to you again, she's not going to Madison's slumber party tonight.'

'Oh no,' Amanda said, her eyes wide with alarm. 'You can't *make* her be my friend.'

'She's not allowed to be mean,' Sterling said.

'She's not mean. She has some new friends, that's all.'

'The cool kids are nobody's friend.' Sterling took me aside. 'Watch a movie with her while I finish cooking.'

In the TV room, I looked for the complete DVD sets Olivia had unwrapped just hours before. I picked one plastic case from each box. When I glanced up, Amanda was tiptoeing toward me. 'Something from the *Harry Potter* series or one of the *Twilight*s?'

'Which do you like?' she asked.

'To be honest, I tend to like vampires better than boy wizards. But I believe *Twilight*'s a love story, so it might be kind of sick.'

'Every love story's sick,' Amanda said. 'And why even have vampires except for especially sick love stories?'

I smiled, thoroughly enchanted. 'In real life, love stories aren't necessarily sick. Some might be, but most are not.'

'Depends,' Amanda said, 'on who you are and what makes you sick.'

I smiled at this, suppressing a laugh.

The movie I'd selected was *New Moon*, which Amanda said was the second in the saga and better than the first.

I sat back, sipping Dewar's. Sterling appeared with an icy long-stemmed champagne glass for Amanda, which she carefully filled with sparkling grape juice bottled like champagne.

Amanda stood still, tasting it. I watched her take two delicate sips before forcing my eyes back to the screen. Then she set the glass down, twirled through the room, and mock-stumbled, landing on her stomach. Her elbows on the rug, chin in her hands, she crossed and uncrossed her ankles, her pink socks worn through at the heels. She glanced over her shoulder at me, before losing my interest (not a chance, but she didn't know that). A minute later, Amanda rose in a graceful column to drink her 'champagne.'

'Whoa,' in a squeaky, high voice, she said, 'the bubbles are filled with helium! They tickle my nose.' Setting the glass on its coaster, she spun and stumbled again, but this time sat up, facing me. 'I'm so happy I feel like I must be drunk.'

Soon Sterling called us to the table. Olivia stomped downstairs wearing a long filmy skirt, Doc Marten boots, a cropped denim jacket, and the hair bow set at a jaunty angle.

Sterling lit candles throughout the dining room. At each place setting was a last present: braided leather bracelets for the girls; a rare translation of Dante's poems to Beatrice for me. And for Sterling, the red gloves Santa forgot to put under the tree.

I sliced rosy roast beef. Sterling passed a platter of twice-baked potatoes and tried making conversation. Olivia answered in monosyllables. Amanda answered shyly.

What had happened to their private language?

Olivia pushed her salad away. 'I hate this.'

'I love it,' Amanda said. She'd never tasted 'on-deev' before.

Sterling offered no dessert, although yesterday I had stood in line to buy little lemon tarts. Olivia slumped in her chair and Sterling asked, 'Are you packed and ready? Because in another ten minutes, I might not allow you to go.'

'You wouldn't dare.'

Sterling asked, 'Are you ready, Amanda?'

Turned out, Amanda hadn't been invited to the slumber party. Sterling and I looked at each other, equally disturbed. But Amanda, apparently, didn't mind. She told us she wasn't friends with Madison and offered to clear the table.

Driving Olivia to Madison's house, I was stupid enough to ask if she and Amanda had grown apart.

'What does that mean, Daddy, "grown apart"? I fit in with this group and Amanda doesn't.'

By the time I returned, Amanda had gone.

Sterling and I sat at the bay window, eating lemon tarts. She said, 'They're mean at this age. But if it doesn't last long, they learn to be friends who really talk to each other, as opposed to the typical male friendship, which consists of fantasy football.'

The real meanie, Sterling said, was Amanda's mother. 'Why can't that woman buy her gorgeous child a pair of skinny jeans? Of course, that would involve taking the girl shopping.'

'Skinny jeans?'

'Amanda doesn't have the right clothes. And among seventh-grade girls in Westchester, wearing the right—ridiculously expensive—clothes is everything.'

'Olivia wasn't wearing jeans.'

'That's beside the point,' Sterling said. 'All Amanda needs is skinny jeans and a pair of slouchy boots.'

I kissed the inside of Sterling's wrist. 'How did you find those Dante poems?'

'Amazon. Secondhand.'

I was halfway upstairs when she called, 'Walter? No meddling!'

'Don't worry.'

I stood at our bedroom window and gazed at the light from Amanda's room spilling onto the asphalt between our houses.

Seven

New Year's 2014

Sterling said she wanted to celebrate New Year's Eve only with me, no one else. Olivia had just announced she was invited to a sleepover by a girl whose parents Sterling knew from the country club—big money on big display.

'Why didn't you tell me, Sterling? I would have booked a suite in the city. You know what? I'll get us a reservation off someone's last-minute cancellation.' Early in our marriage, we used to ring in the New Year by hiring an overnight babysitter and going out for dinner and dancing. Near dawn, we would shake the glitter from our hair.

'No,' she said. 'Let's just spend a quiet evening at home.'

While waiting for Olivia to get ready for the slumber party, I asked what Kevin Dalton was doing for New Year's.

'Visiting his brother in Waterville, Maine.'

'Is he the reason you didn't mention New Year's sooner?'

A bit sharply, Sterling said that she *had* mentioned it—sooner.

I told her then, as I had before, that while I wasn't happy about her spending so much time with Kevin, I trusted her to do as she liked.

What she liked, she said, was snuggling next to me on New Year's Eve.

On the way to a multi-tiered granite mansion, Olivia chatted happily about the sleepover. Everyone at school had been texting about it. She hadn't been invited until today, but wasn't worried. Someone would ask if she was coming and Melissa would immediately invite her—which is exactly what happened. So, Olivia had put together the perfect outfits and had even brought two packs of gold-foil cardboard tiaras, which were either fun or stupid. 'TBD before midnight.'

'I'm sure they're fun, Olivia—at a New Year's Eve party.'

Returning, I backed into the garage and noticed Amanda's light shining in her bedroom. Sterling was waiting for me in a red velvet dressing gown. She had ice-cold Veuve Clicquot Yellow Label ready to open.

She didn't listen to music at home, normally, but had given me a box of re-mastered John Coltrane CDs for Christmas. Coltrane, Eric Dolphy, and McCoy Tyner filled the room with *On Green Dolphin Street*.

We sat on the couch, sipping the champagne. Apropos of nothing, Sterling wondered if we had planted in Olivia seeds of jealousy against Amanda. How many times had we praised Amanda's spirit and sense of fair play, her natural beauty, and her unwillingness to complain—without thinking to compliment Olivia as well?

Soon we returned to the kitchen so Sterling could refill her glass. When she was drinking freely, I held back, not that I ever drank very much. But Sterling loved to drink. It made her feel fun and free. She didn't care if she slurred her words, talked too loud, and laughed even louder. Perhaps if I drank to keep up with her, I wouldn't care. But if she was getting drunk, I wanted to be sober enough to drive, in case of emergency. She drank a second glass standing up and, after pouring a third, sank heavily into her place at the kitchen table. We stared through the bay window at Amanda's house.

Seeing the light on in her bedroom, I recalled the New Year's I was twelve and alone at Exeter. All the other kids were home for winter break. My sister had died the year before and, as always, my parents were traveling. I had sat at my desk, studying mathematical conjectures and the history of zeta functions where non-trivial zeroes were real and trivial zeroes were imaginary. I had spoken out loud just to hear my voice, which sounded muffled. And I wondered if I was non-trivial or trivial.

Sterling guzzled her champagne and regretted the few times she'd mentioned 'Daddy's Amanda fixation' to Olivia.

'Christ! If you think that, Sterling, why didn't you tell *me* instead of her?'

'But I have told you—often. Of course, I should have kept it to myself. One, because you're not *exactly* fixated. And two, if you were ever to hide your fondness for Amanda, she would lose the only affection she gets.'

'"The only affection she gets?" Where do you come up with this stuff?'

'From Olivia. She always used to say, "Imagine how lonely Amanda must feel." So, I did imagine it, and I told her that anyone in Amanda's position would need a father figure. That probably ruined their friendship then and there.'

So, Sterling and Olivia had seen through me. I hadn't realized anything showed. Had I known they would notice how Amanda beguiled me, I would have tried harder to hide it.

Sterling leaned across the table to stick her face right in front of mine. 'Amanda idolizes you, Walter. She seeks and needs your approval. When she and Olivia make up, as I'm sure they will, you must continue being the one grown-up man Amanda can trust.'

'She does not idolize me.'

'She adores you. And you know it! To my mind, if Olivia's jealous, too bad. Amanda needs more attention and Olivia would benefit from less.'

It didn't occur to me then, but if I had paid as much attention to Sterling as I did to the girls, I would have asked my wife if, growing up, she sometimes felt left out. I had the impression her father had worshipped Kaye. I knew he had taught Sterling to think for herself, and he had been a generous and affectionate father. But I doubt Sterling had been a miracle to him, as the girls were to me. Perhaps Kevin gave her a semblance of that kind of attention.

Lost in our thoughts, we watched the clock's minute hand, preparing to kiss at midnight. But sitting at the table, we saw Amanda throw open her window. She leaned out and yelled, 'Happy New Year, Everyone!'

We got the middle window open and yelled back. 'Happy New Year, Amanda!' but received no sign that she had heard us.

I then danced Sterling around to 'Equinox,' until she flopped onto the stairs. I went to the kitchen for a glass of water but, feeling a stirring sensation, looked at Amanda's window. Something was happening in her room and I stepped outside to observe. Gazing up, I saw her feet. She was jumping on the bed.

Sterling called, begging me to carry her upstairs. 'That is, if you *can* carry me. Don't hurt yourself.' I slid one arm under her legs and the other under her back—and managed. She laughed, thanking God I was so strong because she got heavier every year. 'You don't mind, though, do you?'

No, but I didn't want to carry her upstairs again. After settling her on the bed, I whispered in her ear that it didn't matter if she was heavier because her proportions were the same, maybe even sexier. She liked that, and we had ourselves a time.

*

Kevin returned from Maine with ideas for period floor-to-ceiling window frames. He and Sterling spent almost every weekday visiting estate sales. On Sunday, while Sterling was discussing architectural details with Kevin on the phone, Olivia burst in, asking, 'Where has Amanda been? I haven't seen her since Christmas!'

Sterling told Kevin she couldn't talk and hung up. She then told Olivia, 'You were mean to her on Christmas.'

'No, I wasn't. But if I was, she wouldn't care. Look at how mean her mother is.'

Sterling and I learned that Olivia rarely saw Amanda anymore because in seventh grade the students were assigned to different tracks: advanced, average, or at risk. Amanda was in the average track and Olivia was advanced. 'Average is basic,' she said. 'So basically, Amanda's just basic.' Using her thumbs, she rolled up her upper lids, a scary new face. 'Ha-ha. We go to school to learn how to be snobs.'

Later in the week, Olivia stomped into the living room, claiming she was so jealous of Amanda she could scream. Seventh grade average or not, Amanda had just been promoted to associate editor of the school newspaper.

'You should be happy for her, not jealous,' I said. 'It sounds like you're being mean to her again.'

'Daddy, I don't see her enough to be mean. Besides, she has tons of new friends. Luckily, one of them is Madison.'

When we were alone, Sterling mocked me for taking Olivia too seriously. She claimed I had overreacted to what was ordinary give-and-take. 'You're an alarmist,' she said. 'When it comes to the girls, I suggest you mind your own business.'

'I'm Olivia's father. I can take an interest in her relationships.'

Sterling said, 'I have a hunch that your interest is more like an obsession.'

'Really. Well, your hunch sounds like an accusation.' I didn't say what I really thought: that perhaps her hunch sprang from a guilty conscience. She and Kevin Dalton were adding significant mileage to the Volvo.

Another man would have demanded answers. But I didn't want Sterling to lie. Even if they were having an affair (which I more or less believed they were), it wouldn't last long.

In hindsight, however, I recognize another reason for remaining silent. It wasn't a conscious thing, and it shames me now. But because I was working fourteen-hour days, I was glad Sterling came to bed stimulated from being with Kevin Dalton. I appreciated how ready she already was. I liked the expediency.

February 2014

Sterling showed me a glossy catalog filled with antique moldings and chandeliers, mosaics and stained glass. Kevin Dalton would be attending an auction in Albany. She pointed out the items Kevin said were rare, possibly even one of a kind. I crossed out items I disliked, such as mosaics and windows that belonged in a museum. No statuary, no gimcrack, no cupolas, no monolithic pier mirrors.

'Will you come with us? Olivia can come, too, if she doesn't find a friend to take her in.'

'That's an unpleasant way of putting it—a friend to take her in? I'll pass. A three-day weekend with Olivia sounds great. And honestly, you don't want me there.'

'Yes, I do.'

'You, Kevin, and me? No, thanks.'

'Do I detect a smidgen of jealousy?'

I looked at her closely. 'Be careful, Sterling.'

'Can you go two nights without me?'

'Probably. Now that I'm past thirty.'

'You're above jealousy.'

'Don't say that. I dread it so much that I'm practically certain it'll ruin me one day.'

'But you're above jealousy involving me.'

'If you think jealousy is romantic, it's not. When I was at Harvard, I saw people with extraordinary minds lose their careers because of jealousy over a smartass kid.'

'So you're too smart to do that.'

'Stop it, Sterling. We can be good for each other or not. And if not, we won't last.'

The next morning, Friday, after I ran and showered, I was hurrying to get dressed. And Sterling called me back to bed. I declined, saying that I'd be late. She said, just come quick. And I did, very hard and very fast, with a tinge of guilt.

While she lay in bed watching me put on my suit and tie, I told her she'd never find another man like me. Then I kissed her until she insisted I stop.

'All right, but don't forget—I'm rich.'

She rolled over and sighed. 'Oh, yeah. Rich is important.'

That evening, I arrived home after Sterling and Kevin had left for Albany. Olivia pounced from a corner, frantic from trying to reach me. Madison had invited her snowboarding for the long weekend. Her family had a time-share in Okemo, Vermont. She mimed speeding sideways. 'Please, Daddy.'

'Let me call Madison's parents. Do you have their number?'

'Yes, but don't say I've never gone snowboarding. Madison's been doing it since she was three.'

'Olivia, if you want to go, you must take lessons.'

'God, all right!' She'd do anything rather than be cooped up with me.

'Try again, unless you can pay your own way.'

So, she smiled and apologized. She threw her arms around me. I was the best daddy.

'Okay, sweetheart. Let me make that phone call.'

*

Saturday, with both Olivia and Sterling away, I stretched in near-record cold and jogged downhill, preparing for my run. It was then that I saw Amanda pedaling hard up the incline, brown bags strapped to an older, more unwieldy bike than I remembered. Her breath white in the sharp air, she panted 'hello' but didn't stop.

'You could walk the bike.'

She shook her head as she pushed forward. She wore canvas sneakers, no laces—and no socks. The skin of her slender ankles looked blue with cold. Reaching the flat of her driveway, she lifted her head and tossed back her long tawny hair. It flew, bright and alive, across the dreary dead sky.

*

The next morning, I woke early to run the full long loop around Rockefeller Park. Returning, I saw Amanda attempting handstands on the asphalt.

'Hello, Mr. Mitchell.'

'Amanda, either you start calling me "Walter," or I'll have to call you "Ms. Jonette."'

Her bare hands smoothed her long sheaf of hair and held it away from her face. A faint gleam of pink surfaced along her wide cheekbones.

'Let me get cleaned up,' I said. 'And then, if you're not busy, I wonder if you would accompany me to the mall?'

She stared at her canvas-clad toe tracing a circle on the ground between us. 'But you hate the mall.'

'Usually, that's true. But I'm hungry and in the mood for the chicken satay at that Thai place.'

'Are you sure?'

'I could use the company. Sterling and Olivia are away this weekend.'

Half an hour later, I coaxed her into the Mazda. She strapped the seatbelt over her navy pea coat.

Out of the car, in the underground parking lot, she smoothed her hair again and her breath formed white plumes in the dank miasma. I opened the heavy metal door to the escalator area and said, 'After we eat, I'll read my book and you can shop for trendy clothes.'

She looked up at me, giggling. '*Trendy clothes*?'

'Isn't that what they're called? Skinny jeans, someone told me. And you need boots. Also, warm shirts or sweaters.'

She shook her head. 'Too expensive.'

'Not on my charge card, they're not. When I was a kid, one cool shirt and the right pair of Nikes made all the difference.'

'But it'll take me forever to pay you back.'

'I don't want you to. In fact, I won't allow it. You have to promise me you won't tell anyone. It'll be our secret.'

'Oh, man!' She promised, and I promised, and we forgot about the Thai place, even though I had been dizzy with hunger.

Facing the water flowing over the bronze wall, I studied a new collection of Leonardo da Vinci's sketches until Amanda returned, laden with shopping bags and skipping before me. She was wearing form-fitting pale blue jeans, with frayed rips on each leg, a swirling oversized pink and orange cap, and a matching hoodie. On her feet were thick short motorcycle boots. Setting the bags on a bench, she smiled and her shyness opened into real happiness, followed too soon by worry.

'I overdid it,' she said. 'My mother will kill me. Women have to be independent, especially financially.'

'Hold on. This has nothing to do with independent women and their finances. We made a pact. Based on you choosing some clothes, with no payback. If you break your promise, you'll hurt my feelings.'

'I will?'

'Yes. A secret pact is an oath.'

'I know, but I thought the promise was to keep it secret. I don't remember promising not to pay you back.'

'Yes, you do. I told you I can't allow it.'

'But if my mother finds out—'

'I won't tell if you won't.'

She swung around and sat beside me, as bright and happy as I'd ever seen her. Her cap, she said, was beehive-style, and she'd gotten matching mittens. Two thermal-knit long-sleeve shirts, a cardigan, and another pair of jeans, no rips.

'Socks?'

'Three pairs. Two from Hot Sox and the other pair at the shoe store.' She handed me the credit card and pawed through the bags for the receipts. 'I'm really sorry.'

'I believe the U.S. Army supplies more clothing for recruits going to boot camp.'

She laughed. 'The army?' She shook her head and caught her cap before it fell off. She adjusted it on top of her head, angled slightly back. 'The army doesn't have pink- and persimmon-colored sweaters and black, patterned over-the-knee socks.'

'We don't know that. Maybe they use them for special missions.'

In the car, she asked if I thought ripped jeans were silly. 'They last just as long as regular new jeans. The rips are just there to look cool.'

'Well, they do look cool, Amanda. Very cool.'

I turned into the enclave and drove slowly uphill. When I pulled into her driveway, the garage door was open, which wasn't unusual. She thanked me again and although I was suffused with tenderness for her, I forced myself to look straight ahead.

I remained in her driveway long enough to enjoy her elation as she twirled through the garage's empty space in her heavy boots, the outstretched bags adding ballast. Setting the bags down, she slid back to me and stopped. I lowered the window and she whispered, 'You and I are nothing like my mother, Walter.'

I squeezed her shoulder. 'Maybe not. All I know is that for me, giving gifts is often more fun than getting them.'

'I know! My favorite thing this Christmas was being able to give you a real present.' She jumped and turned in the air.

Shifting into reverse, I saw Sterling in the rearview mirror. Home a full day early, she leaned against the Volvo's bumper in our garage. Even at a distance, inside my car, I could feel her anger skewering me.

I parked the Mazda beside the Volvo. And then, inside our double garage, Sterling shoved me hard through the door into the kitchen.

'Walter, have you lost your mind? You are *not* that girl's father.'

'True. But I care about her and whoever her father is, does not.'

In the hallway, she yanked my arm. 'Are you really oblivious to how totally over the top this is? I mean, honestly, how could you?'

'What—buy her warm clothes? It's not a crime.'

'Juicy Couture and Bloomingdale's. Pray to God Olivia never finds out.' She stomped upstairs and yelled down to me, 'I swear, ever since Jimmy Quinn died, you've forgotten where one person ends and another begins. Find the boundaries!'

Sterling, I soon learned, had returned home early because of a bitter argument with Kevin Dalton. 'Leave me alone,' she said. 'I'm in a terrible mood.'

Perhaps her terrible mood explained her outrage over me taking Amanda shopping. I made the mistake of wondering this aloud. And Sterling lit up, almost aloft with righteous indignation—the terrific moral certainty that cheaters so easily summon.

*

That evening, we ate dinner separately. Olivia was still on her snowboarding trip. I was loading the dishwasher when Gil, Madison's father, called. Olivia had broken her thumb at the base. A clean break, he said, but still a bad injury.

While he was talking, Sterling dashed into view, wearing her coat, gloves, and scarf. She shook her car keys in front of my face. Undoubtedly off to see Kevin.

'Excuse me, Gil,' I moved the phone away. 'Olivia broke her thumb,' I said softly to my wife. 'If you wait a second, you can talk to her.'

Sterling didn't have a second.

Gil regretted not going with the girls, but Madison had said to leave them alone. 'I should know by now that "leave us alone" means—stay glued to them.'

'It wouldn't have made any difference,' I said. 'Olivia does what she wants before anyone can stop her.'

Gil said the ER doctors had given her painkillers. 'She's giddy now. But later tonight and certainly tomorrow she'll be uncomfortable.' He expected to have Olivia home midday tomorrow.

Ninety minutes later, Sterling returned, her mood restored. I watched her in the mirror as she took off her earrings, and her face squinted a reflected warning against any questions.

The next morning, when I returned from running, Sterling was up, dressed, and leaving to meet Kevin. They were attending *another* auction. She'd be home after dinner.

'Just so you know,' I said, 'when Olivia gets home in a few hours, she'll be in pain.'

'Well, don't coddle her. She brought this on herself.'

That afternoon, ugly sleet poured down. Gil carried in Olivia's wet bags and removed his boots. Olivia whined and cried when I helped her out of her jacket. I asked her to sit down so I could undo her laces, but she ignored me and clomped into the TV room.

Gil said, 'A broken thumb is maddening. It makes everything—washing, getting dressed, even moving around—difficult if not impossible.'

As he was leaving, Olivia called out, 'Daddy, take care of me!'

I couldn't recall her ever saying anything like that.

Sterling stormed in after dinner and, seeing our daughter on the couch, said, 'How does payback for stupidity feel?'

'Sterling—' I warned.

'What?'

'Let me show you the X-rays.'

She ignored me and stood over Olivia, who asked her to move aside. She was blocking *The Wizard of Oz*.

'Don't tell me what to do! Instead of lying around right now, you should be studying bus schedules, young lady. Because I don't have the time to drive you to the doctor's.'

'What bus schedules?' I took Sterling's arm and, when she shook me loose, I took it again and pulled her into the downstairs study. 'Olivia needs to see a hand orthopedist. If her thumb isn't properly aligned, it won't heal right. Without physical therapy, she could lose mobility.'

'All right, you drive her.'

'Fine.'

Olivia's treatment consisted of six weeks in a hard cast. X-rays to check on the healing process. Three weeks in a brace, during which Olivia would go for physical therapy at the hospital.

Sterling remained furious: furious that Olivia had broken her thumb, furious that she felt sorry for herself, and furious that she exerted herself as little as possible.

And, in case I was wondering, Sterling hadn't forgiven my lapse in judgment regarding Amanda.

'Lapse in judgment. What does that mean?'

'It means you shouldn't have bought her clothes!'

'I've apologized to you. If you're still angry about it, do what you will—to me. Do not speak of it to Amanda or Olivia. And do not ask that Amanda pay us back.'

'Is that what you think? That I'm upset about the cost?'

'Then what?'

She wouldn't say.

March 2014

When Olivia wasn't in school, she lounged on the couch, watching movies or TV.

One night, Sterling yanked her up, saying, 'You'll be sorry, you little brat. Six weeks of playing couch potato. See where that gets you.'

I separated my wife and daughter and pulled Sterling into the study again. 'You cannot talk to her like that! Whatever your personal frustrations are, all she did was act on her usual overconfidence.'

'You have no idea what my frustrations are.'

'Then tell me.'

Sterling walked away.

April 2014

On the first warm weekend, I ran farther south along the aqueduct after my regular Sunday loop and found the winding road to our 'dream property.' The structure—which Sterling had called a split-level eyesore—remained untouched, though we'd gotten knockdown permission nearly a year ago.

When I asked Sterling why no progress had been made, she acted peeved and defensive. There had been backups for new demolition equipment. The electricians were on strike. And the men who were supposed to lay the foundation were building condominiums upstate.

She had quit playing golf and tennis and hadn't hosted (or, to my knowledge, attended) a party since before the financial crash. More and more frequently, she phoned me at work, saying she'd be home late.

One night she said that Kevin had Broadway tickets to a Eugene O'Neill play.

'You know, Sterling, I like Eugene O'Neill as much as the next man.'

'Oh, you do not.' She laughed in a way that sounded as if she might cry.

*

Olivia's cast came off and her doctor manipulated her thumb, moving it back and forth, asking, 'Does this hurt?'

'Does this?'

Everything hurt.

After being fitted for a brace, she was scheduled to attend physical therapy three times a week. After the first week, I learned she had skipped the second and third sessions. Because, she said, instead of meeting professional athletes at the sports clinic, she had to roll Play-Doh into little balls with a bunch of old people.

'If you keep your appointments,' I said, 'you could be all done in three weeks.'

Amanda offered to walk to the hospital with her. More than once, Olivia told me, they had stopped at a tattoo place on the way. The man let them look at the designs but wouldn't tattoo them until they were eighteen.

'But Daddy, I bet if you were with me, he'd do it.'

I laughed. 'What do you want inked and where?'

'That's the big question,' she said.

June 2014

Olivia didn't do well on her Regents exams, and the teacher requested a conference. Sterling and I sat in undersized chairs at eight in the morning. Sterling said, 'You must have noticed Olivia's been depressed. What did you expect?'

'I want you to know it's just a formality,' the teacher said. 'She can still start eighth grade in the advanced track. Then, in six weeks, we'll reconsider.'

'Reconsider what?' Sterling asked.

'The first six weeks are a probationary phase.'

Sterling was incensed—but, for once, on Olivia's behalf. It had been a long time.

When I arrived home from work that Friday, Sterling, Olivia, and Amanda were laughing in the kitchen.

*

School ended for the summer. Madison went to 'oboe camp' in Connecticut. Olivia made a face. 'The oboe's weird.'

Amanda was baby-sitting for twin three-year-old boys, Leo and Theo. Their nanny had quit without notice. The mother, who knew Amanda from the Y, had hired her until she could find someone able to drive and live with them. But Amanda and the twins liked each other so well that after two weeks, the parents offered Amanda a live-in job until school started. Olivia said the parents had a big play-set and lived a few blocks from the park, so during the summer, they didn't really need a driver, anyway.

'Amanda's getting paid a ton and only has to do, like, half the work she usually does. No cleaning, laundry, or grocery shopping. She makes breakfast and lunch but the mother makes dinner.' Olivia also said that when the twins' mother had asked Amanda's mother about her living there, Cheryl had said, 'Great timing!' Because Cheryl and her boss wanted to attend a golf tournament in Wisconsin, at a resort he had invested in.

'What about you?' I asked Olivia. 'Let's make of list of things you want to do this summer.'

'No, thanks, Daddy.' She slammed the front door on her way out to 'hang in town.'

That night, I asked Sterling if there were plans for Olivia's summer.

'We'll talk tomorrow,' she said. I wasn't sure if she meant she would talk to me tomorrow, or to Olivia, but I didn't press it.

The following evening, Sterling cozied up beside me on the living room couch, where I had been reading about the House of Borgia.

'I was thinking I'd take Olivia to visit my mother next week.'

'Next week? Ordinarily, the bank requires a few weeks' notice, but it shouldn't be a problem. I'm overdue for a vacation.'

She took the book and patted my leg. 'Just Olivia and me, this time. Mother, daughter, and grandmother.'

'Don't take Olivia. If you want to leave me, Sterling, let's talk about it. But don't take Olivia.'

'We're visiting my mother for a week!'

I didn't believe her. And when I told Olivia that I'd miss her, she shrugged. 'It's one summer, Daddy.'

The next evening, I arranged to take Olivia to a fancy restaurant for dinner. During the car ride to Millbrook, I gave her two gifts from Grand Central's Apple store: a new iPhone and some expensive headphones. 'Don't worry,' she said. 'I won't be gone forever.'

'I'll miss you, sweetheart.' We sat in the garden, away from other diners. While we waited for dessert, I took her right hand with mine, lifted our clasped hands so our elbows were on the table, and wiggled my thumb. 'Care to wrestle?'

'With my broken thumb?' Her face took on a dubious and particularly feminine expression I had never seen her make before.

'No longer broken,' I said. 'Let's see how strong you are.'

She giggled, her thumb pushing and pressing one way, mine the other. 'Don't let me win,' Olivia said.

I didn't. We called it a draw and laughed.

Tiramisu was her new favorite dessert. When she kissed my cheek, I smiled and squeezed her hand, hiding my anxiety.

The night before Sterling and Olivia were to leave, I lay awake, watching the moonlight traverse one wall and then another.

'Sterling, are you awake?' I saw her eyes open. 'Don't take Olivia from me. If you take her to Maine for the summer, you'll find reasons to stay…which is when you'll ask for a separation that's already occurred.'

'That's not true.'

'Are you in love with Kevin Dalton?'

'Don't be stupid. It's a lot of work to create a beautiful home. And he knows how to do it.'

'That wasn't my question. You've seen Broadway plays together. You've gone on trips upstate and charged expensive dinners to my account.'

'One play, Walter.'

'You and Olivia are everything to me.'

'I'm not everything to you.'

'Olivia is.'

'Stop worrying.' She kissed my neck. 'Nothing's changed.'

It had for me. I had broken through a wall of silence, addressing out loud a menace that had been hovering for too long. Sterling rolled back to sleep. But I couldn't. Saying what I loved and dreaded no longer frightened me. All my life, I had shut out premonitions and denied my real feelings. Why? Denial couldn't save me, or anyone, from the perils ahead.

Sterling had been harping on my state of mind since 9/11. More than a decade later, I discovered an open chamber beneath a thousand layers of wreckage and remnants of death—its lid blown off.

At least since Jimmy Quinn's death, if not earlier, our marriage had been mostly one of convenience. Sterling knew that I didn't care if she wanted to leave. But she also knew perfectly well that I cared about Olivia—that I *lived* for Olivia! She kept me from despair.

I accepted that Olivia would grow up and move away some day. But I was looking forward to her adolescence. Olivia was certain to raise hell. Since rising from her broken-thumb depression, she practically buzzed, as if her whole being were preparing to make trouble.

I simply hadn't foreseen—hadn't thought it possible— that Sterling would take her away. The two of them quarreled constantly. Olivia loved me, and even at her lowest, confided in me.

In fact, I wondered why she hadn't refused to go with Sterling. And then it came to me: Kaye. Olivia loved her Granny and Kaye loved Olivia. Kaye offered the type of feminine nurturing that Olivia needed and didn't get from Sterling.

As much as I would miss her, Olivia would thrive, being with Kaye. Further, I told myself, Olivia during adolescence wouldn't want to spend time with me the way she used to. Better for her to be with Kaye now than with her depressive father and distracted mother in a marriage that was falling apart. And Maine wasn't far; I would visit.

*

I always ran and went to work hours before Sterling and Olivia woke. But that morning, the morning they would pack their stuff in the Volvo and drive away, Sterling slipped out of bed while I showered. In the kitchen, wearing a white robe, she handed me a cup of freshly brewed coffee. 'Want breakfast?'

'No, thank you.'

I was halfway out the door when I turned around and begged Sterling again not to take Olivia.

'You're being silly,' she said.

I begged some more.

'Stop.'

Finally, crestfallen, I left in a hurry. I was no longer worried; I was certain. I had lost my family.

Eight

July 2014

I threw myself even deeper into work. Several years earlier, the bank had tapped me to design algorithms for high-frequency trading. The trading system had been generating small but steady profits. Now they had spiked. This triggered a frenzy for similar systems in other groups, which kept me in back-to-back meetings. My practice had always been to limit risk first, and for the moment, at least, the managing directors seemed to agree. When I spoke about letting profits accrue within a continuum of peaks and lulls, they apparently heard, 'limitless wealth.' Rampant greed stalked the meeting rooms like a feral beast.

Still, I liked the work, and it filled my waking hours. I decided to ask an unassuming associate to assist me. Denise Gold and I worked hard, eating in the late afternoons at our desks.

So, although I came home each night to an empty house, I wasn't unhappy. The first night, I fixed an omelet with four serrano chili peppers from my garden, drank a beer, and listened to Sterling's voicemail. She affected a blasé tone, talking about the drive up and the beauty of Maine's coast. She asked me to call back, but I couldn't stomach the charade of pretending we were merely taking a break from each other. The next night,

I heard her voice on the answering machine and listened only to make sure I didn't miss any news about Olivia.

After a few nights of this, Sterling's messages became plaintive. She said she wanted to talk about our 'situation.' I did not. Sterling began leaving messages at my office, which I ignored. At home, she would call late and demand that I pick up, and when I did not, she would sob and sniffle, promising to try again tomorrow.

*

Olivia disliked talking on the phone, and starting the day they arrived, she sent me texts. I responded, and our little chats kept her close to me. After two weeks she began mentioning Karl, a boy her age, fourteen, who loved Granny just like she did. Karl had a sailboat and he took Olivia exploring. In a grassy, shallow pond, they had discovered tiny frogs and millions of minnows.

Friday evenings, I no longer left the office early. I stayed late. Near the end of July, Olivia's incoming text sounded while I waited for the elevator.

Hey Daddy, Karl showed me a secret spot of velvety green moss Love, O

I texted, *O, does Karl call you that?*

Yep

I like it.

Soon she was referring to Karl as her boyfriend. Karl knew how to swan dive and could play Rachmaninoff on the piano.

On weekends, I ran, cleaned, and picked fresh lettuce, cucumbers, and herbs from our garden. My tomatoes that summer were the best crop yet. One Sunday afternoon, I was eating an excellent salad topped with feta cheese, anchovies, and vinaigrette dressing when I heard Kaye leaving a message on the answering machine, and picked up.

'Walter. Have you met this opportunist? This Kevin person?'

'Many times, yes.'

'And did you know he's renovating Bar Harbor's municipal building?'

'No. But it's not a complete surprise. His brother lives in Maine.'

'The man's a glad-hander! He's not welcome in my home. Susie's lost her mind.'

'Is Olivia there?' I couldn't help asking.

'She's at Karl's. She's fine. It's Susie who's up to no good. Not just with this opportunist, either. She undermines Olivia's self-esteem. She calls my beautiful granddaughter "fat." I've half a mind to boot her out.'

'Don't let me stop you,' I said, but Kaye drew a doleful breath.

'I didn't—' She paused, then said, 'I have to tell you—'

I saved her the distress of informing me that my wife would be staying with the glad-hander. 'It's not your fault. It's theirs, and, to a lesser extent, mine.'

Kaye hung up. She never said goodbye. It wasn't her style.

Even though school didn't begin for another month, I wrestled with the inevitability that Olivia would not be returning for eighth grade.

August 2014

My work continued to be almost gratifying. My systems spread across the bank's trading floors. Glen Engle congratulated me.

In the mornings, I woke with a spurt of optimism. I ran, worked, and slept better than ever before. My dreams filled me with sensations of renewal and freedom.

Then, one Friday evening, Denise and I were analyzing a new risk metric for top management when she asked if she could leave early. Everyone else on our floor had already left hours ago.

'Early? It's late. When I told you not to stay late unless you felt like it, I meant it. You never need to ask.'

She started to cry. Her girlfriend was leaving her.

'Take some time off, Denise. Find out if you can save your relationship.'

'We tried. It's not that I work too much. She found someone else.'

'I'm sorry,' I said. 'I've found that throwing myself into these puzzles offers kind of a buffer. But if I could, I'd find a less exhausting distraction.'

A few years older than me, and the only female quant, she cried for a while. I brought her tissues and a bottle of water. I asked how I could help her, and she swallowed a sad half-laugh. 'You can't help, Walter, but thanks for offering.'

A question appeared in her expression, flickered there, and disappeared.

'Were you thinking of asking me about how I've handled my wife leaving me?'

She said, 'No, no—' but when I laughed, she laughed, too, confessing, 'Yes.'

I told her that I missed my daughter, not my wife. Denise backed away from her own loss, saying that my daughter's absence must be much harder. I told her what we all know deep down but often forget: You can't compare losses or sorrows. My greeting-card wisdom embarrassed me, but Denise hugged me.

I was the only one at the bank who had ever shown any interest in her as a person.

'Go home,' I said. 'Take all the time you need.'

The second I was alone, a foreboding descended. My phone pinged—something from Olivia. She sent photos that she and Karl had taken of each other. He was a lanky, lank-haired boy with acne, and dark heavy-lidded eyes. In one photo, he had his arm around her, their heads touching.

Two days later, she texted to say that she had enrolled in Karl's school for eighth grade. She sent a link for the Connors Emerson School, which boasted of high academic credentials and a concern for ethical behavior. *It's not snotty,* O wrote, *like school there!*

Saddened, I texted, *Happy 4 U, O.* And I was. After months of lying listless on the couch, her hand in a cast, Olivia should live her life. She wasn't obligated to brighten mine.

September 2014

Right after Labor Day, Glen Engle arranged a meeting with me. Big news, he said. The chieftains were promoting me to managing director, putting me in charge of the New York City mortgage traders—fifty or so adrenaline-charged alpha males—in addition to the risk-management work I already was doing. Face-to-face in Glen's austere office, I thanked him—'What an opportunity.' Then I looked at him directly. 'Risk manager and head of trading in one? I haven't heard of that before.'

'We have no doubt,' Glen said, 'that you need a new challenge—a real challenge.'

I nodded and offered another 'thank you.' But I wanted him to know who I was. 'I've always worked with mathematical constructs. Not over-amped gamblers.'

He smiled. 'Take the job. You'll be surprised at how soon it becomes natural.' He added that, as a managing director, I could expect a bonus of five million—and that was in an ordinary year. (This one had been extraordinary.)

Aiming for measured enthusiasm, I said, 'Five million dollars—a year.'

'Minimum,' he said. 'Your skills are renowned. But it's your composure that will make the traders listen to you. They're used to running all over people. But when they stand toe-to-toe with a man who won't back down, they'll do as he says.'

I finished the day's work, taking care not to hurry. On the train, I thought about how there was no need to tell the wife who had left me. No need to tell anyone. The additional millions of dollars didn't scare me. Over several years, if I invested well, I could set up a charitable foundation. Running my own foundation for a cause I cared about would be work I *liked*.

But they had me pegged as someone I was not. Calm and steady on the outside—yes. But I didn't know how to manage people who cannot manage themselves. More to the point, I hated giving orders to another person.

Of course, had I been ten years older with less time remaining to make my name, I might have gone for it. But I was only thirty-three and still hoped to achieve something of merit. I wasn't aggressive. I wasn't mean. And I didn't want to be.

Not long after the cleaning staff finished, I was pushing the button to the elevator when I remembered my phone. Finding it on my desk, I saw that Olivia had sent me a photo of herself on a sailboat. *Hey, Daddy. Karl took this! He says I'm gorgeous! Isn't that silly?*

Not to me, it wasn't. Within the past two months, my daughter had developed curves even her father had to acknowledge as gorgeous.

The next thing I knew, I was perusing the mortgage bundles for the first time in months. I browsed through files from Florida. The raw material of mortgage-backed securities was delivered to me in rough bundles every week but, ordinarily, I had no reason to look at them. The information was online. But just skimming through these Florida mortgages, I sensed blatant fraud: loan documentation that smacked of NINJAs (No Income, No Job, No Assets). Less than seven years after the crash and low-level bankers were already back to the insane game—just to bulk up bonuses, which would have been fat enough without resorting to fraud. By the time these inflated bonuses came in, the poor borrowers would have defaulted on their homes in Florida. True, nobody at the bank was initiating the swindle, but unless I was wrong, we *were* peddling it.

Tomorrow I would track down the sources. And this time, instead of looking the other way, I would do what decency demanded.

*

At home, I parked in the garage and stepped outside. The air was oppressive, humid, and still hot. Clouds covered everything except for the new moon. Amanda's house was dark—I hadn't seen her all summer. School must have started last Tuesday. Yet there was no sign of her.

In the stuffy kitchen, I drank a glass of tap water and considered dinner. But I wasn't hungry enough to expend energy preparing something. Upstairs, I undressed and showered in gloom. After drying off as much as I could in the humidity, I stepped into a pair of briefs before lifting the curtain. Now the light in Amanda's bedroom shone. Perhaps she had moved a lamp, because her bedroom's bright glow bounced off the asphalt and seemed to pool at my feet, causing me to drop the curtain.

In bed that night, I kept falling in and out of consciousness. Even half awake, I felt exposed. Finally, sometime after two, I rose and slapped cold water on my face. The previous year, the barber had talked me into growing my hair, and now it fell in a wave that just cleared my eyebrow. At first Sterling had liked it. Then, she didn't. In the bathroom's fluorescence, my black hair took on a blue sheen.

Back beneath the sheet, I listened to the wind stirring outside. It sounded like indiscernible murmuring, the muffled voices of all who had left my life.

Later, a crack of lightning woke me. Rain beat hard against the windows. I rose and checked that they were all closed. I lay awake while the storm became a drizzle. At four, I quit watching the walls, gave up trying to sleep, and showered. Half an hour later, I heard a car coming up the hill, threw on a T-shirt, and grabbed my raincoat from the downstairs closet. The Jeep Wrangler pulled into Amanda's driveway. I dashed out the door to speak to Cheryl Jonette.

In the last shades of night, I hopped over puddles. Beads of water ran from my hair. I rapped my knuckles on Cheryl's car window. She stared straight ahead at the slowly rising garage door.

I rapped her window again. 'Ms. Jonette, a word.'

The window lowered and the garage light spilled onto my bare, wet shins.

'Is something wrong?' she asked.

'I heard your car and seized the moment. As they say.' My fake smile tightened.

'I wasn't able to be here last week when Amanda started eighth grade. I'm here now.'

'Did she tell you that Olivia's in Maine, staying with her grandmother?'

'When did that happen?'

'A recent development.' I took a deep breath, but couldn't bring myself to elaborate.

'Well, Amanda can fend for herself.'

'Your child is alone up here. Now that Olivia's away.'

Sighing, she got out of her car and stood uncomfortably close to me. Unlike Amanda, with her burnished skin and huge wide-set eyes, Cheryl's skin was slack and her eyes were small and narrow. Even in her business heels, she was shorter than her daughter, but she held herself as if to intimidate. Her dull, saggy face tilted up, fixed on mine.

'What do you mean, she's alone? You're here.'

'I mean no one is taking care of her.'

'If you're threatening to call some agency, Mr. Mitchell, I'll fight you to the death. And I'll win. Our congressman is my good friend.'

Congressman? I didn't laugh, didn't even blink. 'Call me Walter, please. I would never go against your wishes. But look at how isolated Oak Grove Point has become. A few families at street level, and then only Amanda—and me—up here.'

In the watery limbo before dawn, I assumed my calmest aspect. 'I want to be helpful.'

'You mean, you'll check on her?' Cheryl's face became a flat but eager mask. 'Can I tell her to phone you in case of an emergency?'

'Amanda knows she can do that. But you might tell her to call me if she ever needs anything.' Fingering the inside of my raincoat for a business card, I explained that I worked long hours, downtown. I showed her the card, pointing out the phone numbers, including my cell, and my email. 'If I'm unavailable, Amanda should leave a message.'

'Excellent.' Cheryl extended her hand and shook mine enthusiastically.

*

In my midtown office before the market opened, yesterday's dismay slid toward horror as I tracked down the mortgage sources. Brokers in Florida were passing corrupt deals onto us by the hundreds. My group was repackaging them almost like money launderers.

I phoned Glen Engle, who misheard my mention of Florida as a vacation request. 'Just the thing,' he said, 'before stepping into your new role here.'

'That's not it,' I said. 'I glanced at the raw mortgage files last night and mistakes—or frauds—from Florida kept jumping out at me.'

'Troubling,' he said. 'We'll correct the situation in February. Now's not the time.'

'I realize people have already used these to boost their bonuses, but waiting five or six months is sowing misery—in Florida, and eventually here as well.'

'I'm not defending the practice. But there's good reason to wait.'

'Personally, I find it unpalatable.'

'Unpalatable, I like that. If you can learn to wait, you could be running this place before you're forty.' He paused and cleared his throat. 'Walter, don't worry. We'll take care of this early next year.'

'I won't look the other way, not again.'

Another pause. 'All right, don't. Hold onto what you've found, but put it aside until February. For now, leave it alone.'

'I'm going to redo our latest products. Do you have a moment to see me today?'

'Don't do this, Walter.'

'I refuse to participate in ruining more people's lives.'

He cleared his throat a second time. 'Don't say that again and we'll forget this conversation.'

'I cannot allow this.'

'Fuck you, then! Be here at three.'

Half an hour before our scheduled meeting, Glen's boss, the bank's number two, phoned to offer me a leave of absence. 'Glen said six months off should satisfy you.'

'Thank you, but no,' I said.

At precisely three, Glen's assistant ushered me through the door. She offered to bring coffee or tea, hot or cold. But Glen said, 'That's all right, Heather. We have everything we need.'

I sat in one of two chairs facing his desk, a file balanced on my lap. He got up from his desk and sat in the chair next to mine, adjusting it so that he faced me. I handed him the file. After skimming its contents, he glanced at me, frowned, and then gestured—not quite drawing a palm down his face but indicating exactly that—with a sad turn of his hand. 'May I keep this?' Glen held up the file.

'I'd prefer it. And you have my word—I won't speak of this again.'

'I know that. And you have my word. But it won't help.'

'I know that.'

Glen Engle stood up, and then we parted in haste and small sorrow.

*

Pushing those mortgages in Glen Engle's face was akin to handing in my resignation. Why did I do it? Partly because preying on the poor really does outrage me. The last time brokers had targeted the destitute, the whole economy crashed.

But I can't deny that fear of failure played into it as well. I knew I wasn't cut out to run a department of mortgage traders. All my life, I had surpassed expectations with ease. Failing as the head of mortgage trading would show Bank of America and Glen Engle that their estimation of me had been wrong.

So, instead I chose a way to save face. Money wasn't a problem for me. I had more than enough to take my time finding a benign or possibly even an honorable career.

The next few days would be unpleasant as the bank decided what to do with me (though the outcome was certain), but I would continue to go into the office until they fired me. Requesting my fate be delivered via FedEx would make me a coward.

That Wednesday, I left the office at five, falling in with the first wave of rush-hour commuters. Senselessly relieved to find my home unchanged, I undressed and sipped Dewar's with ice.

Wandering upstairs, I soon found myself standing by the bedroom window. With the curtain in one hand, I rattled the ice in my empty glass with my other—and recalled how Amanda's bedroom light had cast a pool at my feet.

The thought disturbed me, and I dressed quickly: jeans, a fresh shirt, belt, socks, and shoes. My glass needed a refill. There, on the bedside table, stood the open bottle of Scotch. So uncharacteristic of me not to have put it away. So convenient as well. I filled the glass. A text sounded.

But it wasn't from Olivia!

Seeing that it was from Amanda, I swallowed a searing gulp.

Hi! Mom said to check in or else you'll call the cops!

I couldn't help smiling at this and tapped a squinting emoticon along with, *Your mother doesn't know we're already friends.*

In reply, she sent: *Promise me that will always be our secret pact!*

Her intimate demand pierced me like a dart. Should I be texting with a twelve-year-old girl, not my daughter? Then she added: *Please, swear nobody else will ever know!*

Miraculously, Amanda's little addition scattered my guilty fears. She needed a protector. *Okay,* I typed, and added a thumb and forefinger touching. Then *it's no secret that I've always liked you. Sterling and Olivia know it.*

She wrote back, fast: *Liking each other is different from being secret friends!*

My fears started to return. But I reminded myself that her mother had encouraged this. And that all girls love secrets. A girl like Amanda, deprived of attention, might very well *need* this secret.

Our secret friendship is sacred, I texted. *So let's check in with each other.*

A goofy smiley face and what looked like a tiny star circling a larger one appeared in response.

Clicking off the phone, I drained my glass. I shook it, sipped again for any last whiskey clinging to the ice, and set it down before lifting the window curtain.

Behold: Amanda was standing within the window frame. Her hair looked wild, as if she'd hung her head over the edge of her bed and jumped up. Smiling, she pointed to her shirt, one that I had bought for her. Bright orange-pink, with a big brown monkey's face on it.

Then, she disappeared from view.

*

No one stopped me from attending the next morning's investment committee meeting. I spoke at uncharacteristic length. Without prompting, I showed my well-grounded projections for a rebound in the housing market. I advocated leveraging all that we could.

Then, to avoid small talk or worse, I waited until everyone left the conference room before closing my laptop and standing up. Neal Patel, one of the senior investment bankers, was waiting in the hallway and matched me stride for stride as we marched toward the elevator. 'I spoke with Glen. Excellent work, catching those Florida properties. I'll be happy to give you a reference.'

'Without mentioning that I yelled *Fire!* much too soon?'

'A superior reference, Walter. You're smarter than anyone here.'

In the elevator, he took out a card and made a note on the back of it. He slipped it to me and said, 'Tell the headhunters to call me at that number.'

I thanked him, wishing I'd gotten to know him better.

Friday morning, my time had come. I knew it and took a last look from my corner office, Times Square in one direction, Bryant

Park in the other. Then, I walked through the department. At each doorway—all open—I paused for a moment. Most people didn't look up. Denise had waited until this week to take me up on my suggestion that she go on vacation. I was grateful that she wasn't there to witness my exit. I had emailed Glen Engle recommending her as a replacement for me, but he responded quickly that Joe Schumacher already had the job. A poor choice, I believed, yet I stopped by Joe's office anyway to congratulate him. When he didn't respond to my greeting, I commended the back of his head and wished him great success.

Marjorie, who had been my secretary for seven years, told me that Claudia Hirsh in HR wanted to see me at 10:30.

'I wonder what she's doing now.'

'Perhaps,' Marjorie said, 'the wait is to encourage impossible hope, which is really just another form of torture.'

'Yes, but what's a bit more?'

Marjorie and I had enjoyed working together. 'Best of luck,' she said.

'Yes, you too.'

She had *The New York Times* on her desk. I asked if she had started the crossword puzzle. She said she never attempted it on Friday. 'Do you want a pencil?'

Taking the newspaper, I pulled a pen from my pocket and she smiled. She'd miss me. Likewise.

I waited on the fifteenth floor on a small couch outside Claudia Hirsh's office. I finished the puzzle in a matter of minutes. Last year, at the winter holiday party, Claudia had gotten so drunk she couldn't balance on her high heels. So she'd taken them off. It had been snowing lightly. Standing beside me in her stocking-clad feet, she had asked me to carry her outside.

'Pardon me?'

She didn't want to ruin her shoes. Her feet were freezing.

Claudia was a big woman. Holding her upright while trying to hail a taxi had been tricky. I was strong, of course, and even stronger in recent years, lifting weights in the company gym. But she was cumbersome on the slippery pavement. Later, she blamed me for causing her to lose her shoes. Supposedly, I had 'dumped' her into the taxi. I apologized but refused to reimburse her for the thousand-dollar designer heels.

'Good to see you,' she said now, opening the HR department's outer door. In her glass office among a dozen other glass offices, she read aloud a note from Glen Engle. My tenure at Bank of America had made a difference. My work during the financial crisis remained unparalleled. My contributions had been first rate.

Claudia cleared her throat and said, 'All right. As for severance—' I would receive my full salary for another year and—this wasn't standard—next year, a bonus equal to what I would have received had I remained head of risk management through December. I signed several documents and two burly young men in suits escorted me from the building.

I knew the protocol. Often, these security guards wear uniforms, including handguns in holsters. So my walk of shame was relatively gentle. Nevertheless, it had a surreal quality as if I were watching myself on a black-and-white screen full of glitches.

The Metro-North train at midday was virtually empty. I sat in one of the seats that faced another, the way Jimmy Quinn and I always had. Those days weren't just long gone—they no longer even felt real to me.

Out of nowhere, a disheveled, obese woman set an enormous Duane Reade bag in the seat next to mine and settled herself opposite me. I angled my knees away from hers. The train rolled from the station into the light. She lowered her head to the empty seat beside hers and vomited. Without a thought, I reached out with a handkerchief, which she didn't use to wipe her mouth but to cover her sick.

'Excuse me,' I said and, nimbly extricating myself, quickly proceeded to the next car. Alone in that section of the train, I stared at the Hudson River. When the train stopped at my station, I completely forgot the Mazda parked in the lot, the municipal permit stuck on the windshield. Mechanically, I trudged up the steep hill of Main Street, proceeding a mile on Broadway before turning right into the enclave and up Oak Grove Point's spiraling lane.

I sat on the middle step of the wrap-around front porch, which Sterling had added to the house two years ago. The sun moved across the sky. When it reached the treetops, I found my keys and opened the front door.

Upstairs, I thought about going for a run—only to realize I was weak with disgrace. I undressed and shoved my expensive suit, shirt, socks, and underwear into one bag; my shoes, belt, tie, and cuff links into another. I would never wear them again, but cleaned, pressed, and polished, some other guy might use them to get a decent job. I threw my watch in after the cuff links. Then, in the shower, I scrubbed off the residue of cold sweat. But a raw indignity stuck. Clean but humiliated, I lay on the bed, aware of a perverse freedom hovering above me. I had never regretted blasting through my education and starting my adult life ahead of the usual timeline, but by now my youthful plans for law school no longer aroused my interest. I needed a few days before confronting the question of, What next? Standing and pacing, I drifted to the window. When I lifted the curtain, coincidence and fate converged:

Facing my house, Amanda throws her backpack on the ground. She tears off a denim jacket and tugs at the white sweater covering pointy little buds on her chest. She stands on tiptoe and extends her arms from the shoulders. I watch her turn cartwheels up and down the asphalt between our houses. Her arms and legs remain straight and symmetrical. She rolls hand to hand, foot to foot, her long tawny hair flying. Her arms and legs trade weight and balance in circling precision. Up the street six times; down the street six times. Face flushed, hair tangled, she stands opposite my window and looks up. She smiles and waves at me. Alarmed, I grab the curtain to cover my naked body before waving back. Then I fall backward into bed, where I struggle against terrible hopes and fears that are one and the same.

3. RATIOS AND PROPORTIONS

Nine

September–December 2014

By the clock I doze only eight minutes, but I wake refreshed, Amanda's cartwheels turning inside me. My cell phone rings.

'That was amazing,' Amanda says. 'Even before I got to the driveway, I knew you were there. I knew you were watching me. Has that ever happened to you? You know someone's close and watching you even though you can't see them.'

'Yes. It's a coincidence.'

'It was more than that. 'Cause I did those cartwheels especially for you—like we were reading each other's minds!'

'Ordinarily, you know, Amanda, I don't get home until 9:00 at night.'

'Really. So it's really amazing, then, that you were here, watching me at 4:30!'

'Yes, except today was a bad day for me.'

'A bad day? Oh no! Want to come over?'

When I fail to answer, she says, 'Or I could come there.'

'Amanda, I need to hang up; I've got another call. Can you call me later?'

'Later, alligator.'

Christ. That poor love-starved child! When she sensed me watching, she reacted with pure joy. In her bittersweet, evanescent

103

childhood, she offers an open heart. I'm here. No one else is. The bedroom phone was ringing and has gone to voicemail. Hearing Sterling's voice, I tap the mute button.

After a moment, I hear Amanda outdoors again. She's cartwheeling or skipping beneath the window. She's either right below me or across the pavement, tossing her glistening hair around. And why not? That's what girls do at her age. Before adulthood demands self-conscious purpose. Amanda is enjoying more heady freedom than she's likely to experience again for decades, if ever.

I burrow back under the bedcovers and imagine the sensation of balancing upside down and tipping from one hand to the next, then hand to foot, and then upright. I'm only half asleep but dreaming: Amanda and I are rolling in parallel spheres. We roll and collide, and our spheres merge. Free of conscious cause and effect, we simultaneously rise together, weightless, defying gravity in a terrifically gratifying release.

Hours after dark, my cell phone startles me awake again. Her voice is quick and bright. 'You said to call again. So I am.'

Instantly alert, I sit up and grasp for something to say. What I suggest strikes me as perfectly appropriate until I hear myself say it. 'Tomorrow's Saturday. Are you free for lunch?'

Amanda gasps in happy surprise. 'Yes.'

*

Most Saturdays, I sleep until 8:00. But today I wake at 5:00, as if it were a workday, which for me doesn't exist anymore. It's drizzling and foggy, but just before dawn I'm on the wooded trail, running fast, taking care to avoid slippery leaves.

Several times, even though I know Olivia's happy in Bar Harbor, I've pressed her to come home for a visit, because

I miss her. But she loves it there. Her new school has no cliques. And she doesn't want me to visit her, a sad mystery I've tried and failed to solve. Even phone calls are too much to ask of her. A daily text—or if I'm lucky, a quick flurry of them—that's all.

I should be stricter. I know that. My failing as a father was the same trait that sealed my fate at work: I excel at self-discipline but have trouble imposing rules on anyone else.

When I realized Olivia was staying in Maine because she wanted to, and not because of Sterling's drama, I set up a PayPal account for her. Money for clothes, music, and movies. I didn't want Kaye paying for her, and I certainly didn't want her depending on Sterling's unstable moods.

Unfortunately for me, Olivia's move to Maine is a milestone in her progression away from childhood, away from me.

Reaching the park's first steep incline, I sprint, spurred on by the truth, which I can't outrun: Amanda fascinates me and becomes more alluring every day. If only Olivia were home, I wouldn't need to worry about my feelings for Amanda. I would be her best friend's father, and nothing more.

As it is, I keep slipping back to my dream of us encircling each other and floating away. Even in my subconscious, I have not—not yet!—strayed too far from decency. I cannot, will not, ignore her. So, here and now, I vow to treat Amanda Jonette with the utmost scrupulousness.

The trees drip. A scant shower hangs in the air but the sun winks through the clouds, making the peak-color foliage shimmer: gold, red, and purple. I race up the highest crest. And, whoa!—hop right and then left between piles of horseshit.

At the house, I drink a liter of water and carry a cup of coffee upstairs. My new emails include a video of Olivia and her friend

Karl playing on the bay. They recorded each other and have made a split screen of the videos. At the end, Karl's holding a phone at arm's length. His other arm rests on Olivia's shoulder.

I'm in and out of the shower, a towel wrapped around my waist, and assembling my shaving things by the sink when my cell phone rings. Without checking to see who it is, I pick up and Sterling boo-hoos into my ear.

'Stop that or I'm hanging up.'

'What the hell happened, Walter?'

'You mean my job.'

'I can't believe it. What were they thinking?'

'Who told you?'

'A woman I used to know at Lehman. By yesterday afternoon, you were topic number one on the alumni circuit.'

'This woman found you in Maine?'

'My cell number hasn't changed. Last night, I left you fifteen voicemails. If you didn't pick up this morning, I was going to ask Mother to try. *Why didn't you call me?*'

'Because I'm not ready to discuss whether our separation is ripe for divorce. But when that times comes, I'll be sure to let you know.'

'God! If only you'd talk to me, Walter! You'd know—no divorce.'

'You sound awfully certain of that. How's the separation going? I gather from Kaye that you and Kevin are living together.'

'He rented a carriage house. And yes, I'm staying there. Mother managed to make me miserable every day.'

'Poor "Susie."'

'What are your plans? You need to rent an office. You can't stay at home—people will suspect. Go to an office every day in a building with several other offices. Nothing has changed except that now you're working for yourself. Day trading or consulting. Oh, and work your contacts. Didn't someone at D. E. Shaw call you last year?'

'I won't work for a hedge fund.'

'It's an investment bank.'

'Doesn't matter. I'm not cut out for it.'

'D. E. Shaw likes quants,' she says.

'I'm not interested, Sterling. Not anymore.'

'Probability—isn't that your forte?'

'I'm adept in mathematics. But I'm not a risk-taker.'

'You know people. You've done favors for them. At least network.'

'I lost my job because I don't beat my chest and shout about being the king of the jungle. And after hours, when people act chummy, my timing's off. I laugh at the things everyone takes seriously. And worry about things they think are jokes.'

'Really. Well, here's some advice: Being unemployed is *not* a joke.'

'I haven't stopped chuckling since they walked me out.'

She says, 'Hold on,' and I hear her murmuring to Kevin.

'Tell him he can go ahead with your dream house.'

It sounds as if she's closing a door. '*Our* house,' she says. 'I don't want to lose you. This is just a temporary thing.'

'It's tedious, Sterling. But I want you to know—we have the money. I plan to take some time off and explore my options, although I'll be surprised if I don't end up going to law school.'

'If you wait long enough, you and Olivia can go together.'

'I wouldn't mind that, but you would. Because, my God, what will people think? Tell them to think this—we have enough money; no need for more.'

'Walter, there's no such thing as "enough money."'

'Don't believe it. I'm done.'

'You're not done with me, though. We'll get back together. I just don't know when.'

'If that's really what you think, then what you're doing with Kevin is extremely risky. Some people work very hard to stay in love and cannot.'

She says, 'That's why we're taking a break. So we don't have to resort to trying,' but there's a waver in her voice.

'Anything but that! A bit of consideration, however, might be refreshing. Don't call to cry on my shoulder. It's obnoxious.'

*

The morning drizzle becomes a downpour while I'm driving into town to buy fresh bread, good cheese, and olives for lunch with Amanda. On the way home, thunder and lightning stop traffic, and the cars inch along.

By contrast, the kitchen is warm and colorful. Big white daisies in a red ceramic pitcher, a blue checked tablecloth, and white china plates—I've gone overboard but Amanda will appreciate it. Hearing her enter the garage, I open the side door. She's luminous in the darkness where Sterling used to park her Volvo. Amanda bends sideways, wringing water from her hair.

'Come inside and get dry.'

She stays in the corner and steps out of squishy flip-flops, apologizing for dripping all over the place. Her jeans are rolled up just below her knees and held there with safety pins. Peeling off her saturated hoodie, she says, 'I lose umbrellas after a few minutes. My mom says if I go without, I just might learn. But I don't. I never learn.'

She's shivering and the hoodie she's holding drips so much water that a small puddle forms.

'Here, let me take that. I'll hang it in the laundry room.' I bring a towel for her feet and another for her hair. 'Why don't you borrow one of Olivia's sweaters?'

Like a gazelle, Amanda bounds upstairs, and I go about setting our places at the table, salad dishes with arugula, cherry tomatoes cut in half, and tiny wrinkled black olives.

She returns wearing a burgundy-colored sweater Olivia outgrew. She's covered her bare feet and legs with red-and-white striped, over-the-knee socks. Her damp hair is fixed in a loose braid.

We're having toasted cheese sandwiches prepared with a long-handled press held over the gas flames. I've buttered the inside of each metal square and cut the bread to fit. And I arrange the strips of Gruyère so the sandwiches will be thick but not too gooey.

'Are those things for camping? Like making s'mores?'

'They might be antiques. Sterling's mother had them in Maine.'

I fasten the presses shut and pass one to Amanda, who holds it too close to the burner.

'Let me take over while you make the drinks. Sparkling water's in the refrigerator, and if you don't mind, I like a dash of pomegranate juice in mine.'

'I love pomegranate juice. Is it okay if I make mine half and half?'

'Certainly.'

Setting the drinks by our plates, she sits at the kitchen table, which was constructed to fit flush with the big bay window. The rain beats hard against the glass. She turns sideways, watching me at the stove where I'm almost finished.

'Walter, what do you think about Persephone?'

The rims of my ears burn, hearing her say my name. 'Persephone? Because of pomegranate juice?'

'Yeah, I guess. The devil feeds her three pomegranate seeds in hell, which means she has to spend half the year with him and half with her mother. Which do you think was worse?'

'Her mother was supposed to be very nice. The goddess of summer and bountiful crops.'

'Don't answer if you think I'm rude to ask, but do you believe in hell?'

'Here you are.' I pry one toasted sandwich from the contraption onto her plate and the other one onto mine. 'Why would I think that was rude?'

'Some people get annoyed.'

'Not me. No living person knows what happens after death. Many people say they know, because their belief is so strong. But it's still just a belief.'

'So…nobody knows!' She beams at me. I'm embarrassed by my preachy explanation, but that's not the reason I look away. Up until a mere three months ago, Amanda was always shy around me. Now she's all high spirit.

She lifts her sandwich and I can't help warning her not to burn her tongue. She sips her red drink, her eyes wide and teasing over the top of her glass, a flicker of pretend obedience. Eating a forkful of salad, Amanda shakes her head—she's never tasted anything like it. 'I try to make salads, but they never turn out right.'

'You shouldn't have to fix salads by yourself. You shouldn't have to prepare all your meals and eat them alone. How often does your mother visit?'

Amanda takes a dainty bite from the toasted sandwich. Eyes closed, she presses her lips together. 'So delicious!' Eyes open, she says, 'You saw her…on Wednesday, right?' Amanda takes a bigger bite and then, 'Cheryl swears it's every month. But something always comes up with her boss. If I'm lucky, I see her every other month. Sometimes every three months. Can I tell you a secret?'

'That's why we have a pact.'

'My mother wants me to act like we're so close that it doesn't matter when or for how long she's here. She believes that and expects me to believe it. But I don't believe it enough.' Amanda falls quiet for a second and looks at me. 'We have an oath, right?'

'I swear to God.'

"Cause I try not to talk about her. If the wrong person hears that my mother leaves me alone, they're like—shocked! Obviously, I say, I was joking. Like, I can't believe they took me literally.'

'Do you know the saying, "Damned if you do, damned if you don't"?'

'It's Cheryl's favorite! You're never going to win. Nobody's going to believe you, so stand back and shut up.'

She takes small bites of her sandwich. The cheese is still warm, and she chews slowly, her eyelids slightly fluttering. She mock swoons, her head touching my shoulder. 'It tastes so good I might faint.'

'You won't faint.'

I nudge her until she's sitting straight in her own chair. 'Will you tell me if I yammer on about Cheryl? So I don't bore you.'

'You never bore me.' (I look away and swallow. I shouldn't have said that.)

She doesn't notice, though, and takes more tiny bites. I wonder if she knows that she's always enchanted me.

'I'd love it,' she says, 'if I could be honest and be guaranteed there'd be no intervention. On TV, they take the daughter away because the mother's an alcoholic or a drug addict or having a breakdown. Cheryl's not like that. But she's mean. And jealous.'

'Anything you tell me, Amanda, is our secret.'

She sips her drink. Her legs swing under the table. 'Maybe that's why I asked about Persephone. In myths, the girl goes to hell. Or gets swallowed alive. Or turned into a cow.'

Her fingers fly over her plate when she talks. And when she stops, she watches me. When I don't say anything, she continues: 'Did you know I was promoted to the advanced group this year? The teachers say they should have double-checked my score last year, because usually I test really high. But last year, I must not have been feeling well. Sometimes, I don't think about how I'm feeling. You know, unless it's so bad I can't get out of bed. Cheryl says I'm not a baby, that only babies need grown-ups to tell them when they're burning up and better lie down.

'I just like to complain, and if I complain too much, she drives off without leaving me any money. Her whole thing is, "Don't depend on anyone." But Cheryl's not exactly "Ms. Total Independence." She's been chasing after her boss forever, always convinced he'll marry her in a month or so. But things happen and their marriage goes on the back burner. She swears he really wants to marry her, though.'

Amanda leans into me. 'But how can she be so sure when she doesn't trust anyone?'

This insight surprises me. 'How did you figure that out?'

'I watch TV shows, or used to, that are all about love and trust. The characters talk and talk about it.' She dabs the napkin against her lips. 'Do you remember Jade?'

'I liked Jade. She cared about you.'

'She loved me and I loved her. Even Cheryl says so.' Amanda reaches under the table and I'm aware of her tugging at the over-the-knee socks. She straightens up and turns toward me. 'After Jade left, she used to call me from her new job—until Cheryl found out. Oh, wait! I learned something about my father. Not really, but kind of. 'Cause whenever I asked about him, Cheryl refused to answer. But on Wednesday, I asked again and she goes, "Here's the thing—" She'd been with this guy for a long time and something happened. She knew he was going to dump her. So, to get back at him, she took up with his friend. A few months later, they both dumped her. But I still think she must know which one's my father. Even back then, it was easy enough to find out. But she says they were both assholes, so it makes no difference. And, that I have to be independent.'

'Your mother's definition of independence is different from mine. Independence, I believe, means taking responsibility. You're free in that you decide for yourself. But every decision has consequences, which you accept and nurture.' I catch my index finger tapping the tabletop and stop it, but I can't stop myself from talking. 'If your mother doesn't trust people, I'm sure she has very good reasons for that. But they're not your reasons, Amanda. Nobody's born independent. And until you're legally an adult, you're Cheryl's most important responsibility. That you're able to take care of yourself is not a justification for Cheryl neglecting you.'

She gives me a look intended to remind me that I promised not to interfere. Yet I cannot help adding, 'You know your mother's limitations and you love her … But when the time comes that someone else loves you, and loves you romantically, make sure the person is ethical. You're smart and perceptive. You'll know who's trustworthy. Never let anyone take advantage of you—even if you like the person.'

Throughout my little lecture, I've been clearing the table and loading the dishwasher. Finished, the palm of my hand finds the crown of her head. She tilts back in her chair, her eyes seeking mine. Blood crashes and crests in my head. 'Want dessert, honey?' I ask, sitting down.

The accidental endearment sends me from the table again and into the living room, where I try to remember if I've ever called Olivia 'honey.'

Amanda tiptoes in and sits on the couch, across from the chair where I've landed. She pulls the huge Leonardo da Vinci book from the coffee table onto her lap. The cover is a glossy collage of his masterpieces, including *The Vitruvian Man*.

'Did you see *The Simpsons'* "Vitruvian Man" episode?'

I confess that I haven't. I ask if she's studied proportions in school.

'We're starting to. Ratios and proportions.'

I tell her about Leonardo's theory of the human body in relation to the universe. 'Cosmological and micro-logical.' Without thinking, I cross the room, sit beside her, and flip to the full illustration.

Amanda's voice drops to a whisper. 'He looks like he's going to cartwheel off the page.'

Momentarily stunned, I say, 'You're right. I never noticed that before.' Our two heads peer down at the picture.

I stand and take a step back, gazing at the exquisite girl who, as of today, has become a conscious obsession.

She asks if we can watch her favorite TV show, *The Real Miranda*. 'Olivia has them on DVDs. But she didn't love it like me.'

'Don't you have homework to do?'

'Of course, but today is Saturday.'

The rain continues to fall outside and the day is losing its light. I don't have the heart to send her home.

While I search through a jumble of DVD cases in one of Sterling's Navajo baskets, Amanda chatters about the pilot episode, which is where she thinks we should start. 'This girl Miranda moves from New York City to Ames, Iowa just before high school. And the first day of high school—in Iowa—she feels like the other kids have superpowers. Except maybe for this one girl, Iris, who befriends her. They collect evidence but can't prove anything.'

She asks if I have a favorite show.

'I don't watch much television.'

'Because you work so much?'

'Not anymore. I'm taking a hiatus.'

'Hiatus like a TV series?'

Murmuring yes, I find *The Real Miranda* and hold it up in ridiculous triumph.

Amanda giggles as I try various remotes.

We sit side by side on the low orange couch, which forces me into a half-supine position but isn't uncomfortable. Amanda's delicate fingers slowly rotate the DVD box.

'*The Real Miranda*,' she says, 'is full of references that I don't know. I look online, but the people on those forums make up shit—stuff, I mean. So, if you watch the first season with me, I'll be able to learn what I've missed. Someone said that the name Miranda comes from Shakespeare.'

'*The Tempest* has a character named Miranda, and I believe there's an Iris, too.'

The show opens with Miranda singing at her bedroom window. She's looking out and we're looking in at her. Amanda says that, instead of one recurring theme song, each episode has its own song. This one's about moving to Iowa. The second verse asks whether Iris has a superpower but doesn't know it.

Amanda swoops about the room, singing along. When the song ends, she looks at me, her hands covering half her face, her big round eyes gleaming into mine. A terrific urge to embrace her possesses me. To suppress it, I focus on the TV.

The actress playing Iris is quick and dark and moves like a ballerina. I ask if Amanda knows that Iris comes from Greek mythology, like Persephone.

'Really?'

'Iris represented the rainbow.'

'So cool.'

I nod like an idiot.

Amanda tries to recall when the kids in Iowa will first demonstrate their powers.

While saying this, she tucks her legs beneath her and sits on her feet—so she can drape her arm around my neck. 'Do you think it's better to be honest about being super-good at stuff even if it sounds like bragging, or better to act like you're ordinary when you're not?'

Staring at my shoes, I say, 'Best to be honest about your abilities and learn to recognize and appreciate other people's strengths and talents.'

'That's one of the theme songs,' she says, tilting back as she shifts position again. 'Everyone's unique but united.' Now she rests on one flank and slowly arcs her long legs and striped socks over my head before resting them in my lap.

Gently, I lift her legs off of me. Gently, I arrange her so that she's sitting up, feet on the floor.

'Why can't we curl up? I know you like me.'

'That's the problem. I like you too much.'

She moves to the extreme other end of the couch, crosses her arms, and twines her legs. Her indignation, and maybe embarrassment too, fills the air.

'A million times I've been told to keep away from strange men. And you're the only man on earth who isn't strange.'

'There's more to it, Amanda. You know that.'

'It's cold and raining. We're happy and cozy. Why can't we cuddle?'

'It's better if we don't, honey.' The endearment, which so upset me earlier, sounds exactly right now. In fact, from now on, whenever I have to deny Amanda anything, I'll sweeten it with 'honey,' which hurts no one.

*

She pouts and fidgets. The fine line I'm walking is no more substantial than a silken thread and I'm too far along to turn back. If I tried, she would take it as rejection. And besides, the mere attempt would send me into a free fall.

The pilot episode ends. Amanda clicks on a cartoon. Subdued, she says, '*Futurama*'s all reruns now, but I still watch it.'

Then, in an overreaction to distant lightning, she startles into the air, and ends up with her head resting on my chest. Tilting her chin, she asks, 'Okay?'

'All right.' She shifts her head higher. Her hair, mostly dry now, is coming loose from the braid. Strands fan across the front of my sweater and tickle my neck. She shifts again. I concentrate on remaining still.

For nearly an hour, I restrain myself—I cannot and will not touch her shoulder. I will not trace a finger from her delicate earlobe to the base of her throat. I ache everywhere. She wraps

117

an arm around me, her fingertips fluttering against my ribcage. I regulate my breathing but cannot slow my heartbeat, which pulses hard in my chest.

Finally, she sits up—and, thank God, moves to pick up the remote. She selects a sitcom punctuated by loud, abrasive commercials. When she sits down again, it takes all my self-control not to guide her head back to my chest. Music blares, and she cups her hands around my ear, whispering, 'Do you like this?'

Not for a split second do I imagine she's asking about the TV show.

'I like it so much that you must go home now.'

'But why? The show's not over.'

'Wait here and I'll get you some rain gear.'

I find a pair of red rubber boots Olivia has outgrown. 'Try these. No, keep the socks.' The waxy raincoat I lend her is too big. She makes a face at the hat but keeps it on nonetheless, her smirk irresistible and a bit forgiving.

'Once you're inside, honey, flick the lights, so I'll know you're safe.'

Ten

The next morning, Sunday, I return from my run and she's standing in her doorway as if waiting for me. Walking toward her, I ask, 'What are you doing up so early?'

'I don't know. I'm just awake.'

Reinforcing our roles as adult and child, I ask if she'll let me see her homework sometime.

Amanda's eyes widen. 'You want to?'

'I'm interested, yes.'

She smiles and says, 'How 'bout tonight after dinner?'

That wasn't my plan but it makes sense, so I spend the day cleaning the house and preparing tomato sauce for pasta. Fixating all the while on our lives being misaligned by two decades.

At the first dimming into evening, I stroll outside, listening to the mild September wind blow through the trees. They have grown considerably since we moved here, and now blend with the natural forest. This lends Amanda and me shelter, and isolates us from the rest of Oak Grove Point.

I hop onto the front porch and go inside. The phone rings. She breathes softly but cannot disguise her anxiety.

'Amanda, is that you?'

'Dinner's ready!' She bursts out with this so abruptly that I laugh without thinking.

'What's so funny? We're having hamburgers. Can you bring over some sparkling water and pomegranate juice?'

'But I made dinner for you.'

'No, please! I made dinner!'

'Amanda, it has to be at my house, or we cannot do it.' My words sound sharper than I intend.

'Come on, I vacuumed and everything.'

'If I enter your house, while you're there alone—well, I might seem like an intruder.'

'Do I seem like an *intruder* when I enter your house, and you're there alone?'

'I can't explain the difference, honey. But you must come here. I cannot go there.' To me, the difference is critical. Setting foot where she bathes and sleeps, wakes and dresses is forbidden. And after yesterday, maintaining my balance with Amanda has become life or death.

Perhaps five seconds pass.

'Walter, what's wrong?'

'What if we bring the meal to my house and eat in the dining room?'

She mutters in annoyance but agrees.

At Amanda's front door, I take a platter with two uncooked hamburgers and buns from her arms and remind her to bring her homework. She grabs a jacket and two notebooks.

Back in my kitchen, I review several pages of math functions while Amanda arranges the food on the counter. 'Excellent work.'

A shy smile and she asks if she can fix the same drinks as yesterday. I nod and turn to her weekly journal.

'We're supposed to write about our families,' she says. 'But I write whatever I want. The teacher said fine before I even finished explaining…'

She trails off and I lose myself in her journal, which describes yesterday's thunderstorm as a flashy, just-passing-through kind of guy, who deliberately vanishes the moment the grass and the trees, the earth, and even the sky want more.

While I broil the hamburgers with scallions from my garden and toast the buns, she sets the dining room table. I suspect she bought the most expensive ground beef she could find: sirloin. I slice a just-picked tomato and cut a crisp bell pepper into strips. 'Want a piece of cheese melted on top?'

'No, thanks. But do you have any brown mustard?'

I smile at her and spoon it into a tiny flat bowl with a matching spoon. It's nearly 8:00 pm by the time we sit down.

I light Sterling's entire collection of candlesticks and the room glows like a church. Amanda's eyes are dazzling in the candlelight and she whispers, 'So romantic, Walter.'

In my mind, I hit hard against moral rock-face and soon reverse my earlier resolution not to sit on the couch with her and watch TV. Amanda needs the warmth and reassurance of human connection. If the brief, silken contact between her skin and mine stokes anything improper in me, I swear she will never know—no matter what.

For, as well as anyone, and certainly better than most, I know the toll of being required to fend for yourself too soon. It would be wrong for us to live parallel lives, performing similar motions inside our houses. If I were to fail to give this child the consideration she's due, it would be criminal.

But my reasons are far from altruistic. Without Amanda, life would feel grim and stale. Without her bright tenor, I'd fall flat.

*

Employed or not, I wake every day at 5:00. Without a morning train to catch, I run for an hour and a half. Upon reaching the aqueduct, I walk to cool down. But at Oak Grove Point, I sprint to the top for the foolish satisfaction that comes from 'conquering the hill.'

On schooldays, at 7:15, I'm dressed and drinking coffee by the window. By eight, Amanda skips past my house without looking up. My hand is raised and I wait until she reaches the road to drop it. She's dancing down the spiraling hill in Olivia's old red rubber boots. Her lithe body flows and her silken, tawny hair waves behind her.

I spend the next few hours studying my Renaissance art books. Later, I start dinner, usually a pot of soup. After lunch, I lift weights while listening to jazz.

At the afternoon's peak, I brush my teeth again. I shave thoroughly, including my neck, and change into a clean casual shirt. I've found the one I bought when Sterling took up with Kevin Dalton. It's a blue-gray button-down of heavy silk and cotton twill that makes me feel sleek and strong.

To my surprise, Sterling had noticed it. She said, 'Don't wear that when you're trying to be invisible.'

The remark was far from mean but she had intended it to hurt me, because the subtext compared me to Kevin. It hadn't hurt at all, however. What did hurt—a little—was discovering that Sterling could no longer hurt my feelings. Because I don't love her like that anymore. Whatever Sterling thinks about a shirt or a house or a man doesn't concern me.

Amanda Jonette concerns me. And I, who have always been risk averse, will risk all decency to give her a fraction of the love she deserves. Impeccable attire that looks like ordinary casual clothing will lend me refinement, and maybe even padlock the wild animal rattling the cage.

Each day at 4:00 pm, I stand in Olivia's bedroom, watching from the window. In fifteen to thirty minutes, I see Amanda tossing her backpack high in the air, twirling beneath it, and catching it. She proceeds up the hill in crisscrossing arcs. When she rounds the last bend at the top, I step across the hall and watch from my own bedroom window. She reaches her front door and rewards me with a curtsy, a smile, and a pretty little wave before disappearing inside her mother's empty house.

Two hours later, she rings the doorbell. We have dinner. I review her homework and we watch television.

Amanda thinks our 'snuggling' is what fathers and daughters do. Except, she's never met her father. And no daughter demonstrates such mad devotion. Amanda is strong and capable, yet she cries for cuddling and cooing as urgently as an infant.

This cannot last. But, for now, I crave the splendor stirring the air that surrounds her. She presses against me, nestles and squirms. The thrilling pleasure she inflicts cuts straight through me. For which, I'll gladly suffer whatever lies ahead.

Eleven

By mid-October, the oak and beech trees in Oak Grove Point are denuded and the wind blows hard down from Canada. Tonight, Amanda arrives shivering in the oversized hand-me-down sweater of Olivia's and tan corduroy jeans rolled up to her knees. She steps out of the rubber boots and her delicate feet and ankles are chafed from the cold.

My impressions become jumbled. She talks faster than her mouth moves. Her voice trills while her face conveys a cunning loveliness.

She takes my hand and asks if we can sit down for a minute.

'Is something wrong?'

'I want to cuddle.'

'After dinner, while we watch TV.'

'Okay, but can't I have a hug first?'

Seeing my hesitation, she rolls her eyes. 'A hug hello.'

'All right.'

She throws her long slender arms around my neck. Pressing into me, her head at my heart, she looks up and asks if I missed her, because she missed me.

'It's only been about twenty hours,' I remind her, but Amanda doesn't let go. I hate doing it, but I do—I remove her hands and ask her to pour us sparkling water with orange bitters, something new. 'See if you like it. Just a shake or two, though. It's an acquired taste.'

Stirring a pot of minestrone, I remind her that she should drink milk with dinner.

'Do you have skim?'

'Do you remember Sterling?'

'Oh, yeah. So you do.'

Minestrone and homemade bread with Jarlsberg cheese, after which I make ginger tea to go with the baked apples, which she's never tasted.

'Who invented these?'

'Someone who didn't have time for apple pie.'

'Yeah, that's what it tastes like.'

While she clears the table and loads the dishwasher, I look at her homework. She's completed pages of elementary matrices and written a short but interesting description of life in New Amsterdam.

She sits and shifts her chair so that she's facing me. She tilts her head and asks, with a tinge of shyness, if I think she's smart.

'Yes,' I tell her. 'You're so smart that I can't believe you don't know it.' I attempt a lighter tone and ask if she has a boyfriend.

She tosses her napkin in exasperation. 'You must have forgotten how juvenile middle-school boys are. Stupid show-offs. Anything—and I mean anything—for attention.'

'You and Olivia said that right after starting middle school, remember? But in Maine, Olivia's best friend is also her boyfriend, a skateboarder.'

Amanda widens her eyes. Sarcastic or genuinely impressed? 'Ooh, a skateboarder. That's insane.' (Sarcastic.)

'Her grandmother likes him.'

'Maybe Maine's different.' In middle school here, Amanda explains, the gossip and practical jokes are so brutal that the kids have to attend anti-bullying sessions.

I close her notebooks and stare out the window. Behind me, she leans down and wraps her arms around my shoulders. 'I know that when you were an eighth-grade boy, you weren't like the buffoons in my class.'

'Maybe that's because I was never in eighth grade.'

'Why not?'

'I crammed five years of school into one.'

'Because you're a genius.'

'No, I'm not. I wasn't then, either, but I studied nonstop rather than contend with loneliness. And because my parents were important scientists, the school administrators found special tutors for me. I was allowed to soar past my age group.'

'Do you wish you hadn't?'

I smile because it does sound that way. 'I don't regret it. I wouldn't have gotten away with it if I were conceited, although teachers aren't always the best judges of that. But I wasn't conceited. I had reasons for wanting to race ahead even if doing so left me with social gaps. I thought then, and still think, that if I had followed the usual route, I would have ended up with more serious troubles.'

Amanda says that I sound like a genius to her. She's circling around and I glance at her bare legs and feet.

'Go borrow some more socks, honey.'

'Are you sure?'

'If Olivia left them here, she doesn't want them.'

Amanda goes upstairs and I lean back and close my eyes. Without meaning to, I recall my life before being sent to boarding school. I played soccer and basketball and lived at home with my sister, who was in high school.

Emily loved me. She drove me to the ice rink for hockey practice and attended all of my games. She bought my clothes and fixed my meals. She knew my friends' names. We went to the movies once a week—films that we could laugh at together. Just before my eleventh birthday in December, she was picked up by the police for acting up in public. She had taken psychedelics and gotten separated from her friends.

My parents could not tolerate an unruly, law-breaking daughter. Emily might tarnish their reputations in the scientific community. Although I never learned the whole story, I have always believed that their intolerance killed her. So, no wonder I'm lenient. No wonder I'm *too* tolerant.

In whatever institution my parents placed her, Emily was a prisoner. No phone calls, no mail. And I was promptly shipped off to Exeter. By February, Emily was dead.

The headmaster took pity on me. My parents paid my tuition and board through vacations, glad to fund extra courses as recommended. Studying sealed me off from grief—and from myself. Physics and math kept me from pondering unsolvable problems like life and death. I studied mathematics at Yale when I was fourteen and was accepted into a Ph.D. program at Harvard when I was sixteen.

Over the noise of the dishwasher, I don't hear Amanda return to the kitchen. But then I feel her presence beside me. She taps my knee and I open my eyes.

'Walter, you look so sad.'

I say her name but am not sure if she hears it. Time rushes even as it freezes solid.

'Sometimes,' Amanda says, 'I'm so happy for no reason I think I'll die. What I feel is so much—so much more—than just me.'

This arouses such terrible affection in me that I stand up and pace, making my way to the back door, to avoid looking at her beautiful, bewildered face.

Outside on the deck, I search for the moon. Inside, Amanda's sitting on the couch, ready to start a new season of *The Real Miranda*. I enter through the sliding glass doors and she says, 'Just until ten, then I'll go home and flick the lights.'

*

At daybreak, I charge through a high-splashing, ankle-deep mud puddle, jump over some small ones, and skirt others. Today I'm running the ten-mile loop at Rockefeller Park, which is mostly level, unlike the eight-mile circuit with its loose scattered steps, or the five-mile steep grade that descends to a pond. I have decided not to do anything about work or school for a year.

Having shot past the phase of youth when you think your day will last forever, I now wish *these* days could last forever. Despite the anxiety, I *want* to plummet through endless mirrored tunnels, hand in hand with Amanda.

When I'm ready, I'll get a law degree and work toward a position that allows me to help regulate banking. I know how investment bankers scam the system. I know every tranche and trick on the bond-trading desk and want to see bank fraud defined as the crime it is. With commensurate, mandatory punishments.

But right now I'm living in, and for, the present. Within a year, Amanda will start high school and leave me behind. This unnerves me even more than my struggle to protect her—from myself.

Two strides and I leave the park, crossing the highway onto the aqueduct, where I race through sunlight. Home, filthy but refreshed, I leave my muddy, drenched clothes in the laundry room and dash upstairs to shower. I'm dressed and considering breakfast when the phone rings, and—for once!—it's Olivia.

'How are you, sweetheart?'

She doesn't answer but I hear worry within her shallow breath. Before long I learn Sterling has told her to 'ask her father' if she can skateboard with Karl and his friends. I tell her, 'Yes' in a heartbeat, followed by, 'Wear a helmet.'

She says, 'Without fail.' Karl will make sure. 'I'm the only girl in the group.' Karl and his friends skateboard at events. She's learning just enough to keep up when they're traveling on flat pavement.

'I'm Karl's disciple.' She giggles at that. 'Next week I'm meeting his father, who's a famous skateboarder. He and Karl's mom are divorced, too.'

'Your mother and I are not divorced, Olivia.'

'But you will be.'

'Did your mother tell you that?'

'No. But Granny says it's just a matter of time.'

'Is she there?'

'Yeah, hold on.'

'Wait. Talk to me first. I miss you.'

'I love you, Daddy. But I'm happy here.'

I hear her handing the phone to Kaye, and in my head, I shout after my daughter, 'I love you, too.'

Kaye stays quiet for several seconds, before saying that Susie knows she's running away from her greatest blessings: Olivia and me.

'What do you think, Walter? Do you think she's been a good mother?'

'Is Olivia still there?'

'Of course not. Susie will regret this. When the pieces finally hit the ground, I hope you'll visit me.'

'Do you approve of Olivia skateboarding?'

'Yes. She's not the daredevil she used to be, and a sense of freedom is essential to her right now. That's why she's here. Susie may have brought her here to rile you, but I think, deep down, she knew it would be good for Olivia.'

Kaye says she loves seeing her voluptuous fourteen-year-old granddaughter act like a tomboy.

I laugh at that.

'An old lady's vision,' she says.

'Let me guess. Sterling disapproves.'

'Skateboarders aren't student council material. But I bet Karl plays it both ways.'

I say nothing about broken bones but Kaye tells me not to worry. (Although, maybe she means don't worry about Sterling.) In any case, I tell her that hearing from her reassures me. 'That's good, Walter,' she says, and she hangs up.

Twelve

Each night, I try to forestall turning on the television. I use Amanda's homework to lead us into discussions—about anything; her curiosity is boundless. Amanda's shyness as a little girl sometimes camouflaged her superior intelligence. Now her mind is expanding at a fantastic rate.

Tonight, when I remark on this, she says, 'I know!' Anything she needs to know is just available to her the moment she needs to know it. 'Without looking stuff up,' she says, 'the answers line up inside my mind, waiting for me to use them.'

'It's exciting when nothing's missing. All the pieces fit.'

'That's exactly what it's like!' It amazes her that I accept her experience as real.

I have also introduced reading aloud to each other after dinner. This new routine began when I insisted she hear the original Hans Christian Andersen stories behind the Disney movies we've watched. We sit in the living room armchairs. The large furniture makes us feel significant. Amanda declares that *The Snow Queen* isn't at all like *Frozen*. She can't comprehend why anyone connected them. And, the *Little Mermaid* is so sad! It was never her favorite movie, but now the cartoon version insults her, because it 'totally insults the real Little Mermaid!' The story makes her cry. I comfort her and her tears dampen my shirt. After a second's hesitation, I stroke her head.

Our voices resound throughout the house and possibly into the night. Tall trees on the other side of the road are visible through the windows. The living room light is soft. Facing me, she takes my hands and presses them against each side of her face. Her hands stay on mine, yet the temptation to stroke her impossibly soft skin besieges me. (My palms and fingers burn for control.)

And she says in a very deep voice, 'Look into my eyes.'

'No.' It's the right answer, I think. She's teasing. My hands slip free and my eyes shift from hers. We laugh. And I tell her that she can't hypnotize me. Nobody can. I'm resistant.

'That's just like you, Walter! Nobody can hypnotize you because you won't let them. So, you'll have to hypnotize me. Come on—make me enchanted.'

Shaking my head, I laugh. 'You know, I lost my job because I refused to try to control people.'

She nods. 'But that was at work. Isn't it different between you and me?'

'Different how?'

'Because,' she says, 'we care for each other.'

Up and pacing, I look away and suddenly suggest that tomorrow evening we stay in our separate homes. 'Just once. For a change.'

Amanda laughs and stands. Hair sweeps across her forehead and she extends her arms toward me. If she hasn't been acting beyond her years ever since Olivia left, she certainly is now.

'Shall we pretend our front yards are an ocean, Walter? Shall we reach for each other across half the world?'

I suspect she's imitating an actress, but if so, not one I know. She pouts, either as part of the act or for real. Her damp lower lip and welling eyes bewitch me.

'Give me a minute.' I go upstairs, fill the sink with cold water and put my face in it. If our magical circle of two is so magical it never changes, I'll embrace the limits. But all magic is a trick. I can love and protect her but only briefly, only while we remain here, the two of us alone.

Face dried, hair combed, I return to the living room and say I didn't mean it. 'About staying in our separate houses. That's stupid. But what about this weekend? Don't you want time with your friends?'

'I see them all week long, Walter.' She and Madison work on the newspaper before school. Madison's family, she says, has their own secret right now. The older sister, Margo, is taking a year off from college. Nobody knows why.

'Does Gil—I mean Madison's father—know that Olivia's in Maine?'

'I don't know.'

'Our pact exists so that I can take care of you. It's no reason to avoid your friends.'

'Why can't we keep things the way they are? Just you and me.'

'We can do our best, honey, but things change. Did Cheryl call this week?'

Amanda waves her hand as if waving away the question. 'She *says* she's coming home for Thanksgiving.'

'For a week?'

'She plans to stay from Thursday through Sunday. Please don't tell her she needs to spend more time with me.'

'I won't, not specifically. But I need to explain the situation, honey. Your mother must realize what's going on.'

I manage to convince Amanda that if I can talk to Cheryl first thing, I'll explain her new clothes and the streamlined new blue bicycle, for which nobody owes me a dime. (I couldn't stand watching Amanda struggle with the rickety hand-me-down and its ill-fitting chain.)

Ever since I was fired, I've been contemplating the best way to tell Cheryl Jonette that my feelings for her daughter are dangerous.

Thirteen

The Sunday before Thanksgiving, I'm a month overdue for a haircut and stop by the barbershop. Hot towels cover another customer's face. A timer sounds and the barber, Leonard, lifts the steamy wraps—and it's my old friend, Wayne from the firehouse.

'Walter,' he says, 'long time.' He pats his pink cheeks and asks how he looks.

'Smooth. You look smooth.'

He laughs. 'Ya think?'

Leonard clips Wayne's eyebrows. Neither of them asks about my family or my job. Everyone knows that Sterling, Olivia—and Kevin Dalton—are in Maine.

Whenever I oblige Sterling by picking up her call, she mixes weepy confusion with a plea that soon becomes a command: Get to work. Before I hang up or she resumes crying, she describes some perfect little office space that her friend Nina Malloy has waiting for me. Why don't I open a 'consulting practice'?

'If nothing else,' she says, 'get an office and hang a C.P.A. shingle.'

While in graduate school, I acquired C.P.A. licenses in three states. I've worked hard my whole life—until Bank of America fired me. Because of that and my immoderate compensation at the bank, along with consistent, careful investments, I've left my trust fund untouched. I never mention, and rarely even think about, my inheritance. Last year, my mother sent documents showing that vast sums from my parents' share of drug patents have been added to the trust, which I keep for Olivia.

But Wayne doesn't even ask what I've been up to, just, 'How ya doin'?'

'Good. How 'bout you?'

'Busy,' he says. His kids are growing up.

Just then, Amanda and Madison ride their bicycles past the barbershop. Amanda sees me and I see her, although she ignores me. Immediately, the girls are gone.

Wayne's fifteen-year-old son thinks Amanda's hot. 'Amanda Jonette,' Wayne says to my surprise, 'makes us proud.' The middle-school faculty, the school board, and the P.T.A. (of which Wayne's wife is president) are proud of her transformation.

'Transformation?'

'Until recently, she was "at risk." Or so my wife says.'

'Really. She was always my daughter's best friend.'

'Well, with Olivia at your side,' Wayne says, 'nobody looks lost.'

I laugh, genuinely pleased. 'True. Olivia's no waif.'

His wife pulls up and honks the horn. Wayne sees her and waves. 'Just so you know, Walter, you're welcome to drop by the firehouse any time. I'll tell Dennis and Pete—'

'Tell them hello for me.'

Wayne pays the barber and bumps his fists on my shoulders. His wife honks from the car again, and he's gone.

*

After watching *The Real Miranda* together, she rests her lovely, quick fingertips on my thigh. I should probably move them, but

136

Amanda's playing Inch-Me, Pinch-Me. Her fingers travel inch by inch up my leg and onto my stomach.

'Inch-me and Pinch-me went out in a boat. Inch-me fell out and who was left?'

'You tell me.'

She flashes that irresistible grin and mock-swoons, her hair sweeping over me.

'Amanda.' I say her name in warning but it sounds more like awe, which she takes as encouragement to continue pressing her fingers against my stomach and chest.

'Come on, Walter. Who was left? Inch-me or Pinch-me?'

Her fingers land high on my leg, prompting my eyes to close. But I resist and manage to grab her hand. She laughs and escapes my hold. 'Pinch-me!' she says, pinching my inner thigh. 'Now you do me.'

'No, honey.'

'Walter, please.'

'I'm sorry but it's unthinkable.'

'Nuh-uh—*I'm* thinking it.'

My breath is low and slow. And Amanda's saying, 'Tickle, tickle on the knee, if you laugh, you don't love me!'

You cannot imagine the sensations, despite thick jeans covering my kneecap. I shiver and remember playing this game at the beach when I was nine. I tickled Cecilia de Grazia's smooth, bare knee, both of us digging our toes deep in the sand.

Amanda tickles my knee, up my thigh, my torso, neck, and—bam! I trap her shameless fingers beneath my chin. She squeals and her warm, fast breath moistens my cheek. No! Absolutely not! Relax one cardinal rule and the rest become elastic.

'No more tickling. Let's go look at the moon.'

Since October, I've been walking outside with her before she goes home to sleep. Our first breaths in the cold air appear as ghostly plumes. The moon is full and rising over the northeast line of trees. We walk toward the woods beyond the Point.

'Walter, can we hold hands in the moonlight?'

I start to take her hand but draw back. 'Aren't you afraid we'll turn into werewolves?'

'You're making fun of me.'

Amanda's indignation is so beguiling I almost want to tease her more. But I apologize. It was a stupid joke. Still, she refuses to hold my hand, claiming it wasn't a joke but an excuse.

'That's not so. If I could, I would always hold your hand.'

'Unbelievable,' she says, and cartwheels in a wide circle around me. The feat exhilarates her. Her hair is tangled and her energy so high, she laughs. Ha! She hugs me and I'm forgiven.

I resist the urge to lift her in the air. Instead, I step backward and kneel on one knee. 'Please, give me your hand.' I kiss her knuckles goodnight, making her giggle. She's still giggling when she runs to her front door, calling, 'Stay there and I'll flick the lights.'

*

While running before dawn, I ponder Wayne's easy friendliness. He knows I lost my job. Nina Malloy has no doubt told everyone that I'm not doing any business anywhere. So, Wayne knows I'm idle and absent and had the courtesy not to mention it.

Following our brief conversation in the barbershop, I can't help wondering if he suspects I'm caring for Amanda. And, granted, this is radical speculation, but perhaps by saying that Amanda makes him proud, he was implying approval.

He and everyone else around here have noticed the difference: A magician waved his wand and the poor shivering urchin became the smartest, prettiest girl in town.

Yet, she won't ride her new bicycle to school—too many questions. Besides, she likes walking. She meets Madison on Main Street for breakfast. For lunch, she takes a sandwich she fixes in my kitchen.

This morning, she slices homemade bread and spreads it with almond butter and tamarind chutney—a treat she discovered in my refrigerator.

I ask, 'Do you ever buy yourself dessert, a brownie or some candy?'

Her sandwich and two tangerines in a brown bag, her white ski jacket on, Amanda covers her mouth, and I realize: Those dainty bites and careful chewing? She has a toothache.

From the bay window, I watch her skipping down the hill. Midway, she moves in a crisscross, tossing her backpack in the air, which until now she only did uphill, coming home. I see her look and wave, although she can't possibly see me from where she is.

This extra little dance springs from anxiety, because she knows that on Thursday I intend to speak with her mother. That's the plan, anyway. Up until this week, Amanda claimed Cheryl was visiting from Thanksgiving morning through Sunday. Then, last night, out of the blue, she said, 'Don't blame me if she doesn't show up until Christmas.'

*

After dinner, while I load the dishwasher, Amanda hops on the stool near the counter and swings her legs. I ask her if Cheryl actually said she might not return until Christmas.

'No, but I'll bet you.'

'When was the last time you told her that I need to meet with her as soon as possible?'

'I say it every time she phones: "Don't forget, Mom. Walter needs to tell you about our situation." And Cheryl says, all right, but if something's wrong, I'd better warn her. And I say, nothing's wrong. You just want to talk to her.'

'Nothing is wrong, honey. But she really does need to understand the situation.'

Amanda sulks. 'Just what's the big, bad situation, anyway?'

'Your mother needs to know she can't ignore you. And leaving you here with me has led to all kinds of heightened feelings. She'll know what I mean.'

'What's wrong with that? We share the same feelings.'

I lean against the counter, watching her feet move in midair. 'It's not that simple, honey.'

'Because you think I'm a child, right? But I do a lot of stuff most kids I know will never have to do. They live in a garden of verses. I don't. I've always had to figure out what my feelings are and what to do about them. Like, I used to be scared all the time. And then I found out I could use my fear like nervous energy, to get stuff done. Like when I asked the man at the Y if I could help out there. I was so scared, I was shaking. He told me I was too young. So, I nodded and thanked him, and then I walked down the hall and into the girls' locker room, where I picked up all the wet towels and heaped them in the laundry bin.'

'And then what? Did someone come in and tell you to leave?'

'Nobody noticed me. Except this little girl, probably about three, who'd been whimpering. When she saw me, she began wailing. And I remembered right away—when I was that little and someone forgot about me.

'I knelt in front of her and wiggled my thumb between our faces. 'Cause I used to pretend my thumbs talked to each other, like those thumb puppets, remember?'

I nod, trying to not appear enrapt while encouraging her to continue. She doesn't seem to notice, but keeps talking, offering me a personal history I doubt she has ever revealed to anyone else.

'So, don't laugh. In my "thumb voice" I asked to meet her thumb. Why? Just to say hi. Her thumb bent and wiggled. She stopped sobbing and her squeaky thumb explained that "Brianna" can't find her socks. And was it okay if her thumb rested inside her mouth. I said, "Great idea." And, "I don't know why thumb-sucking bothers grown-ups so much."'

'Amanda, do you suck your thumb?'

'No, I've moved on.' She looks at me until I blush.

'Don't you want to know where?'

'No!'

'And I don't want to tell you, so there! Anyway, back to my story. Little Brianna was sucking her thumb but pointing to her locker. I found her socks and shoes in her backpack and put them on her chubby feet. After that, while she was still sucking her thumb, my thumb asked her thumb to come out. My thumb wiggled and said, "Let's hold onto each other and go outside in case someone's waiting for you." And someone was—her mother or nanny or someone—and they said, "*There* you are, Brianna! What took you so long?"'

'After two more days of me showing up, the man at the front desk stopped reminding me I wasn't a member. And when I asked the cleaning lady if I could help her fill the dispensers, nobody cared if I filled a bottle of shampoo for myself, a bottle of conditioner, and a bottle of body wash.'

I gently rest a hand on Amanda's shoulder, without rearranging her hair or pulling her close. 'Let's sit down in the living room.' She snuggles next to me but I prod her to sit up, saying, 'The summer before last, you told me that you were helping out at the Y.'

She nods and drops her head so it rests on my arm. 'The swimming director, Ms. Zayas, reminds me a little of Jade. She checked the locker rooms at closing and saw what a difference I made. So, she offered me private swimming lessons, saying she'd hire me to be a lifeguard. Then, she found out the Baxters needed a babysitter. Ms. Zayas said she'd get another lifeguard, because I'd make a lot more money babysitting for Leo and Theo. And I did.'

'So by overcoming your fears, good things happened.'

'Yeah, even without anyone caring about me.'

'The swimming director, Ms. Zayas, cared about you. She taught you lifeguarding but recommended you for a better job.'

'That's true.' Amanda sighs. 'She was really nice to me. But that's not the same kind of caring as you and me. We have feelings for each other.'

'I know, honey. But maybe I should learn from your example. Instead of sitting around the house waiting for you to come home from school, I should make myself useful. Help kids get scholarships. Volunteer for literacy programs.'

She tilts her face to see mine. 'You sound sad.'

'I'm not sad—just selfish. I want this time to read, exercise, daydream. I won't do it forever. But I'm responsible for my feelings, even if they're not as good as they should be. I try to be careful, something your mother is not. I don't know what she tells herself. She wants to be your mother but she doesn't want to stay here and be with you. She's eager to have me act as caretaker even though she knows it's not right. I'm going to tell her she has to be more responsible.'

'But we have a pact, and Cheryl's not part of it.'

'She needs to know how I feel, honey. I care for you more than I should. Most of the time what I feel is good. But too much of any good thing makes you sick.'

'Come on! We're not talking about ice cream. If you "care too much," then what's "just right"? What's the perfect amount, Walter? Because having you care for me "more than you should" makes me happy. Until you, nobody cared about me except for one random person who let me pick up towels in return for swimming lessons.'

She stomps off into the TV room. I follow and take the remote before she can switch on something loud and distracting. Beside her on the couch, I say, 'Don't be mad, honey. If I don't talk to Cheryl, we'll all be sorry.'

'I want you and me to stay like we are. If you tell Cheryl, who knows what she'll do? We might never see each other again.'

'That's why I need to talk to her. Because she's more likely to do that—take you away—if I *don't* make sure she understands.'

Amanda starts to pout, but then throws her arms around me and whispers, 'I'm making you a Christmas present.'

'You are?' I kiss the top of her head, fast. 'Tell me what you want.'

'I want us to stay like we are.'

*

At the base of Oak Grove Point, only three townhouses are occupied. Nobody drives up here. Nobody walks among the oak trees but Amanda and I.

In bed, at night, the temptation I've stifled for hours batters me. Even Jesus was tempted. Who's to say that when the devil's promise of a fabulous city failed, the source of all evil didn't lift a spellbinding thirteen-year-old girl onto the Savior's lap?

A voice in my dreams shouts, 'Blasphemy!' While I sleep, the voice screeches that my devotion to Amanda is depraved. Then, another dream-voice, which might be the same one, tries to rationalize. Feel all the devotion you can, it says, providing you quell your lust.

And yet, this whole predicament is more Cheryl's fault than mine. Not that I'm blameless. I'm guiltier by the minute. But the woman has never taken responsibility for her child.

Perhaps if she made regular visits, I could regain some moral ground. If she spent just a weekend with Amanda every month, I might sustain a respectful position. My hidden, vile struggle exists in large part because of Cheryl Jonette's disregard.

Of course, I have to make a delicate case. I'm not obligated to describe specifics. Such as how my fingers tremble to stroke the hair flowing down Amanda's back and linger among the soft strands. Or that what I want even more is to slide my hand between Amanda's hair and neck—and with my palm at her scalp, run my fingers up the back of her head, onto the crown.

Another man might do exactly that, casually: touch her head; stroke her hair; and even press his hand up the back of her head. But his touch would be lukewarm, not ardent, not ravening. A thousand times a day, my fantasies mix with reality—heaven with earth. The result of which may very well be hell.

Every night, we sit together with the TV on. I have set up strict rules for physical contact: side by side only (*not on my lap!*); she can rest her head on my shoulder, but no lower. Yet Amanda squirms, wiggles, and laughs, always in motion. And with each shift of her body, I am forced to readjust myself, maintaining a distance half a step from the brink. And thus our attention flows back and forth between us. Hours later, when she has returned to her own house and flicked the lights, I'm exhausted as well as inflamed. Amanda does all she can to give and get love. She's too intelligent to be completely innocent, and yet at the same time, she's light years away from what I want. Obviously, then, I detest myself for wanting it.

More than anything, I want Amanda to stay exactly as she is. Even at the distended extreme of my discomfort, I want her to remain at the pinnacle of girlhood. If it were my call, I'd keep her there for another few years. Especially after witnessing my darling Olivia revel in hers for scarcely a few weeks. She's happy now. She's spending Thanksgiving with Karl, who's competing at his father's indoor skateboarding park. But Olivia's childhood ended when Sterling took her away.

*

Speak of the devil, then! Sterling phones and, because it's after midnight, I answer. She's sniffling as usual, but for a second, I panic. 'Is Olivia all right?'

'Of course. Skateboarding with a boy whose father was a skateboarding legend. What could be better? You've been out of work for nearly three months. Have you contacted any headhunters?'

'You already know I'm not interested, Sterling. Do you need money?'

'Very funny. I'm sorry, no. You're more than generous. My concern is what have you been *doing*?'

'Ask something else, because that's *not* your concern.'

'Please, don't be like that.' She blows her nose and tells me that Kaye's dating a man who teaches *Walden* to senior citizens. 'Mother knew him in grade school. He moved back here.'

'How nice. What's his name?'

'Roy Emerson.'

'How fitting.'

'Do you care about me or not?'

'What do you think? We've been going in circles for months.' Like her mother, I hang up.

*

Thanksgiving morning, Amanda phones to say her mother isn't coming. 'Because of work. Her boss.'

Five minutes later, she's at my kitchen door, flouncing about in a colorful flared skirt and fitted ribbed sweater. My plan was half-formed, but seeing her in her new skirt reveals it in full.

'Are you hungry? Because if we eat soon—and you're interested—we can go ice skating downtown from four to six, when most people are giving thanks and spilling gravy.'

She flies to me, arms open. I turn sideways and hold her down. But she's shrieking with glee and doesn't notice how I'm thwarting her spontaneous leap into my arms.

'That sounds like a yes.'

'It is,' she says. 'Yes times infinity.'

Last week, Amanda found a figure-skating channel on television. Girls in sequined leotards performing dizzying spins, double twists, and astonishing jumps off an angled blade. As we watched, instead of nestling into me, she lay prone on the floor. 'Did you see that? Look—slow motion.' She tries balancing near the floor, one leg extended. 'Except they're on ice skates and spinning so fast all you see is blur.'

I haven't skated in twenty years, but if it's like riding a bike, I'll remember how to do it—I was good at hockey.

Amanda cuts cucumber slices just thick enough to crunch. Now that she's not restricted to butter knives, the only kind in her house, she creates crisp, delightful salads.

'Amanda, have you ever had wild rice?'

She hasn't.

'It's dark and nutty. I like it on Thanksgiving, but if you'd rather, we can have potatoes.'

'If the rice is really wild, I'll love it.'

No doubt. Chicken breasts are marinating in the refrigerator. On the top rack is a pumpkin pie that Madison's sister made.

We both knew her mother wasn't coming. After all, this morning was the first time that Cheryl phoned in two weeks. 'Christmas, though,' Amanda says. 'She always comes at Christmas. And today she was nice enough to apologize for being away so long. And, she even asked how I was getting by. I told her, great, thanks to you. Cheryl goes, "I suppose you've been mooching off him like a shameless beggar. Well, tell your friend Walter I'll sit down with him first thing. But if you've been wheedling extras, Amanda, those are your debts."'

The woman makes sure her daughter's aware of how much her existence costs. Amanda's been taught to add up what people spend on her. So, although she knows I love her—in fact, she wields the power of the beloved so effectively that at any minute I'm liable to fall apart—she remains anxious about what I plan to say to Cheryl.

'My business with your mother has nothing to do with money.'

'She won't believe that. And I guarantee you, she won't pay you back. I'm not even sure she could. After all, Walter, you've spent oodles on me.'

'Oodles?'

'Madison's sister Margo says "oodles" all the time. She learned it in college.'

Earlier this month, Amanda adopted a new routine. Each day, she comes home after school and rides her bike to Madison's house, where she stays until 6:30 or 7:00. I worry about her riding home in the dark, and have offered to pick her up. She says not to risk it.

'What's the risk? I like Gil and he likes me. At least, I think he does.'

'Yeah, but Margo can't stop wondering why I'm spending so much time making a Christmas present for my neighbor. And Madison says it's because I don't have a father. I tell them that you're nice to me and so I want to do something nice for you. Besides, giving is better than receiving. They laughed at that. "Sorry," Margo said, "but it's such a cliché."'

'It is a cliché. But clichés are generally true. That's why they're clichés.'

Amanda giggles. She'll tell them that.

The table's set. We apply finishing touches to the meal. In the dining room, Amanda insists on candles even though it's sunny and midday. We keep the lights off, and she's right. The sunlight outside and the candlelight inside fill the room with magic.

I lower my head. 'Thanks. Praise. Amen.'

She swings her legs inside the tall black boots I chose for her. 'That's a good Grace.'

'Nobody's ever complained.'

She loves wild rice. The salad's delicious. Fork in the air, she compliments me on the chicken. 'It's so…tangy.'

But I notice her wincing when she chews. It's that toothache again. 'We're taking you to a dentist, young lady. Tomorrow, first thing.'

'Cheryl won't like that.'

'Then it'll be part of our secret.'

She brightens again. 'Walter, the most obvious thing! You know how I was so afraid that Cheryl would be jealous of all the beautiful clothes you've bought me? It's like…man, oh man, why let her see 'em? She's only here for a few days. Can I put them in Olivia's room?'

I start to agree, but the thought of Amanda's clothing in the bedroom next to mine makes me feel faint. 'You should put them in our garage. That will be…safer. In fact, new rule: Upstairs is strictly off-limits. Okay?'

She puts her hands in her lap and bows her head. 'You don't trust me.'

'Of course I do. It's myself I don't trust.'

'But you put limits on everything.'

'Not everything.'

Her head pops up. Her eyes shine directly into mine.

'We have cuddling limits,' I say. 'And I know you understand they're serious.'

She tilts her head and bites her lip. 'I tease you. But I thought we both liked that.'

'I like it too much, Amanda.' I've said this so often that I quickly amend it. 'Of course, I'd rather feel too much than not enough.' (*Why* am I telling her this? Do I expect the child of my twisted dreams to absolve me?)

She exaggerates a sigh of relief. Or maybe it's real; I can't tell. 'Walter, you and me, we're different from other people.'

If only I were the dispassionate man I once was. But I believe she's right. With Amanda, I'm not the person I've always been. I

149

often feel almost free from gravity. For now, I'm here. She's here. And never will I regret one second with this exquisite girl.

We clear the table. I load the dishwasher. She finds dessert plates, saying, 'If you're sad, I'm sad. And if I'm happy, you're happy. We share our feelings. It's not a coincidence. It's amazing!'

'So amazing we probably shouldn't talk about it too much.' I slice a piece of pie for each of us.

A solemn cast alters her expression, but then she nods. 'We should just feel. Not blab about what's happening inside of us or we'll lose some of it.'

We return to the dining room and eat our pie with scoops of vanilla ice cream.

'Man, oh man, doesn't Margo make the best pumpkin pie?'

Fourteen

Before running home to change into jeans for skating, Amanda glances back and winks. She stretches out her arms, and turning, pulls them in close, like a figure skater.

And here she is already, eager to go. Circling the kitchen, she's wearing a poppy-colored sweater beneath the white ski jacket. I lower my eyes to conceal my pleasure at her every gesture. You would think I had never glimpsed her burnished beauty before.

'Are you wearing good socks?' I ask. 'They need to be very snug.'

She lifts her jeans to show me new socks that match her sweater. 'Have you heard from Olivia today? Because I just sent you a video she sent me.' As the words leave her mouth, Amanda realizes that, of course, I haven't seen the video, and dashes upstairs for my laptop.

But I'm faster and catch her on the landing. Sending her back to the kitchen, I say, 'New rule, remember?' And, 'Give me two minutes.'

In my bedroom, I pull on a thick black cashmere sweater and glance at my reflection in the bathroom mirror. I gargle and spit out a bit of mouthwash, grab the laptop and bound back to the kitchen.

Amanda fixes me with her amber-gold eyes at full smolder, a heightened torment aimed at me for imposing rules. If protecting her, nurturing her, weren't more important than anything else, my willpower would crumple like an empty husk.

I open the laptop and show her the rink at Rockefeller Center. 'What do you think? It'll be crowded. If you want, we can find a quieter skating rink.'

'But I've seen this one in movies. Please, Walter? We've got to go there.'

All right by me. First, however, she wants to show me the video of Olivia. I open my email. We watch Karl skateboard back and forth as he instructs my daughter to roll down a concrete slope. Olivia's skateboard drops from an embankment onto the sidewalk and she lands on it nicely.

'She promised—no stunts.'

'That's why she sent it to me and said, make sure he notices the helmet.'

I smile and send Olivia a text: *Brava, sweetheart!*

Driving south on the Saw Mill Parkway, we listen to *Real Miranda* songs. The best one features Iris and the sound of chimes.

'Walter, will you watch the start of the new season with me on Christmas night?'

'What if Cheryl's here?'

'Shit. We'll have to wait till she leaves.'

I resist asking if she's dispensed with: 'Man, oh man.'

'Olivia calls me almost every week now to make sure you're not lonely.'

'Why doesn't she call me?'

'She likes being independent.' Amanda leans over to nudge my shoulder. 'Not like Cheryl's kind of independent. More like

Karl's her best friend and they both love Granny, who tells Olivia that it's *your* job to worry about *her*. And that, of course, you're *not* worried, because you know O's happy living in Maine.'

Impulsively, I take Amanda's hand and tell her that I'm the happiest I've ever been.

She says, 'No shit?' (Guess 'shit' is the new word.) 'I thought so and hoped so, but, you know—grown-ups.'

'I want you to promise you'll be honest with me, Amanda. If you're ever … uncomfortable or just want time away from me, promise you'll say so.'

'All right. But that's not gonna happen.'

'But if it does?'

'Yeah, of course. I tell you everything.'

I find a parking garage and we walk a few icy, windy blocks. At Rockefeller Center, the buildings block most of the wind. The tree is up, but not decorated with lights yet. The evening glows cold but soft and clear. I find the door to the seasonal ice-skating shop. Inside, I pay the cashier for the session and rent skates for us. They're bright blue and stiff, with dull blades.

We find a bench and I say, 'Let me do the laces.' Amanda pushes her blue jeans up, pulls on a skate, and lifts her leg, but I shake my head. It's better if she stands on the floor. Crouching before her, I pull the strings taut and tie them tight at the instep, then double wrap them around her ankle before crisscrossing them through the clasps to the top. I tell her to make sure the skate's supportive but not so tight it's uncomfortable. Then, I lace the other one.

My skates feel weird, but I've never worn figure skates, only hockey.

A crowd surrounds the small rink, watching the skaters. Amanda steps onto the ice, falls, and scoots on her butt away from the entrance. I struggle for balance, managing to stay upright. Other skaters, more interested in taking selfies than skating, have moved to the supporting walls. I glide to where Amanda's hanging onto a railing with both hands.

'Let me warm up with a few laps. Then I'll be able to teach you.'

Halfway around the rink, I find my rhythm and speed up. After two fast laps, I come to a surface-scraping stop next to her. She pushes forward, grabs the ledge, pushes ahead, and almost falls. 'I thought I'd be better at this.'

'Shift your weight to one foot and push off with the other.'

Hands free, she wobbles a little and stumbles into someone's photo-in-progress before falling onto her flank.

Helping her up, I offer to skate backward while she holds my hands.

'You can do that?'

I nod and take her gloved fingers. Her hat bobs forward.

We skate slowly. I turn my head, watching where we're going before unconsciously moving beside her and wrapping one arm around her waist.

She leans into me as I gently cup her elbow, my fingertips steadying her. Amanda and I skate together by concentrating entirely on the other's motion. The focus required is intense and, after a while, I suggest a short rest. She declines, saying she loves this.

She presses into me and we glide along without incident. I love holding her close, protecting her from other skaters, lifting her slightly whenever her glide lapses. I swivel in front of her, skating backward again so that I can touch her cheek, which is cold on the surface but hot deeper down with effort and enthusiasm. She stops long enough to say how much fun this is.

For two hours, we skate side by side, my body supporting hers among a whirl of other bodies. No one minds our purposeful contact. No one stares.

*

The morning after Thanksgiving, I phone my dentist at nine. His office manager confirms that he's working until 3:00, and that several people, who thought they'd have dental work done on their day off, have called to cancel.

I explain that I'll be paying for Amanda out of pocket, and will settle with the insurance company later. The office manager makes an appointment for 10:30. My dentist is in the city, on Park Avenue. Traffic seems oddly heavy, but I rarely drive into the city, except at night. Nevertheless, we arrive ten minutes early.

On an upholstered couch, Amanda fills out the new-patient form. When she rises and returns it to the manager, she smiles and asks, 'If you have time, can you look up Walter Mitchell's record? He hasn't seen the dentist in years.'

(I must have mentioned this while persuading her to see my dentist, although the logic of doing so escapes me now.)

The office manager checks her files. 'Walter, your last visit was seven years ago.' She excuses herself for a moment, and then returns to tell me that I'm in luck. The dentist will treat Amanda and me simultaneously.

She escorts Amanda to one room and me to another, around a corner. After several minutes, the dentist enters and, before examining me, reports that Amanda has two large cavities in her back upper molars. He's given her a tiny cluster of Novocain injections on one side and wants to allow time for the numbing to reach its peak before drilling. Later, he'll repeat the process on the other side.

As for me, it's a different story. My X-rays reveal a deep cavity beneath a heavily patched bottom molar. Extensive drilling but no tiny cluster shots for me. Rather, two huge needles. The dentist asks if I want to watch TV during the procedure, but I brought headphones—Chick Corea will do. He leaves to fill Amanda's cavity and administer the next round of Novocain.

When he begins his work on me, my face is rubber and my tongue is huge. Nevertheless, the drill sears my nerves. I hope Amanda is not enduring similar pain. When he is finally done, the dentist asks me to remove the headphones, and tells me Amanda has saved me from a root canal. 'Don't wait so long between visits.'

My permanent crown will be ready next month. And, he tells me, I should set up an appointment for Amanda with his colleague. Minimal orthodontia can correct her bite, reducing future cavities. 'No longer than six months for braces. Then a retainer at night.'

Returning to the waiting area, I pay for our treatments and arrange for Amanda to see the orthodontist when I return for my crown. Reading Amanda's new patient form upside down, I see that she turned thirteen on November 3—without saying a word.

Here she comes, looking slightly addled. In the elevator, we're both hot and uncomfortable.

'You know what?' My swollen tongue makes me sound cartoonish. 'Let's go ice skating in Central Park till we're back to normal.'

The day is bright and chilly, and the sidewalks full of shoppers. I had forgotten about the pre-Christmas hysteria of 'Black Friday' sales, but Central Park is peaceful. We skate at Wollman Rink with four others, two of whom leave early. Amanda's balance is better than before, yet she clings to me tighter. Afterward, no longer numb or in pain, just exhilarated, we eat lunch at Dean & DeLuca. I ask why she didn't tell me about her birthday.

She shrugs. 'I thought you knew.'

'Amanda.'

'You'd just given me the bicycle. If you knew how many birthdays I've asked Cheryl for a new blue bicycle with a white basket, you'd understand—you already gave me the birthday present I never thought I'd get.'

'No white basket, though.'

'Three speeds and a helmet. And, I stopped wanting a basket when I turned ten.'

'If I had known, we would have celebrated.'

She leans over and kisses my cheek. 'It was the best birthday I ever had.'

*

Saturday, she wants to go ice skating again. I tell her yes, but we must go to different rinks. I have a list.

Sitting on a stool, swinging her legs, she asks why.

'If anyone really looks at you, Amanda, he or she will never forget you.'

'What do you mean?'

'Partly, I mean people who see us together, if they're paying attention, will see I care for you in more than a fatherly way.'

'You mean that?' A rush of energy shoots her into my arms. Her legs wrap around my waist, her hands grip my shoulders, and her breath moves through my ear canal, stirring debilitating

157

lust. Caught off-guard, I press my lips against her head. I circle around, out of my mind, one hand in her bright, tawny hair, the other beneath her butt. We spin into the TV room and we fall back onto the couch. I slowly lift her off my lap and fall forward. Faint with sensation, I press my face into my knees.

She strokes my head. 'Am I too heavy for you?'

I laugh and sit up. 'No, honey. But my feelings are more intense than yours.'

'No, they're not!'

'The way men feel, Amanda, isn't always nice.'

She scoffs. 'You're not like that. You're always nice.'

I shake my head. 'Don't jump on me like that again. I mean it.' An odd delay to my panic—it's still breaking from the thrill of the moment—heightens everything. I'm trembling and don't dare to look at her. 'Excuse me.' I hurry from the room.

She calls after me. 'I'm sorry. Walter? Sorry.'

*

Although it's been gradually happening every evening since the autumnal equinox, darkness falls noticeably earlier each December evening. It's dark by five o'clock. Concerned about Amanda riding the dimly lit mile from Madison's house (where she's making me a Christmas present), I offer to meet her with the car, one block away.

'Why? We'll seem so guilty.'

Home safe every evening at seven, she parks her bicycle in the garage and lets herself in through the kitchen door. She does her homework for an hour while I finish making dinner. Usually, she's happy to let me see her work. Once or twice, she wants to revise something after dinner. Either way, we are soon nestled together on the couch, watching TV. More and more, I'm afraid, I'm the one hoping (not aloud, though) that we'll watch just one more show. Aware of this, I pay strict attention to the time. To get enough sleep, Amanda must leave here at ten.

One evening, before turning on the TV, I mention that she has a first-rate mind. She reaches for my face while crossing and uncrossing her eyes. 'You will continue to believe that until I snap my fingers three times.'

'Is that so?'

'You're actually easy to hypnotize. Like people who claim they're not ticklish.'

'It's true. I'm compelled to do whatever you want.'

'Then why do you push me away?'

'Because we can't change age. Or time.'

*

On weekends, we ice-skate. I have found every ice rink within reasonable driving distance: Elmsford, Yonkers, North White Plains, Rye. In mid-December, Amanda convinces me to return to the Rockefeller Center rink, and afterwards, we visit the Metropolitan Museum of Art. I show her my favorite Renaissance paintings, and the collections inspire her. She says, 'Everything connects to everything,' which I tell her is a line from Leonardo's *Notebooks*.

After our trip to the Met, however, I decide against returning. Because I observed that there are two types of men, my age or older, who take girls in early adolescence to museums. The first are divorced fathers, and their sorry attempts to connect with their daughters remind me that Olivia now relates to me, for the most part, through Amanda.

The second are slick, artistic types who think they're still young. The men are generally close to my age and sport tousled hair or watch caps with skimpy dark sports jackets. Also, bright, new basketball shoes—all the better to hop about their *Alice in Wonderland* girls grown large—girls who could be nineteen or just as likely twelve. Either way, these girls are innocence exaggerated: hair-bows and matching satin sashes tied around flowery, smocked dresses. Some walk as if in line for Communion: hands folded, faces lowered as they stare at their feet in white anklets and black patent leather shoes.

Not surprisingly, I've never noticed these couples before. Perhaps they're a figment of my guilty conscience. Except I see others stare at them, too. The men speak in low, unintelligible rasps. The girls blush, suppressing giggles. So, even though I've never seen them before, I'm certain that they (or variations of them) have traipsed through museums for centuries, parading a pretend interest in art.

*

Amanda's winter vacation starts on Friday. Her mother is expected Saturday morning, Christmas Eve. I am determined to speak with Cheryl immediately. I remind Amanda of this, and tell her that even if her mother listens to me, which is unlikely, our routine won't change. We'll continue eating together every night at my house. I'll check her homework and we'll watch TV until bedtime.

What I don't tell her is my secret hope that Cheryl visits Amanda for an occasional Saturday and part of Sunday, so that I can restore my resolve. All my life, I've been practical, hard-working, and proper—it's who I am. Or, rather, was. Now, I just want to be with Amanda. I want the impossible.

160

Fifteen

I don't know how much Amanda knows—or what she thinks she knows or what she pretends to know. Add to this my intimations, fears, and brave assumptions.

We agree that when we're together we share the same feelings. We think the same thoughts. Amanda knows that I adore her but regards my need to reproach her mother as a threat or possibly a betrayal. 'Please,' she begs, 'just forget about her.'

But she knows I'm not forgetting anything.

She doesn't seem seriously worried yet, but I suspect she's hoping to persuade me not to confront her mother. Staring into my eyes, she crosses and uncrosses hers. 'You're getting sleepy, Walter. So sleepy. Now close your eyes.'

She presses her forehead against mine, which always gets to me. Her hands grasp my knees, and with my eyes closed, I'm acutely aware of how close her face is to mine. I feel her breath and the warmth of her skin. Even my mildest longings disgust and thrill me.

She makes her voice a croak. 'Keep your eyes closed until I say you can open them. Do not—you must not!—run outside when my mother drives up on Christmas Eve morning. Do not get in her car. Do not open your mouth.'

One Saturday afternoon, she stands on the step stool as if addressing a crowd. 'Hear ye! Hear ye! Pro talking to Cheryl? Anyone?' She jumps down to participate in the imaginary audience. 'Boo!' Stomps her feet. 'No way!' and hisses. Back on the stool, she says, 'Thumbs down all around, Walter.'

She appears to grow taller and more commanding. 'Now then! All those *against* talking to Cheryl!' She falls from the stool as if blown down by the crowd's violent, unanimous agreement. 'Hear that, Walter? They're going wild!'

I smile, and by the end, we're both laughing.

*

School ended at noon today, and the two-week winter vacation began. It's Friday. Tomorrow is Christmas Eve. We skated at Van Buren Park until dark. Now we're tired and content. For dinner, red lentil soup and endive salad, which Amanda eats with her fingers, having read that it's like asparagus. For dessert, hot cider mixed with tea and gingerbread cookies from Madison's kitchen.

I build a fire in the living room. Amanda's looking at Leonardo's sketches for pumping water. Firelight glows behind her. Her high cheekbones are a wonder. She stands and, backlit by the flickering light, tips into a 'roundhouse' cartwheel, meaning she lands on both feet. This makes the wheel so narrow she can do it indoors. No one else makes me feel so free.

But funny, sunny Amanda isn't smiling. Tomorrow's the day. She's attempted to charm me, yet nothing's changed. I haven't consented to ignore her mother.

She's in the TV room staring at the backyard through the sliding door, the glass etched with frost. I touch her shoulder and she turns, lifting her face, waiting for me to speak.

I smooth her hair. 'If I could skip the tête-à-tête, I would.'

'What's a tête-à-tête?'

'It's a French idiom, meaning head-to-head, or, more accurately, face-to-face for a private chat.'

'Well, a tête-à-tête sounds fun. Not like having "a word" or giving someone a piece of your mind.'

'Amanda, when I worked at the bank, I dealt with professional negotiators. And I often won.'

'So what, Walter? Cheryl will agree or disagree, but either way she will keep doing what she does. All *you're* doing is giving her reason to hurt me, and she doesn't need reasons.'

'Hurt you, how?'

'You know how! Nothing that shows. In fact, nothing physical anymore now that I'm taller and stronger than her. She's just mean as hell.'

'I'm sorry, honey. Come here.' We sit together on the couch.

Amanda has some sense of what happens to me when she glances at me over her shoulder. I've seen her testing the effect. A glance from her and I'm moved in every direction at once. She gets me going like that and kneels on the couch. She cups her hands by my ear and whispers, 'This thing with us, Walter, is supernatural.'

She turns on the TV and I wrap an arm around her. She moves her hair and finds my hand, pressing it along the length of her neck. Her lashes flutter. Her eyes meet mine, and I can see her wondering what it would take to stop me from talking to her mother.

So, I tell her again why it's an obligation—and still she doesn't understand.

If her head continues to rest against my heart, my distress will beat so hard, she'll hear it. I ask if she would mind fixing us sparkling water and pomegranate juice.

Freed of the stirring caused by her physical presence, I review what I'm going to say to Cheryl. What I believe to be necessary is this: If Amanda can make *me* dangerous—me, the nice, quiet father of her daughter's erstwhile best friend—consider what the next guy might be like!

Possibly, Amanda's realized her displays of affection are part of the problem. Because my sublime tormentor, who so relentlessly sneaked past all my barriers, has withdrawn.

'Here.' She hands me a glass of sparkling water.

'Where's yours?'

She shakes her head before throwing herself onto the floor. Turning to look at me, her feet crisscrossing in the air, she says, 'I'm not thirsty.'

'Will you sit beside me?'

'I'm comfortable like this.'

'All right.' She stares at the TV, unable to understand why I'm doing this to her.

'Your mother needs to know she's already caused you harm, but if she continues, people will start to take advantage of you. I need to tell her that, Amanda, for the record.'

She rises onto her knees and faces me. 'Cheryl doesn't keep records.'

'Honey, what if instead of me, some other man wanted to take care of you?'

'No other man is going lure me into his clutches, if that's what you're worried about. Do you think I don't know the world is dangerous?'

Amanda stands up and I edge forward on the couch, but stop—uncertain what's right. She hasn't jumped on me all week. She's obeyed all the rules! I'm seeing the real Amanda—the part of her that never changes, whether she's presenting a startling insight or watching cartoons and whistling to match the characters' vocal patterns.

'Why don't you say something?' She pushes me back into the couch by my shoulders, which fills me with pleasure even though she intended it as a rebuke. When Amanda's angry, her complexion radiates a shimmering heat.

I stand up, estimating the space between us—not too near, not too far.

I cannot quiet the storm inside me. When did Amanda's eyebrows become so dark and dramatic, framing her eyes, which seem impossibly wide apart? They were always the rare and beautiful color of glowing amber, but now they're almost painfully sharp and deep.

'We're not like other people, Walter. And we're especially not like Cheryl. Have you forgotten that? The whole reason we have a pact is because we're not like her!' She turns away, but not before I see her gorgeous eyes brimming. Without her jacket, she runs outside and across the street. I wait in the kitchen, as always, but she doesn't flick the lights. After a minute, I flick my kitchen lights. Another minute and I flick them again. Finally, she flicks her bedroom light once, and then her house is dark.

I text: *JSYK, I would never tell anyone what we share.*

I haven't had alcohol for months, but now I reach for the bottle of Dewar's. Then, suddenly, I'm asleep on my feet. Several minutes later, I'm crawling into bed. And when I close my eyes, I see—and feel—Amanda's head resting in the palm of my hand. I see, too, that my constant desire to support her head is necessary. Her neck is like a flower stem; her head is like the sun.

The real Amanda seems unreal to me. While I—I just seem insane.

Sixteen

The clock reads three in the morning. Unable to sleep, I find myself downstairs wearing only my underwear. I slide open the TV room's glass doors and stand outside—alone in the stark cold backyard. Alone in the dark silence. A halo surrounds the moon. Coating the flagstone beneath my feet are layers of ice on which my bare soles stick and slip. It's ghostly cold. My heart beats a plea to the earth and sky: Do not let my passion warp her. *Do not let me harm her in any way!*

The longer Amanda and I persist like this, the more my fantasy—that she wants what I want—infiltrates unguarded moments. And even thinking of this soon becomes an evil meditation.

Amanda's keenly aware of the unique emotional lines and arcs connecting us. What happens now could determine much of her entire life. And so, I vow and vow again: I will never hurt her. And yet, an awful aspect haunts me.

After a shivery pause, watching my pale breath disperse into the freezing black atmosphere, I resolve not to distance myself from her just because a vile distortion lies beneath all that is good in me. For if I grew cool now—which I cannot imagine—Amanda would never forgive me. I would never forgive myself.

And so—just what *do* I tell her mother? The rush of Amanda's affection exhausts me. Yet without it, I would die. Amanda knows this. She knows, too, that I love her much more than is defensible. I've told her this. But I pray that's all she knows! Let her never suspect my struggle to keep my sick longings locked inside my feverish fears and dreams.

What if Cheryl does, in fact, listen to me? If she suddenly became present and attentive to her daughter, it would shatter me. But then sooner or later, I must be shattered. And that's exactly what I should convey to Amanda's mother. That despite a disciplined nature and a mostly pure heart, some of my feelings are perverted.

Indoors, I drink a sobering glass of Scotch but cannot get warm. I take a long hot shower and fall asleep, wrapped in towels beneath the blankets.

A few hours later, I'm running Rockefeller Park's longest loop. In the receding night, the bitter air renders everything— the ground, trees, steps, dead leaves, droppings, and boulders— incorporeal shadows. I'm layered in thermal winter running gear. From beneath my woolen cap, sweat streams down my face and neck. The wind's against me and I started too fast. Returning, I slow my pace and enter Oak Grove Point at a fast walk. And instead of sprinting to the top as usual, I practically stagger around the final turn.

Amanda's sitting on my front step, shivering in flannel pajamas, her skin bright from the cold, her long honey-colored hair heavy and wet down her back.

'Why aren't you inside?' She knows the door's unlocked. 'Are you trying to *make* yourself sick?'

'Don't be mad, Walter. I'm already sick for being such a brat.'

'You're not a brat.'

She's brought two big grocery bags, which I lift, one in each gloved hand, and set on the kitchen counter. Amanda's phone pings. It's Cheryl. 'Yeah, okay. Mom? I love you.' She stares into space and looks dispirited. She sighs. 'My mom will be here in an hour.'

'Has anything changed, honey? Because while I want your mother to know what's happening in case I get caught—'

Almost comically, she gasps and covers her mouth. '*That's* it? *That's* why you want it on record?'

'—I can't imagine what I'd do if she took you away. Do you know if that's likely to happen? Is she getting tired of chasing her boss?'

Amanda whoops with relief and joy. She flies toward me, and this time I open my arms and her legs wrap tight around my waist. We spin into the living room and she's singing. She thought I was tired of taking care of her.

All my conjecture—that she knows her power over me—was wrong. Amanda's experience hasn't prepared her to be adored.

Sinking damply into the couch, I try to slow my heart. 'How could you think that, Amanda?' My chest heaves now that I've lifted her off my lap. She pulls off my cap and her fingers comb my sweat-soaked hair. I stop her by pressing my fingers on top of hers. 'I need to shower and change. And you should go home and get dressed. Do you have a hair dryer?'

She hates hair dryers. I'm ushering her through the kitchen and out the door when she looks up and says, 'I've always been afraid you'd get tired of me. But I'm much more afraid, so much I don't let myself think about it, that you'll get in trouble.'

'I won't get in trouble for being a good neighbor. But your mother needs to know that. It's the reason I have so many rules.'

For once, Amanda approves of this. She says, 'See you soon.'

I shower, shave, and dress. When I come downstairs, Amanda's in the kitchen, wearing an oversized gray sweat suit and dirty canvas sneakers without laces or socks. Before commenting, I remember—all her nice clothes are hidden.

Her grocery bags contain cupcake ingredients. 'Madison's family has this tradition of red velvet cupcakes on Christmas.'

'What are red velvet…?'

She's on the phone with Madison, saying the recipe calls for 'cake flour' and all she has is regular white flour. 'Will that work?'

It will. They, like everyone else, hang up without a goodbye.

I offer to measure and mix the dry ingredients. Amanda blends butter, sugar, and eggs in the mixer. When she adds the buttermilk, baking soda, vinegar, vanilla, and two ounces of red food coloring, the batter sprays all over. She shrieks and turns off the machine.

I tell her not to worry. It'll be easy to clean up, and start to dip a finger into the bowl but she grabs my wrist.

'It's got raw eggs in it. You could get food poisoning.'

I tap her head and step back, letting her take charge. Then we hear Cheryl's car, and we both turn to the window as a new cream-colored SUV pulls into Amanda's driveway.

'Wait here.' I run outside and waylay Cheryl, who has yet to unbuckle her seatbelt.

Without asking permission, I circle around to the passenger side of the car and hop in. 'Ms. Jonette, Cheryl—Merry Christmas,' I say.

And she screeches. My hands are red with food coloring.

'Whatever that shit is, don't get it on my new car. Greg gave me this for Christmas.'

'It's cupcake batter with red food coloring. It'll come off with a little soap and water. We need to talk. I take it Amanda's warned you.'

'Warned me? She didn't warn me of anything.'

'Your daughter grows more wonderful every day, and I love seeing her blossom and mature. But, as I've tried to explain to you before, I don't always trust myself around her. Because, even though I've known her since she was three, she doesn't always strike me as the child she is. A lot of the time—and we spend a lot of time together, Cheryl—it's as if…as if…she's thirteen going on thirty.'

Cheryl tilts her head back and approximates a laugh. 'Of course, she is! I couldn't work upstate most of the week except that Amanda copes as well as any adult.'

Most of the week? My dripping red index finger taps the top of the dashboard. 'My problem has nothing to do with Amanda coping. Last time you were here, my family had left. Not long after that, I lost my job. So, I'm restless and alone up here with your daughter, who is equally alone and more alluring all the time. Not deliberately, Ms. Jonette—'

'I hate being called Ms. Jonette.'

'Cheryl, then. If I'm unnecessarily formal, it's because alone with Amanda I struggle to remain—circumspect.'

She smirks.

'Respectable,' I clarify.

'Oh, please. You're perfectly respectable.'

'I care about your daughter.' My finger pounds the dash harder and faster. 'Nobody else comes up here.'

'Your secret's safe.'

'My secret?'

Cheryl snorts as if amused. 'Not that it *needs* to be secret. You're like a father to her. And she's like a daughter to you.'

'Except, I'm not her father and she's not my daughter.' I've rehearsed this conversation using every conceivable variable, none of which sounds right. Plowing ahead, I phrase it as well as I can. 'There's no *biological* taboo between us.'

'That's what's so great!' Bracelets jangling, Cheryl lifts her hands like hallelujah. 'That's why you two get along better than any real father and daughter ever could.'

I try again. 'It's difficult, because my feelings are such that I should stay away from her—for her sake. If I could, I would leave. But if I did that, she'd be alone, and that—well, that would be criminal. To abandon her, I mean.'

Cheryl's whole body quivers in what I can only assume is outrage. Her voice shakes. 'Don't you dare tell me what's criminal! We've discussed this and you agreed to watch out for her. Winter has stranded me, I'm afraid, but once Greg and I are married, Amanda will have a real home.'

'Do you understand what I'm afraid of?'

In a furious stream, Amanda races from my house and slaps the roof of the new car. Time's up. Cheryl opens her door to greet her daughter but at my insistence shuts it again. I try to ignore Amanda's frantic, pleading expression.

'We haven't settled this.'

'Oh, I think we have, Walter. If you care about Amanda at all—'

'When I'm with her, I can't control my feelings. I'd die before allowing myself to take advantage of her, but she's all I think about.'

There. That's blunt enough. So blunt, in fact, that I catch a glimmer of comprehension in Cheryl's small dull eyes. But the faint, fleeting light disappears as she refocuses on her own agenda. 'Nonsense! You'd never take advantage of her.'

'How do you know that?'

'Well, Amanda knows you wouldn't. And, she knows how to take care of herself, so there's no need to get dramatic. Give me a few months. In the meantime, I'll do my best to get here more often.'

Short of grabbing the monstrous woman's shoulders and describing everything I yearn to do to her daughter—impulses I refuse to articulate even to myself—what else is there to say? Am I ethically bound to admit that I desire her thirteen-year-old daughter in every conceivable way? That I love Amanda to the exclusion of all else?

I unfold myself from the car, but before crossing the driveway, I glance at Amanda, who's no doubt overheard more than she should have. She hugs her mother and strokes her fur hat. I recall an early secret Amanda told me—she loves her mother. Mean, neglectful, even abusive, the woman is still her mother.

Seventeen

After cleaning up the splattered red-velvet cupcake batter, I eat a sandwich and two flavorless oranges. Lift weights to a playlist of jazz trumpeters and read a long essay on the history of Mideast wars. I do the laundry and a few other chores. All of which only adds to my restlessness until I decide to attend the Christmas Eve service at the Episcopal Church, which Sterling joined for social reasons. I wear a suit I bought last year but have never worn. After having it tailored, I realized it was slightly too bright for work.

The church is crowded. Walking in and out, it's 'Merry Christmas' all around. Everyone seems to know me, although their names elude me—it has been years since I met these people at Sterling's cocktail parties. I nod politely when they ask after her and Olivia, and promise to pass along everyone's best wishes.

Outside after the uninspiring service, I see Nina Malloy and tell her she looks great. I kiss her cheek and do not discourage her from chatting a while, despite the cold. My impulse is to suggest we get together sometime. But, recognizing that I'll never follow through on the gesture, I don't mention it.

When I return home, all the lights are on in Amanda's house. How strange that I find this alarming.

*

Christmas morning, I run, shower, get dressed, and eat. Having straightened everything in the house, I roam from room to room, staring through the windows. Soon, I'll make my way to church for the noontime service. Wearing a suit last night bordered on a new experience. That's how far I've come from my earlier life. Today I select a different suit, a subtle dark check that also wasn't quite subtle enough for me at Bank of America.

*

When I see Nina after this second service, I tell her I didn't realize she was so religious. She laughs and says she was going to say the same thing to me. I kiss her cheek again and start to walk away, but turn back. 'Are you and Sterling still friends?'

Her tired face awakens. 'I was thinking of asking you the same thing.'

'We're still married and still friendly, which isn't the same as being friends, but please don't tell her I said that.'

'Walter, she doesn't deserve you.'

'Don't be too sure.' My tone is teasing and she blushes. 'Merry Christmas, again.' I regret ever having been cold or critical toward her. I simply didn't know better.

At home, I check my phone and find that Olivia has sent a photo of Karl and her dressed up to see *The Nutcracker Suite*.

For Christmas, I sent her four tickets to the ballet in Bangor. Also, a black velvet dress that's a little too tight, but that's how she likes her clothes to fit—so every curve shows. For his part, Karl wears a white T-shirt topped with a maroon smoking jacket. I'm still looking at the photo when she phones and says that Karl found the jacket in a vintage shop in Bath, which is where his dad's indoor skateboarding park is.

'You may not like *The Nutcracker*, sweetheart, but I wanted to give you something you wouldn't choose on your own.'

'We're flipping, Daddy. Karl's been playing Tchaikovsky on the piano instead of Rachmaninoff. And, we watched a DVD of the San Francisco Ballet performing it. Most of all, though, I love the dress. All I got you is a book.'

'That's a book in the package you sent? I was afraid it might be socks.'

Olivia giggles. 'Mommy gets you socks. The book is about Lehman Brothers going down. The author writes for *Rolling Stone*.'

'I've heard it's supposed to be great.'

'Except you already know the story.'

'Not even half. I had a great boss at Lehman, who told me upfront that I wouldn't be able to change the culture and not to bother trying. So, now I'm thinking of going to law school.'

'Karl says banking crimes are so complicated, nobody can figure 'em out.'

'The people committing them know what they're doing. Did Karl read this book?'

'He read the part of it that was in *Rolling Stone*. I just sent you another photo.'

'I see that. You look beautiful, both of you. Are those new shoes?'

'Granny gave them to me.'

'Does Mommy approve of your wearing high heels?'

'Of course not. Daddy, did you know Granny has a boyfriend? She and Professor Emerson went to Palm Springs for Christmas. You wouldn't like Chill—Karl's mom's boyfriend. He smokes weed all day while Amy works. She's an emergency room nurse and works long shifts, double sometimes. Chill fools with his grow lights and watches old Westerns. "Classic films," he says.'

'Who's driving you to Bangor?'

'Amy always drives. But first, we're eating dinner at a fancy restaurant.'

'Will you call me next week, Olivia, for New Year's?'

'I'm calling you now, Daddy.'

'Can you visit? When's your next vacation?'

'I can't come for spring break. I told Amanda. I'll come when school gets out.'

'Summer's a long time from now.'

'I love you, Daddy. And I love my Christmas presents.'

I say something agreeable and we hang up. It makes me sad that Olivia won't call next week (and she's made it clear I'm not to call her), but perhaps I deserve it. I first thought of tickets to *The Nutcracker* and a black velvet dress as presents for Olivia when a fashion catalog arrived in the mail for Sterling. A girl Amanda's size modeled the dress. I spent most of an afternoon imagining zipping it up Amanda's lovely warm back, holding her hair in one hand and then pushing the pearl button in and out of the loop at her nape. We would have loved going to the ballet together. But I'm doing my best to keep things—appropriate.

Five minutes later, Sterling phones. She and Kevin are staying at Kaye's house while she's in California with Roy Emerson.

'Thank you for the antique tiles, Walter. Kevin says they're from the late nineteenth century. He thinks he's seen them before.'

'I'm glad you like them. Just don't use them around food.'

'Why?'

'They used to use uranium to make that color.'

'I'm not worried. They're beautiful. You and I are going to have a remarkable home and everything in it will refer to us.'

'You know how I hate that.'

'You won't hate our home. It will be refined, not ostentatious. Have you opened your present? I hope it inspires you.'

'The dollhouse?'

She sighs. 'It's an architectural rendering, but fill it with dolls if you want. At least you'll be doing something.'

'You have no idea what I do.'

'You read about Leonardo da Vinci.'

'Goodbye, Sterling.'

'Wait. I'm sorry. In a few months, I'll be home.'

'I miss Olivia. You and I might be able to start over—or we might not.'

'Don't be so negative. When I come back I'll make up for lost time.'

It's always been easy to ignore Sterling's provocations. But I've changed. 'Have *you* ever considered going back to work? The banks are in desperate need of your assistance.'

'What's that supposed to mean?'

'You were great at your job, Sterling.'

'After fifteen years I doubt I could just pick up where I left off.'

'You had a significant presence. And you still know people.'

She's crying, and it sounds as if she may start wailing. I'm about to hang up when she says, 'Wait!'

So, I wait.

'Without me, Walter, you might never do anything again.'

'Merry Christmas to you and Kevin, and see you in the spring, perhaps. In the meantime, remember who's providing all the money to fund your lifestyle up there.'

'I'll call you next week.'

'Let's get through the winter. Then we'll talk.'

'You need me, Walter. You think you don't, but you do.'

I hang up and take another shower.

Eighteen

Christmas afternoon, I receive a FedEx envelope. Inside is a winter greeting card—moonlight on snowdrifts. Printed in pen is a quote from Leonardo da Vinci: *He who does not punish evil, commands it to be done,* legibly signed, Glen Engle, who hopes to see me in the New Year. Glen Engle didn't send this. He doesn't want to see me. And nobody I worked with would connect me to Leonardo da Vinci.

Then I remember that Heather, Glen's assistant, once worked at Lehman and was Sterling's friend. Chances are, she asked Heather to send this in the hope that I would phone Glen and make amends. Unlikely perhaps, but Sterling is as upset now about me being out of work as she was the day after I was fired.

Downstairs, I admire the four oversized cupcakes I baked yesterday with the remaining red-velvet cupcake batter. Contained in fluted green paper, they smell delicious. Their rich dark red tops are full, rounded mounds. The aroma reminds me of Amanda.

I'm reading the frosting recipe when she sends a text.

Cheryl's cramming years of mother-daughter stuff into every minute! We've already had two screaming matches!

I text back: *I'm here if you need me, honey.*

A minute later, Amanda phones. 'I'm locked in the bathroom,' she whispers. 'I might have to hang up any second. Did the red food coloring stain your kitchen?'

'The cleanup was easy.' I don't notice my lie until I've said it and quickly tack on a happier truth. 'There was enough batter left for four cupcakes. They're very tempting.'

'Will you wait for me? Cheryl won't leave until tomorrow. She wants to go now, but if she did, it would mean she was a bad mother.'

No trace of irony.

'Of course, honey. See you tomorrow.'

*

The next morning, when I return from my run, all their lights are burning. Hours later, just past noon, Cheryl charges from the house dragging her luggage. She turns around screaming, but Amanda closes the door. Cheryl doesn't care. Inside her new car, she turns around carefully before peeling away.

Five minutes pass and Amanda appears at my door wearing pajamas.

'Get your clothes from the garage, take them home, and come back dressed as usual.'

'Can't we pretend it's Christmas morning? We've been up all night too excited to sleep.'

'No. From now on, I'm on heightened alert. Your mother laughed at my *talk*.'

'Told you.'

'Yes, you did. Hurry so we can exchange presents and frost the cupcakes.'

She knows what I'm giving her—white figure skates. She saw me buy them at the White Plains ice rink. So, she admires the silver wrapping paper and red satin ribbon before carefully peeling away the tape. Laughing, she laces one of the skates and stands, balancing on her bare foot. She arches her back and reaches up, over and behind to grasp her raised ankle, her leg forming an arc. I'm amazed she can do this. Almost immediately, she topples. She steadies herself on the one blade, her fingertips, lightly grazing the floor, helping her to balance.

'Nobody can spin on a rug, Amanda.'

She shakes her head and pulls on the other skate.

'Wait,' I say. 'We'll have someone at the shop check the fit.' They have a machine there that stretches the leather. 'Leave the guards on, though. The blades are very sharp.'

Sitting beside me on the floor, she hands me a flat, square package wrapped in tissue paper and decorated with stick-on stars. Instead of kissing her, I kiss the wrapping and set the present on the coffee table. 'I'm saving the best for last. Let's see what I got myself.' I rip red and white paper from a large box.

'Hockey skates, Walter! If only I had gotten them for you!'

'Anyone can buy skates. I'm guessing that you're giving me something that very few people, if any, can buy.'

She nods, bright and happy. 'Nobody can buy this.'

While I carefully unwrap the flat package, Amanda sings under her breath. It's a classical song in German. Before I ask about it, however, I'm unfolding a long tightly knit scarf of blue and gray.

'It's herringbone,' she says.

'It's beautiful, Amanda. You didn't make this, did you?'

She did. Jade taught her to knit straight stitch when she was six. 'I never made anything, but I remembered enough for Margo to teach me how to make this.'

Spreading it between my hands, I say, 'It's so soft—and perfect.'

'The yarn's alpaca,' she says. 'Margo's mother gave it to me from her store. It's supposed to be very warm but lightweight.

The knitting isn't perfect.' She points to two tiny holes. Margo, who has enrolled to study poetry at Sarah Lawrence College, wanted Amanda to go back and fix her mistakes. But she barely had enough time as it was.

'It's the finest scarf I've ever seen.' I move to hug her, but she climbs into my lap. I push her off as if she's on fire, because I am.

Sometimes, when I push Amanda away, she acts hurt. But this afternoon, she uncurls her long lithe body and rolls onto the floor, saying, 'We feel the same.'

'Maybe our rapport is deeper than that. Feelings change over time. But you and I…'

'I know.' Amanda's voice is low and ripe with potential.

What the hell is wrong with me? Talking to her like that! I stare out the window for a second, composing myself, and then leave the room.

She finds me sitting at the kitchen table, facing the bay window. From behind, she wraps her arms around me and lays her head against my shoulder. 'Don't be sad.'

My fingers touch hers, layered over my chest. 'The rink in Elmsford is open until six. Want to go?'

*

The shop adjusts our skates. Amanda can't get used to her super-sharp blades. She clings to me the way she did that first time we went skating, but then, skating is our excuse to cling together. At closing time, nobody's in much of a hurry. I'm faint from hunger and buy pistachios in the shell from a vending machine.

Halfway home, Amanda pulls a bottle of greenish-black nail polish from her bag. 'Margo gave Madison this but their mom won't let either of them wear it. She's so strict, it's stupid.'

'I have to agree with her. You're too young for Goth.'

'It's just a little nail polish.' She tosses the bottle behind her, into the back seat.

'You know those girls who spend their time on Main Street?'

'The ones who wear lots of make-up and not enough clothes? Say what you mean. Are you afraid I'll look slutty?'

'Damn it, Amanda! How can you say that?'

'Because you're warning me not to look like the slutty girls on Main Street.'

'That's ridiculous. My worst thought, if you must know, is a wish to keep you a girl forever. Is that sick enough for you?'

'Oh, please.' She plays a phantom violin and hums a lugubrious tune. She continues to play, and at a stoplight, I nudge her shoulder. 'I'd cry but I forgot my handkerchief.'

*

Tonight we eat a quick dinner. I load the dishwasher. Amanda makes the frosting, following Madison's recipe, and I fix a pot of tea. We drink orange pekoe and eat our cupcakes while watching the season opener of *The Real Miranda*.

A character named Sam has shown up with the best superpower: bilocation, the ability to be in two places at once. The twist is that Sam is a pretty girl when she hangs out with the girls. But around the boys, Sam is all bro and basketball. The camera shows Sam laughing, fighting, and bro-ing out at one end of the cafeteria while simultaneously showing off a floaty new skirt with an asymmetrical hem at the other.

Amanda says, 'They use minimal computer imagery. Multiple cameras, hair, make-up, and clothes help. But mostly, it's the actor's gestures and expressions.'

'The acting is excellent.'

'Does that mean you like the show?'

'Very much.'

'Is bilocation possible?' Amanda asks.

'Lots of impossible things,' I tell her, 'can be proven to be possible—in theory.'

'But not in reality.'

'Not yet.'

Nineteen

It's Amanda's first day back at school and she refuses to accept a ride, even though the temperature has dropped below freezing. After watching her skip down the hill in her white down jacket and knee-high leather boots, I put my coffee cup in the sink and get my coat.

At the New Rochelle Honda dealership (not the one in nearby Mount Vernon, where I test drove the car last week), a salesman shakes my hand. 'The Accord rates higher for gas mileage than any other car this year—in any price range.'

'I just want something reliable and generic.'

He murmurs approval. 'A vehicle like this blends in. You'll save on traffic tickets.' He leads me to a metallic gray sedan, New York plates, black interior, and lists its selling points.

I interrupt. 'For a fair price, I'll pay in full. Today.'

'Ah.' He straightens his tie and signals for the branch manager to join us. For full payment, the branch manager says, he can include 'an incredible deal' on a high-end sound system.

'Yes, but I want the car for transportation, not parties.'

'You never know…'

The salesman gestures to his colleague—he's got this.

The next day, after Amanda has danced her way down the hill, I call a taxi to take me to New Rochelle to complete the transaction. An hour later, and I drive away in the new gray Honda Accord.

Thinking I should prepare Amanda for this, I park it in the backyard, behind the tall hedge. But at 4:30, after she has tossed her backpack uphill and thrown it on her front steps, she runs to my front door.

She grabs my hand and pulls me in her excitement. 'Walter! Wow! Come on!'

At the backyard fence, she opens the gate, and runs to the car. 'You bought this for us!' She swings open the front passenger door, slides into the seat, and flips the windshield's sun flap. 'We're going incognito!'

I laugh and stand back. And—Christ! She flies into my arms. Her legs wrap around my waist and her lips fill my ear with sweet bated breath. 'I love it, Walter! I love you.'

Her hands at my neck nearly bring me to my knees. I stagger, rushing with desire from her delectable weight and warmth and extraordinary joy. It astounds me that I'm able to contain the upwelling inside me. My vision blurs as I pry her loose and set her on her feet.

'Amanda,' I tilt her chin.

'The car is awesome and you bought it just for us. We can go anywhere now and not get caught!'

'Caught driving around?'

'Oh, you know. Someone sees how much you drive me around in the Mazda and starts wondering.' She slaps my arm. 'You *know* that.'

I step back, and I don't know what else to do: shake my head? Put up my hands? I recall her looking through me when bicycling past the barber shop, and how her apparent total indifference stung me more than I dared to admit. Now she's hugging and thanking me, and I smooth her hair.

'Of course, I know, honey. That's exactly what this car is for. So that we can go places and do things—without people jumping to conclusions that are none of their business.'

4. PLEASURE AND PAIN

Twenty

January–May 2015

On a fiercely cold Saturday, we drive north to Bear Mountain. And are the only ones ice-skating, buffeted by a harsh wind. Within the bone-chilling blasts, we cling to each other even more than usual. I slip behind her, nearly delirious from contact. Holding her shoulders, I lean forward, brushing my face against her beehive hat. 'Let's go to the Lodge and get warm.'

Amanda twists around and shouts above the gale, 'Not yet! We still have an hour.'

So we keep skating as fast as we can, staving off frostbite.

Inside the Lodge, feeling nearly weightless without our skates, we relax in the narcotic warmth. I find a brochure about a glassblowing workshop here on the grounds. Amanda questions the young man at the front desk, while I linger behind a Christmas tree left up too long, the better to watch her. She's stuffed her hat and mittens inside the sleeve of her jacket, which trails after her on the carpet. Her hair swings one way, her body the other.

Amanda skips toward me, displaying a glossy magazine, *Bear Mountain Lodge, Then and Now.* Flipping to the magazine's 'Now' section, she shows me ads for the dining room upstairs and a downstairs café.

As if we're still on the ice, she starts to take my hand but withdraws it, fast. 'Oops.' She shakes her head and jumps onto the staircase. The dining room has twenty-one tables with white tablecloths. A waiter seats us beneath a huge leaded window framing a snowy field. The menu includes prix fixe meals as well as à la carte. We order chili, cornbread, and hot cider.

Amanda reads to me from the magazine. 'Every room includes a sheltered balcony, allowing guests to appreciate the winter wonderland.'

'*Winter wonderland?* It says that?'

'No, but it should. Snow glowing in the moonlight. The immense white mountain against the black night.'

I laugh and ask to see the page. 'Each room has a sheltered balcony, Amanda. That's all it says.'

'But wouldn't it be cool to stay overnight? No school on Monday, remember. It's MLK Day.'

'Honey, we're an hour from home.'

'That's perfect,' she says. 'Nobody will come anywhere near here.'

'That's not what bothers me.'

'We can get separate rooms. On separate floors.'

I sputter at this. 'Separate floors? What, in case I'm Jekyll and Hyde?'

'*In case?* Walter, you always act like a murderous madman could burst out of you at any second.'

'Slight exaggeration. And, how do you even know about Jekyll and Hyde?'

'It's something people say.' Amanda lifts a spoonful of chili and wrinkles her forehead while blowing on it. She takes a taste and puts the spoon down. Looks around and sighs wistfully.

Her gestures reveal both her question and my inevitable answer. (*Can we just peek at the rooms?*)

(*No.*)

She pushes her red lips together and lowers her eyes, her thick lashes brushing against her cheeks.

No doubt she hasn't a clue how her pout emphasizes that, with each passing week, her mouth looks more like a woman's and less like a child's.

Similar expressions arise on weekend nights when we watch TV later than usual. Amanda sometimes asks if just once she can sleep in Olivia's room. Her house—Cheryl's house—she claims, might as well be haunted.

Early on, whenever I denied her, Amanda's eyes would fill. She would turn away so I wouldn't see, although, of course I did. These days, she's the one who upsets me, but she's long accepted that I always say no.

Now, in this variation of the game, she leans back in her chair, radiating all of her wild, innocent beauty. I blink. She smiles and shifts sideways, crossing her legs and twirling the top ankle. 'You're a hard man, Walter, blaming a girl just for asking.'

We laugh at that—her movie-starlet dialog.

I pay the bill. Back outside, we huddle together against the wind, hurrying along the trail to the glassblowing workshop.

In a clearing, tarps are strung on poles. Bleacher-like seats are set at a careful distance from two roaring furnaces, one closed, one open. I know from the pamphlet that the white-hot fire in the closed furnace burns at nearly 3,000 degrees Fahrenheit. Set up just inside it are sacks of molten glass that serve as raw material. The open furnace, known as the glory hole, is where the glassblowers deposit the worked glass to cool down.

Two artisans welcome us. My guess is that they're about my age, although their manner makes them seem younger. Brian tells us that besides being glassblowers, they're musicians. Luke plays keyboards, Brian guitar and vocals. But they're serious about glass. They wear leather aprons, wrecked jeans, and faded T-shirts. Brian has a trimmed goatee and mustache. Luke has a tattoo of barbed wire circling his neck.

The furnaces draw trickles of sweat from my skin. I unzip my jacket and pocket my wool cap. Brian invites Amanda to help him make a paperweight. They'll use a long pipe to spin the glass. Blowing through the tube is advanced stuff.

Luke is already blowing a small bubble of glass through a narrow tube. He's added pigment to make it red. It will become a little rose in the paperweight's center.

Brian retrieves a molten blob from the furnace and calls to Amanda. She must slip between his arms to turn the pipe with him. She ducks beneath his bare bicep and I shift to see him cover Amanda's hands with his before spinning the tube. He turns his head, so that I half hear him make a harmless comment: 'You thought it would be heavier, didn't you?'

But Amanda doesn't respond.

Luke pulls the red dollop from the cooling furnace and drops it onto a steel table. He uses tweezers to shape petals.

Backed into Brian, Amanda calls, 'Daddy! Come and see.'

I stand up and Brian releases Amanda to insert the spun glass into the cooling furnace. 'You're her father?' he asks.

'Her mother swears on all that's holy.'

'I didn't mean it like that. It's just—aren't you my age?'

'Thirty-three.'

'Exactly.'

Staring at the ground, muddy from melted snow, Brian kicks one boot with the other. I'm certain he guessed both my age and Amanda's on sight. For as graceful and lovely as Amanda is, nobody would mistake her for an eighteen-year-old. Nevertheless, he's more intent on her than on the molten glass. At the steel table, he says, 'Over here, little girl.'

Amanda rolls her eyes at me but does as he instructs, dropping the clear blob onto Luke's tiny rose. I ask how long before we can take it home, but Amanda says that I should make something for 'Mommy.'

Brian sits beside her, swinging his leg, while Luke directs me in the creation of a yellow starfish. Before Luke drops the yellow blob on the steel table, Amanda puts on her mittens, says, 'I'll wait in the car, Daddy,' and takes off.

In a hurry, I go ahead and shape the spun yellow mass with tweezers. It's comically uneven, but good enough. When I pay for our lessons, Brian suggests I write down our address and he'll mail us the paperweights. 'Or, you can come back next weekend. We're always here. Next time, you'll be ready for some real glassblowing.'

'Okay,' I tell him. 'See you then.' He mutters at my back, knowing we won't return.

Amanda's waiting in the car. 'What a jerk!'

'He didn't know what to make of you.'

She shudders. 'Yes, he did.'

I shudder too, although it probably doesn't show. 'You did the right thing, then. Don't be afraid to tell someone off, if they're giving you unwanted attention.'

Twisting her hair, she says, '"No" means "no." Thing is, sometimes I'm not sure what's happening until after the fact.'

'Don't wait to make sure, Amanda. If you feel the littlest bit uneasy, say so and leave. If someone accuses you of being rude, tell them you don't respect people who don't respect you.'

'All right! I will.'

'And honey, I would be honored if you thought of me as your father.'

'Don't say that. It's disgusting.'

'Why?'

'In public, I might say it 'cause it's just easier. But you totally are *not* my father, Walter. The idea's enough to make me puke.'

Twenty One

In February, I receive another FedEx greeting card from Glen Engle, again quoting Leonardo da Vinci: *There are three classes of people. Those who see. Those who see when they are shown. Those who never see.*

He hopes for a meeting. Of course, the message isn't from Glen Engle but from his assistant, Heather, who has signed the card, 'Soon.'

Baffling that Sterling would imagine I could be so easily fooled. In the silence that accompanies unspoken communication, I recall another line from Leonardo's *Notebooks*: *Learning is the only thing the mind never exhausts, never fears, and never regrets.*

*

After dinner, my confused wife phones. I let it ring but tell Amanda I'm going upstairs to find out what Sterling wants.

'Whatever it is, you don't want me listening.'

'No, honey, it's the other way around. I don't want Sterling to know you're here—it's none of her business. And she's calling because she wants me to return to work for my old boss.'

Anxiety constricts Amanda's pupils and her eyes glow like dark gold, but she continues putting away the dinner things and singing.

In the bedroom, I phone Sterling and ask what's up.

'Remember my friend Heather Crosby?'

'Glen Engle's personal assistant.'

'Well, guess what? He wants to start a hedge fund—and he wants your help.'

'Did you tell them to send me Leonardo da Vinci quotes?'

'Did he really do that? Cool.'

'*She's* doing it and signing his name to greeting cards, which she sends FedEx. Christ, Sterling! If *you* want to work for Glen Engle, please do. In fact, you *should* work for him. But do not give Heather, Glen Engle, or anyone else pointers to manipulate me. It makes us both look stupid. Furthermore, I've told you more than once—my Wall Street days are over.'

'He's inviting you to set up an honest fund.'

'Honest? That won't hold up for ten minutes, so stop bothering me!'

'He wants you to devise a foolproof risk-management plan. Nobody else can do that.'

'Anyone who's honest can do it.'

*

Downstairs, Amanda waits for me in the hallway. 'Can you tell me what's happening?'

'Of course.' And I relay the conversation in full.

Amanda shifts side to side, not looking at me. 'Is Sterling coming back?'

'No. That is, not anytime soon.'

Relieved, Amanda throws her arms around me and I stroke her hair. We drift together until my mind swims.

Our physical contact still requires all my resolve. And yet, my base desires no longer frighten me, because our interaction has acquired a predictable, and therefore reassuring, pattern. We start with give and take, give and take, push and pull, until—stop right there!

Naturally, my dreams race and nightmares rage, often interchangeably, all night, every night. But when Amanda's with me, I keep my torments so well hidden they seem almost dormant.

*

Late in March, the Wednesday before her spring break begins, Amanda bursts into the kitchen and discards a pair of worn flip-flops. Her hair is wet and her legs are bare. Technically, spring began ten days ago, but our trees have yet to bud. The ground hasn't thawed.

I'm making risotto, ladling broth from one pan to another. From the sound of things, Amanda is furious. She dumps her homework in the small study we never use and closes its decorative windowed door. Meaning, she brought it here, but does not want me looking at it.

She storms back into the kitchen like a menacing whirlwind. I'm slowly stirring the not quite simmering risotto, but stare at her heels lifting until she's balancing on her toes. Seconds later, she's pulled the Dewar's from the top shelf. And begins pouring it in a glass full of ice cubes.

Stupidly, I ask, 'What are you doing?'

'Fixing you a drink.'

'No, thanks, Amanda. Just pour it down the sink.'

'No.' She hands me the glass, which I set on the counter.

'What's wrong, Walter? Are you afraid a sip of Scotch will rob you of all your inhibitions?'

Hearing her say 'inhibitions,' I feel my head shake in amused denial. Because I prefer to think of it as not letting anything blur our amazing affinity.

'If I'm wrong,' she says, arms crossed, 'drink that down.'

'Honey, I can't.'

'Then I will.' She grabs the glass, but instead of chugging the Scotch, coughs half a mouthful onto the floor.

'You see?'

She runs into the living room. I turn off the stove, leaving the risotto to turn to glue.

Amanda lies prone on the rug and pounds her feet in an angry rhythm. I crouch beside her and wait. After a while, I bend close to her ear and whisper, 'What's wrong?'

'Nothing.'

'That's not true.'

Teasing her, I ask, 'Is this the first time you've lied to me?'

Her body jackknifes up, her feet planted in the carpet, and her fists pressed her hips. 'You think *that's* a lie? What about all the lies you tell me?'

'I'm sorry. What lies?'

'Maybe you really are so warped,' Amanda says, 'that you want to be like a father to me. You and I who—were—so special we weren't like anyone!'

'Come here.' I move to hold her but she sidesteps me. 'I'm sorry, Amanda. The way I see it, we are who we are, with or without labels.'

She backs up and stamps her bare feet. 'I knew it! I knew you'd end up treating me like everyone else does.'

'Honey, sit down and talk to me.'

Angrier than ever, she drops her voice to a near growl. 'I'm the only girl in eighth grade who hasn't gotten her period.'

No urge to smile or cringe—I'll talk about anything with Amanda, and wish I could reassure her. But, obviously, I have no credibility here. In fact, a glance warns me against saying anything other than, 'Let's sit on the couch.'

'And talk about what? How people lie? That maybe I'm *not* the only one? Or that you personally can't speak from experience, but maybe a storm of hormones is affecting me minus the bloody evidence.'

I take her fingers and smile. 'Look into my eyes.'

Not funny—I should have known better than to joke. She flees. I move slowly and carefully, reaching the threshold just as she opens the front door and slams it behind her.

I've known since this started that Amanda will break my heart. It cannot be otherwise. But this isn't the end. Not yet. Did I slight her without realizing it?

Uncertain of what else to do, I salvage the dinner and text her. I pace and wait for an answer that doesn't come. After nearly two hours of runaway panic, I phone, knowing she won't pick up, which she doesn't. Sitting at the kitchen table, I stare out the bay window until she flicks her lights.

Twenty Two

Her house is dark at midnight when I step across the driveway and set her homework behind her crooked storm door.

I wake every hour, stand up, pull the curtain, and stare at her dark house and darker bedroom window.

Before dawn, I run through the park and, returning, continue past the aqueduct and onto Main Street, which ends near the river. The sun rises behind me and the first rays curiously illuminate a flower shop window. I marvel at roses that are a color I've never seen.

Except in dreams. They're Amanda's color, like persimmon, but less orange.

I sprint home, afraid my lost time will have cost me the sight of her skipping down the hill to school. But an hour before she leaves, I'm waiting at Olivia's bedroom window. In my deliberate insanity, I desperately will her to appear. Finally, there she is, charging down the hill. She does not toss and catch her backpack in her usual crisscrossing dance. But she does stop halfway, and instead of waving, knowing I'm watching, she extends her middle finger and dashes to the right, out of sight.

I shower and dress. All I can stomach are a few swallows of orange juice. I clean the house and lift weights, wondering about those roses. But I'm unable to phone the florist or leave the house. If I buy them for her, it could mark the beginning of the end. But how can I *not* buy them? Of course, they probably don't even exist—roses that color.

It's only 10:15. I'm staring at the ceiling, half asleep. The house phone rings. I pick up without checking the caller. A man's voice—Madison's father.

'Gil?'

He says the girls need to be at the school, dressed for the concert by 7:00 this evening. Madison asked him to drive her and Amanda, so if I'm willing, he'll drop them off and drive back to my house. Parking will be scarce, so why use two cars? His wife is attending Margo's poetry reading at Sarah Lawrence. He'll pick me up and we'll go straight to the auditorium.

'Concert?'

'Amanda didn't tell you? Madison says she was afraid to invite you. She thinks it's a lot to ask of a neighbor. Amanda's the soloist tonight. Schubert's *The Trout*.'

'What if she doesn't want me there?'

'She does.'

'I—'

'Walter, the girl doesn't have anyone else, and it's her big night. Cancel whatever plans you have, and I'll get Amanda the same flowers I'm getting Madison.'

'No, let me get them for her. And thanks, Gil. I'd hate to miss this. Amanda's always been shy with me but with Olivia gone… Sometimes she leaves presents for me and disappears when I try to thank her.'

'Buy the lovely soloist some roses. I'll drop off the girls and come back for you.'

I look outside for a minute before jumping in my old Mazda and driving to the Main Street florist (nobody in town has seen me in the Accord). Passing the middle school, I listen for her voice. Why didn't I notice she's been singing *The Trout* all winter?

The florist says, 'Good morning, Mr. Mitchell.' When I ask what her name is, her eyes narrow and I have to apologize and tell her I'm terrible with names.

'Helen.'

'Walter.' She nods. She's known my name for years. Of course, everyone in this little town knows each other.

I describe the roses I saw at daybreak and we share a vision. She says that perhaps the first light cast a hue over the yellow roses. Or maybe I'm clairvoyant, because a remarkable new hybrid comes close. She opens a catalog to a vivid, half-pink half-orange long-stemmed rose. Her Scarsdale store has some, if I don't mind paying extra. They're rare.

'Can I get a dozen delivered in a long white box this afternoon?'

She phones the other shop and then nods. Still talking on the phone, she writes the price of a dozen on a Post-it. She looks up, sees my expression, and asks the address. I give her Amanda's, which for a second I hope is close enough to mine not to arouse suspicion. Either way, the florist, if not the whole town, will know all about this.

Back on the phone, Helen says, 'Local, this afternoon,' and to me, 'Between four and five?'

'Perfect.'

She adds the delivery fee to the price and hands me the Post-it.

'Thank you. That's great.'

Phone still in hand, she asks what to write on the card.

'To the star soloist,' I say, 'from her admiring neighbor.'

She repeats my words to her partner in Scarsdale and hangs up. 'Amanda will be thrilled! If you don't mind my asking, are you attending the concert tonight?'

'Yes, Madison's father reminded me that Amanda has no one else.'

Helen tells me that the middle-school choirgirls all receive the same bouquets backstage. She expected Gil to buy Amanda's along with Madison's.

'No, Gil and I agreed that I'd get Amanda's.'

'It's small,' Helen says. 'Little white lilies and purple asters.'

I'm signing the credit card slip when Nina Malloy enters, looking heavier and pastier than when I saw her at Christmas. Swinging beside me, she takes my wrist, and then my hand, telling Helen, 'I noticed Walter here from across the street.'

I take her other hand. 'It seems like years.'

'More like two months. Where have you been hiding?'

I know just what to say and don't mind saying it. 'To be honest, Nina, I was wondering if you'd been hiding from me.'

Her mouth opens before making a pleased little smirk. She drops my hand and I drop hers. Now she's tracing little circles on my shirt.

'If you keep doing that,' I say, 'I could end up in trouble.'

'Why not tell Sterling she can't have it both ways?'

'I do tell her that. About once a week. Maybe you can talk to her.'

'Maybe I will.'

Helen finishes wrapping the small bouquet in cellophane, ties it with a satin ribbon, and asks me to write a card, then stores it in a box with many others.

Nina says, 'The middle-school concert—Amanda, right? What a nice neighbor you are.'

I smile as if we share a secret. Why did I find her so obnoxious before? I'm more attuned to people after all these months of being alone and out of work—and struggling with my feelings.

I know now that Nina's delighted by my attention and expects nothing more. She's already waved goodbye.

Before I can even ask, Helen is handing me a big yellow rose plucked from a metal bucket.

'You read my mind, thanks.' I give her five dollars, she protests, but I'm outside.

Nina's crossing the street and I call her, a hand behind my back. Can she advise me on a matter of taste? Curious, she walks toward me.

'What's your opinion of showy gestures?'

'That depends. Oh, well—' She laughs. 'Absolutely.' Rose to her nose, she thanks me and walks away, hips swaying.

*

Back at home, my anxieties mount. What if Amanda doesn't want me there? What if the roses embarrass her? On the low orange couch, I sink into a warm pool of sunlight. I'm sleeping there when she runs in from the kitchen. 'Walter, look! Look, come on, look. I can't believe this! I love you!'

We find a vase. She starts to apologize for last night.

I touch the top of her head. 'Hush, honey.'

'Are you really coming tonight?'

'I wouldn't miss it for anything. Besides, Gil invited me.'

She puts each rose in the tall vase, naming one, 'Amazing,' another, 'Magnificent,' and so on...

She asks if I've smelled them. I lower my face to the half-closed petals. 'A soft powder and, maybe, melon? Definitely intoxicating.'

Her face bright with pleasure, she says she's never smelled anything like them. She must get ready and jumps up to kiss my cheek before carrying her roses home.

When Gil pulls into her driveway, I'm watching from my bedroom window. Amanda runs outside, dressed in a flowing black skirt and fitted white top. Her hair is twisted up on her head and lovely curled tendrils frame her face and neck. She's hopping up and down. Laughing, she lifts her skirt a bit to show bare feet. A particular ache tells me I'll remember this sight of her, dressed for the concert, all my life.

Amanda runs inside and Gil gets out of his car. So does Madison, a nice-looking, round-faced teenager with short dark hair. She follows Amanda, who won't let her in. Within a minute, maybe less, Amanda returns, lifting her hem again, showing off little black shoes like ballet slippers. Still no sweater or jacket, though.

Twenty minutes later, as I'm scrutinizing myself in the mirror, Gil returns from dropping off the girls and honks. I'm wearing a simple-looking pale gray shirt of woven raw silk, black slacks, and short black boots with hiking soles.

Do we have time to drink a beer first?

No, Gil wants good seats, and with time to spare, he pulls into the middle-school parking lot. Faculty members meet us in the hallways. Each one says hi to Gil and asks me about Olivia. The teacher who told Sterling and me that Olivia would start eighth grade on probation says being in Maine should keep her independent streak within safe bounds. This town is too close to New York City and too full of kids with unlimited funds. I wholeheartedly agree and wonder why I didn't realize this myself. After asking about Olivia, each teacher tells me that Amanda's work is outstanding. They praise her talent and achievements in one subject or another. They're all so proud of her. What a good thing I'm doing—wait until I hear her sing.

I once heard Barbara Bonney sing this part in concert with Yo-Yo Ma. But Amanda's young, natural presence enlivens the happy melody. Her voice is splendid and joyful. Her shy curtsy conveys that nobody's more surprised than she is at the applause.

Everyone congratulates her. Everyone, I'm certain, feels just as I do. Later, when I tell her this, she swats my shoulder. 'You love to think I'm shy, because when I was little I was afraid of you.'

Twenty Three

The middle school held the concert on Thursday evening because many families start their spring vacation Friday morning—Gil, his wife, and daughters included. But after her sublime solo, Amanda is eager for a regular school day.

Before leaving, she knocks on the door. Will I look after her roses while she's gone? For a second, I think she's teasing, but no. Would I please change the water and cut the bottom of each stem slantwise?

Yes, and my sister Emily used to put a drop of apple cider vinegar in the water to fight bacteria.

Smiling, she skips outside and I follow, standing in the road while she does cartwheels around me. The air has turned mild overnight. Amanda hugs me before scooping up her backpack. She wobbles her head and grins. 'See ya around four.'

Inside, the phone rings and I answer without looking.

Sterling says, 'Nina called last night to say you bought her roses.'

'One rose. She stopped in the florist's while I was there.'

'I know that. But she went on and on about how charming you are. Handsomer than ever. Kind, witty, and wise. So, tell me, Walter—since when?'

'Since always.'

'No, I mean since when are you kind to Nina?'

'She caught me in a good mood.'

'It certainly sounds like it. Are you seeing someone? That was her guess.'

'No, but you suggested that, remember? While you're seeing Kevin.'

'I didn't mean it. Nina says everyone considers you the perfect gentleman, going to hear Amanda sing.'

'How's Olivia?'

'She's spending the week at some god-awful skateboard competition. Apparently, I'm the only one who minds her traveling with her boyfriend.'

'Does Kaye approve?'

'Yes, because I don't.'

'Is that why you called?'

'Nina talked about you like you're the Second Coming. If you refuse to work, at least walk around town and say, "Howdy" to everyone. Or soon they'll start wondering if you're a deviant.'

'A deviant?'

'It's abnormal to do nothing, Walter. Until last night, nobody saw you for months. But they saw Amanda, looking more gorgeous by the minute.'

'So what.'

'So if you continue to stay holed up, people will wonder. She was spectacular and you were gracious. But in a small town, you can't stand out too much. Like, popping into glorious view and then disappearing. Today, you're a hero. Tomorrow, you'll be suspect. Unless you get out and about—see and be seen.'

'Maybe I should walk up to people and just announce I'm not a deviant. Such as, "Whatever you may be thinking is all wrong. I'm Mr. Normal."'

'Shut up and get a puppy. Make it your best friend.'

'Actually, Sterling, a puppy's a good idea. Thanks.'

'You're welcome. Also, I'm happy to remind you not to worry. You've always been fascinated by Amanda. I watched you watching her for ten years. And, you're no more deviant than I am.'

'What a relief.'

'It should be. I'm coming home soon.'

'You've been saying that since you left. But if and when you return, Sterling, you need to know—I don't feel the same way.'

'Don't decide that until I get there.'

Twenty Four

After school, Amanda drops her backpack at her front door. I stand outside, watching as she does another series of cartwheels, this time describing a square. Whereupon, she stands feet apart, and straightens her green and brighter green striped sweater over skinny black jeans. Her long silky hair is a dazzling stream that flows around her in the late-afternoon breeze. Her eyes find mine.

During the next few seconds, Amanda once again undoes everything I've ever assumed about thirteen-year-old girls. She smiles at me and it's clear she'll always possess the same delicate beauty. Even time won't undo her.

We go inside and she sits at the kitchen table, where her roses have opened, halfway to full, heady bloom. She finds her iPhone and takes a close-up photo of them. The rule is—no photos of me; no photos of us. Although, I now have a photo of her and Madison on my phone, taken after last night's concert. Handing me her phone, she asks if I'll take a picture of her with the roses.

After several shots (which I resolutely resist sending to my phone), I ask if she'd like seltzer and bitters.

'Do you? Let me fix it.' She's up and moving, her vivid new Adidas leaving an after-image as she glides across the floor. I balance on the stool that's her favorite seat.

'Cheers,' she says. 'To a whole week off.'

'Cheers.' Seven days together—nine, including next weekend. 'Have you spoken with your mother recently?'

'She called me at lunch but when I told her about my "Trout" solo, she had to go. She won't visit, don't worry. She didn't even mention spring break.'

'How would you like to visit Briarcliff's animal shelter? It closes at six.'

Her drink on the counter, she leaps up, squealing, and pulls me off the stool, into the TV room.

'Really, really, really?' She pushes me onto the couch and, facing me, slides her thighs against the sides of mine, her knees pressing against each of my hips. She's not allowed to sit like this. She's not allowed on my lap. But she's holding my face between her hands, her forehead tipped against mine, and I cannot at this moment order her off. Her sweet, thrilled breath overwhelms me. And I focus all my might on not touching her skin or hair or placing a pulsing palm behind her head. All of which does nothing to impede the rush of every forbidden impulse.

Amanda's voice is a whisper. 'Walter, this is serious!'

The excitement I feel running through her compounds my own. And I demand: 'Be still!'

'Just tell me.' Her fingers push through my hair, against my scalp, and my neck falls backward. Several delirious yet static seconds pass.

'Do not move.' My voice is guttural.

And Christ—I am beyond overwhelmed. My mind leaves my body. Thank God, she obeys. Thank God, she does not move. We've gone through this before, but never with this urgency. Never have I drifted to this hairsbreadth brink. Perhaps she detects my desperation—Finally, I'm ready to speak. 'You have no idea, honey. Let me up.'

'First, tell me,' she rests her fingertips against my temples, 'are we getting a puppy?'

'Yes. We're getting a puppy.' She slides off me and I shoot up, halfway out of the room before I call over my shoulder, 'Don't move, Amanda. Or wait, no—watch TV.'

Upstairs, I lock my bedroom door. Trembling, I select clean underpants, jeans, and a long-sleeved V-neck. No shower, but a thorough washing at the sink. I dress quickly, check myself in the bathroom mirror, and shut off the lights. To calm down, I alternate slow, shallow breaths with long, deep ones. Nevertheless, my blood is racing. Once I'm confident I appear calm, I grab my wallet and keys before leaping downstairs. The shelter is forty minutes away. But they're expecting us.

'You changed your clothes.'

I look at my shirt as if it decided to wear me. 'We're going out. You look lovely unless you want a jacket.'

She doesn't. We hop in the new Accord. The traffic is sparse for a Friday evening—all the schools are on break. She sings a *Real Miranda* song. Always before, she sang these songs like the actress, note for note. But now she plays with vibrato and sends her soprano skittering into a dusky contralto.

'Isn't it strange that nobody on *The Real Miranda* has a little wonder dog?'

Scarcely thinking, I say, 'A cute, smart dog might be distracting. My guess is that before long, Iris with Miranda in tow will save someone whose superpower fails. In the end, they'll learn that their classmates' superpowers aren't as reliable as friendship and loyalty.'

'Yeah, I know. But what about Sam's bilocation? They have to keep that.'

'In history, several Christian saints worked miracles using bilocation. But as far as miracles go, it's probably easy to fake.'

'Walter,' she swats my thigh. 'Don't say that. A wise man once told me a lot of impossible things are possible in theory.'

'I doubt he was wise, honey, but even so, there's an enormous difference between theory and reality. Now—,' I turn onto a lane that becomes a long driveway leading to a huge stone house. '— this is it.'

Inside, a woman in overalls shakes my hand. Her name's Michelle.

A door opens and a young man wearing a Rasta tam pulls a leash connected to a growling, tiny black puppy. The young man's name is Trevor and he calls the dog Skipper, but he says the pup knows that's not his real name. 'He's little but smart.'

The animal shelter task force found him in a ditch on the parkway.

'A baby!' Amanda cries, and the puppy breaks away to jump into her arms.

Michelle says that Trevor's the 'animal task force' for all of Westchester.

The puppy is licking Amanda's face and Trevor says it's best if she keeps him on the leash. She nods and tucks the thin coiled line beneath the little dog, while cooing and stroking its fur. Cradling the animal in her arms, she goes outside while I sign some forms, receive copies, and make an unrequired but generous donation to the shelter.

Strapped in the car, Amanda's holding the dog in her lap. 'At first I wanted to call him Sam but that's not his name. Samson is.'

At Chester's Paw, a pet shop in a strip mall, Samson is welcome to try out different cages. The store's proprietor, a man named Mike whose crevassed face reveals a lifetime of sorrows, professes his belief in Jesus but takes the subject no further. I give him the papers verifying that Samson's had his shots. Mike raises scarred eyebrows and extends his hands.

'May I?'

Amanda hands over Samson, who whimpers as he leaves her hands. Mike sets him on the counter, rubs him, tugs his legs and ears, and presses several points on his belly. The puppy is now calm and quiet and Mike pokes around inside his mouth. 'Name any of your household breeds and this little guy belongs to their tribe. He's a super mix. You can't do better than that. But you'll get him fixed, no?'

'The shelter has him on their calendar,' Amanda says. 'They do it for free.'

'Briarcliff.' He approves.

I buy a heavy metal crate for Samson's 'dog house' (the only way to housetrain him, Mike says). Also: a plaid red bed that fits perfectly inside the crate; a month's worth of designer puppy food; a stiff metal brush; a red leather collar and a woven leash; rubber dog toys; rawhide chews; and a training manual. Mike puts on Samson's new collar, whose shiny metal tag is imprinted with 'Samson Jonette,' a county I.D. number, and Amanda's address and phone number. Samson is not used to walking on a leash, so Amanda holds him while I sign us up for puppy school every Monday and Thursday evening, seven to nine.

'Right here,' Mike says, 'side entrance and up the stairs.'

I make two trips carrying the stuff to the car while Amanda skips beside me, holding Samson. 'Puppy school, Walter!'

In the car, she buries her face in the puppy's fur and murmurs. At a traffic light, she leans over and kisses my cheek. 'Thank you. Thank you so, so much.'

When we reach Oak Grove Point, Amanda and I need to eat dinner but she's coaxing the puppy to trot beside her as she walks between the driveways and up the pavement to the turn-around. They play in circles and I scan the twilit sky.

She's laughing and Samson's barking. I unload the car. With the metal crate balanced in one arm against my chest, I open the kitchen door and set it down. Then I go back outside. Amanda stands with one hip cocked. Samson's twined the leash around her ankles. She steps free easily and for a second it's as if I'm the ground beneath them. Then I'm the wind in the air and the first few stars in the darkening sky. Amanda calls my name.

Indoors, Samson, like Amanda, is not allowed up the stairs or even on them.

Before we eat, she unfastens the leash and lures him into his crate by dropping one of her socks inside. She sets the table barefoot. The roses sit in the bay window.

When we're ready to watch TV, Amanda pleads for Samson to join us. The puppy engages all our combined attention. Playing with him is tactile, freewheeling, rough-and-tumble, and, blessedly, harmless.

Twenty Five

Amanda wants Samson to sleep at her house, which she says is so lonely it's like being in a horror movie.

It's past midnight when I carry the dog's crate and food into her kitchen. The house is so cold I can see our breath in the air. She says she's used to it. The light is soft but clear.

Oh, she explains, she covered the fluorescent tube lights with pink gels from the middle school's theater. The walls need paint. Above a flimsy table and chairs, a pale blue has been scrubbed away in patches. Her kitchen is small, with one window over the sink, facing spindly evergreens.

'How much time do you spend cleaning, Amanda?'

'Not so much anymore, because you cook for me. I can take care of Samson, you'll see.'

'That's not why I asked.'

We go outside to walk the puppy once more. She's holding the leash and seems to be hurrying away from me before I can ask anything more about maintaining that house, which she's kept in decent shape with minimal help for most of her life.

We traipse through her yard and mine and then around the Point. The first time I bend down with a plastic bag to pick up Samson's mess, Amanda says, 'Let me. I want to be responsible for him. Except when Olivia comes back. Then we'll trade back and forth.'

'Is she coming back? Have you talked to her?'

'Texted. She'll definitely call you after spring break.'

(Definitely? Is Amanda urging my daughter to stay in touch with me?)

'Let her know she can bring Karl.'

'Sterling won't agree.' Staring up at me, Amanda adds, 'Olivia and Granny disagree with Sterling.'

I don't know what my face is doing, but Amanda says, 'You miss her.'

I know she means Olivia, not Sterling. 'Yes, and I'm worried she won't come back. If she's happier living in Maine, I have to accept that.'

Amanda reaches up to hug me while Samson runs around our legs. 'I miss Olivia, too,' she says and I quickly kiss the crown of her head.

Now that Samson's eliminated all he can for the night, we return to Amanda's kitchen. She pulls a chewed sock from her back pocket, drops it into the crate, and pushes the puppy in there with it. He whines and thumps his tail but she won't look at him.

Instead, she steps beneath the gel-covered light and stands tall, focusing on me. In her concern, she appears more grown-up and therefore even more desirable. She stares in the middle distance before returning to the here and now. Then, she exhales audibly and asks, 'What about Sterling? Do you miss her?'

'You and I probably shouldn't talk about that. But no, I don't.'

'But she's coming back with or without Olivia.'

'She thinks she is. But I've told her it's not that easy.'

A silent spell falls and I step closer to Amanda, who's radiating anxiety. It's like a ghost that roams her house.

Gently, I lift her chin to see if I can guess what's happening behind her beguiling, wide eyes. Their amber hue has never been so fiery. Her expression is taut and I can feel the tension rising beneath her skin. She looks away.

'Honey, don't worry about Sterling.'

She sighs and sits at the cheap little table. 'I know. I know—I should be happy for these past months, this night…everything.'

I hover behind her. 'Trying to be happy means you're not happy at all. When I say not to worry about Sterling, I mean she's my problem, not yours. That's how it should be, anyway. Everyone only gets so much time before things change.'

She drops her head and after a long pause suddenly twists around, and kneels on the chair, facing me. I anticipate—in fact, I hope—she'll fly into my arms.

Seeing this, Amanda taunts me with a little grin and then matter-of-factly walks me to the door and outside, where I ask her to flick her lights once I'm inside my own home.

'No. This time, you flick your lights to show me you're safe.'

I do that and she flicks hers back.

*

Before dawn, I enter Amanda's kitchen through her garage. We had agreed that I'd walk Samson first thing, because I have been running at 5:30 every day for fourteen years. But when I open the door, Amanda's dressed for the day and sitting on the kitchen floor, nestling Samson in her lap. 'Hi.'

She stands up and walks toward me. The dog's claws scrape the floor as he scrambles after her.

Amanda stands on top of my running shoes and reaches up. 'Come here.' She folds her hands behind my neck. I'm determined not to lose myself in her eyes or study her mouth too intently. I shut down any—and every—response to her touch. I resist her inherent luster and she releases me. Then, as if from far away, I hear her saying, 'Walter, thank you. Just—thank you.'

Walking the puppy in the eerie light before dawn, she says, 'Go for your run.'

'We agreed we'd train him together.'

So she leads the way and says—sounding shy—'You, me, and Samson are like a little family.'

Stepping beside her, I take and swing her free hand, 'You're right. Except I've never felt like this before.'

'That's because you're like me. Your family wasn't dependable.'

'That's true, and it has become true again.'

Before I run off to the hills, I carry the dog crate to my house, because I'd rather Amanda and Samson wait there. If the puppy stains or chews things, let it be in my house and not Cheryl's haunted one. Amanda sees her roses on the table and leans her face into the petals. 'I practically forgot about my beautiful flowers. That's how much Samson hogs my attention.'

'He'll need just as much attention when those flowers are dead.'

'Don't say that.' She stands as if shielding the roses.

'Honey, they seem just like you to me. Except, they're very temporary. Cut hot-house flowers will droop and fall apart in three or four days. Samson is yours for a long time.'

'I know that!' she whispers. 'I love the flowers, Walter, but not like I love Samson. I say, I *love* this, I *love* that. But love means a million different things.'

She's right, of course. It's a shame our language is so inept. But words are both the cause and effect of our thoughts and feelings. So, the shame is on us, not our words.

*

An hour later, returning up the hill, I visit the abandoned playground, where the equipment is weathered and damp. All evidence of night has fled, but the sun remains invisible behind low cloud cover. I stretch and reach my wrists halfway inside the metal basketball hoop. For months, I've been doing metaphysical cartwheels beside Amanda. Monstrous impulses still plague my unconscious, but I'm no longer appalled. Because I know—and continue to affirm—that I will never hurt her.

For a minute, I'm high in the sky, rolling through celestial cycles. Back on the ground, I remember to listen for Jimmy Quinn cheering me on. And he is. He always is.

Twenty Six

The spring air is fresh and sweet even when it's not warm. The outdoor skating rinks are beginning to close for the season. During Amanda's break from school, we've been walking the puppy around and skating at indoor arenas. We've attended two sessions of puppy school. During these classes with three other dogs and their owners, Amanda calls me 'Dad' and sometimes 'Daddy.'

Friday morning, after walking Samson around the pond at Rockefeller Park, we agree to try the Palisades Ice Arena across the Hudson. Amanda says the rink hires a deejay on the weekends. 'But because it's spring break, they're having a deejay every afternoon.'

Wary of a wrong turn taking us into New Jersey, I memorize the directions. Because on Monday, Amanda's enthusiasm and my blind devotion to her led us into sudden legal danger. We were going to an indoor rink in Danbury, Connecticut. Not until I saw the exit sign did it occur to me that entering Connecticut would constitute 'transporting a minor across state lines.'

After taking the exit, I needed to pass through two lights before I could get on the highway going west. So, I 'kidnapped' her for approximately ten minutes. She didn't ask why I changed my mind, but we arrived at a rink in Newburgh, New York in time to spend twenty minutes clinging to each other without jackets and mittens.

This afternoon, we arrive at the Palisades Arena just as public skating begins. The deejay mixes disco, soul, and hip-hop. No waltzes, no staticky speakers.

Amanda and I skate in time with the layered tunes. She's become steady on the ice and a fantastic magnetism propels us with increasing speed and precision. Driving home, we're happy and hungry.

She showers at her house and then joins me in my kitchen, kicking off her shoes, while I prepare dinner. In footless tights and a short tunic, she balances on one leg while stretching the other high and to the side, her thumb and finger clasping her big toe. She holds this pose impossibly long, then stands straight and folds in half, clasping her ankles. I do not even try to look away as she unfurls slowly up, her hair alive in the air, and presses her palms together. She bows her radiant head. '*Namaste.*'

'*Namaste,* yourself.'

'Do you meditate?' she asks.

'I use a breathing technique to counter stress. Sharp, fast inhalations and long, slow exhalations through the mouth.'

'How come you know everything, Walter?'

'I don't—know everything. And can't remember when I started the breathing thing, but it helps me calm down.'

Samson has stopped whining, and his tail thumps inside his cage. Amanda fills his ceramic bowls with dog food and water before opening the cage door. He behaves at Amanda's command, not mine.

The first buds have appeared in the garden. We linger over dinner, watching the April sky fill the open bay window as it slowly develops into an evening of brisk green breezes.

*

On Sunday, our last evening of Amanda's spring break, the puppy behaves so well, I try slipping him a bit of steak at dinner.

Amanda objects. 'You'll spoil him!'

After loading the dishwasher, we walk Samson around the Point before watching TV. Between us on the couch, the exuberant little animal squirms from my lap to hers. He gets up and starts barking and running around the house. I check on him but he's just scampering through the hallways.

He returns and crouches on the floor, then flips over and lays panting on his back, his little canine body squirming. Amanda and I drop onto the floor to play with him. But he immediately gets up, sniffs around, and settles into a corner.

Lying on the rug, we watch the next-to-last episode in *The Real Miranda*'s third season. The commercials promote a denim jacket I bought Amanda two weeks ago, when ads for it pursued me wherever I went online. Traditional metal buttons and pockets, but the back has a latex image of Miranda's face, her bright pink mouth a surprised 'O.'

The image struck me as so garish that I searched Disney shops in various cities until I found a 'distressed' version of the jacket in San Francisco. No worn or torn patches, but the oversized, oversaturated actress's face is significantly faded, as is the denim. Like the standard version, her name is scrawled in heavy script, a fat heart dotting the 'i.' The jacket arrived yesterday.

Amanda loves it—much more, she says, than the regular version, which the whole cast is wearing in a commercial. Before I notice, she's ducked from the room and returns, prancing around me, the jacket dangling from one shoulder while she mimics Iris's quick little dance steps. She hums one of the songs and twirls. Stretched out on the carpet, balanced on my side, I watch without staring, a distinction I'm forever trying to master.

Samson wakes and growls. Amanda stops. The jacket falls. And Samson pounces, tearing into my back.

'Bad Samson! Bad, bad, bad!' Amanda stomps her feet and swats the air just above the dog's head. Samson whines, his spine hunched with guilt, his tail between his legs, before bounding onto the couch. He settles into the far, padded corner, covers his snout with his front paws, and seems to fall immediately asleep.

On the edge of the couch, her hands on her knees, Amanda asks, 'Are you okay?'

'I'm fine, honey.'

'You have to admit he's cute,' she says.

'Very cute.'

While the puppy sleeps, we stretch out on the floor, hands cupping our chins, our eyes fixed on Miranda gazing from her bedroom window. The actress sings *what good is telepathy without a leap of empathy?* Amanda sings along, anticipating the words, lying on her stomach, her feet up and crisscrossing. Twisting, I grab the high arch of her foot. She pulls it free and I fall forward.

'Walter, my God!'

Frantic, she urges me to sit up so she can see my back. And then: 'May I?' Gasping, she carefully rolls up my ruined Italian-knit polo shirt over my head. Moving around on her knees, she touches the tops of my naked shoulders, fretting, 'Oh, my God, oh, my God! The only reason you're not gushing blood is that the gashes are very deep.'

'All right, let me go upstairs and take care of it. You wait here.'

'No way, Walter! You've got three deep, terrible slashes just beneath your ribs.'

'I'm okay, honey. Just give me back my shirt and I'll tend to them later.'

'We should go to the emergency room.'

'No, we shouldn't.'

'You need stitches.'

'Cuts from animals contain too much bacteria.'

'At least let the emergency room doctors irrigate the wounds.' She tells me that last summer one of the Baxter twins sliced his ear where it meets his head. It was impossible to suture it so the doctor flushed the area with distilled water followed by a jet stream of liquid antiseptic.

'Please, honey. I'm fine.' Then I sink into the carpet, stupid and woozy.

Suddenly I'm exhausted—also shirtless and prone on the floor. I mumble, 'Please don't take advantage of the situation. Upstairs or anywhere else.'

'Me?' Her laugh sounds like a bell.

She returns holding a red metal first-aid kit and hydrogen peroxide from the linen closet upstairs. I turn my head. She hovers at the room's threshold. Within seconds, our rituals slip into a precarious, new intimacy. To tend to the scratches, she straddles my waist.

'They're puffing up,' she says.

After cleaning them, which stings enough to make my eyes water, she carefully slathers them with ointment, and stacks gauze over them, covering the edges with medical tape. Amanda stretches over my patched-up but otherwise naked back and whispers in my ear, 'Do you love me, Walter? Do you?'

Each cool, sweet word surges through me. 'Do you,' she asks, 'love me like I love you?'

'Yes, Amanda.' Unwisely, I turn over to stare up at her. 'You know I love you.' I lift her off and sit up. My fingers touch her chin and stroke the sides of her neck. 'I love you more than is morally defensible.'

She breaks eye contact. I'm not sure if she sighs. But I'm not sure of anything anymore.

'That bad dog—I can't believe it. Lie down, Walter. I'll rub your shoulders. I do it for Cheryl all the time. It's the one thing she likes about me. The way I rub her shoulders.'

'But she's your mother.'

'There's nothing wrong with me rubbing your shoulders.'

So, God help me, I drop my forehead onto her denim jacket that's folded like a pillow, and close my eyes, my heart beating so furiously I'm prepared to die. Amanda's knuckles push deep into my upper trapezius muscles, which are like rock. Deliciously, she drags her elbows around and between my shoulder blades repeatedly—until I'm nearly asleep. Finally, her fingertips brush against my skin like wings, soothing every nerve in the region. So I'm calm and steady enough—even as her long, girlish thighs squeeze my waist and her little butt perches on my sacrum. My mind shuts down because after all, she's right. Nothing we're doing is wrong. In contrast to everything I feel—*that is evil!*

She won't get up until I agree to her rubbing my shoulders again tomorrow night.

None of this is going to quit.

Twenty Seven

Today Amanda begins her last twelve weeks in eighth grade. During my run, cresting the first steep hill, I calculate how much time escapes me every day. As if that were the problem. When, in fact, the problem is this: Amanda and I are hurtling ever closer to the end.

Running very fast through the whole long loop, I stop before Oak Grove Point and watch the early sunbeams falling upon the ground. It's 6:45 or so when I enter the kitchen. Amanda's standing there, because today marks our first appearance walking Samson on Broadway—a girl on her way to middle school matching strides with the man who lives across the lane, walking his new rescue puppy.

She hands me a frosted glass of fresh-squeezed orange juice. One sip and I shut my eyes. The flavor invigorates me to the point of confusion and I sink into a chair. It's as if I've just drunk something I wasn't aware I desperately needed. I extend my legs and give in to the waves of gratification carrying me higher and higher with every swallow.

'How,' I ask, 'did you do this?'

Amanda puts her face near mine and crosses her eyes. 'Your credit card. How else?'

'Where did you get the oranges?'

She hops onto the stool. 'I bought juice oranges from the farmers' market just before they packed up yesterday. You can't use the regular kind, so I raced over on my bike before dinner.'

It's scary how much she delights me, and breathtaking how each little pleasure magnifies the others. 'Why didn't I think of buying a juicer?'

'Because you never buy anything for yourself.'

'That's not true.'

'Yes, it is.'

I sit up straight—never to admit that I buy the finest, sometimes even tailored, casual clothing. Only an expert could see that they're not ordinary men's weekend wear. Who, no matter how rich, goes to such lengths? Probably only other men hoping that they'll appeal to a girl at the apex of childhood. (Although, Amanda's past that already. Which is really yet another reason for me to look impeccable.)

We stand up and Amanda tops off my orange juice. She lifts a glass of her own. We clink icy rims and Samson lies at our feet, his tail thumping.

Before I parade around with Samson to prove I'm the world's most regular guy, before I can even shower, Amanda needs to assess my wounds.

'Funny thing,' I tell her, 'by this morning they were scratches, not gashes.'

'I don't believe it. I have to see for myself.'

Without thinking, I say, 'be my guest,' only to panic when she indicates for me to take my shirt off. I step into the laundry room, peel off the saturated synthetic top, and toss it in the machine. Half-naked, I step into the kitchen, plant my elbows on the counter, and drop my head. Her fingertips travel along my spine, dabbing at beads of sweat.

'Don't do that, honey. It's embarrassing.'

'No, it isn't. Three little Band-Aids? I don't believe it.' She pries one edge and all three limp, sodden strips fall into her hands.

'Just drop those, Amanda. They're disgusting.'

But she opens the cabinet under the sink and carefully deposits them in the wastebasket.

'It's a miracle. Last night they were gruesome lacerations. Now they're topped with that goo that turns into scabs.'

Goo? It makes me queasy.

Amanda stands on tiptoe and kisses the place between my shoulder blades where a pool of sweat has collected.

'I love the saltiness.'

Where in Christ does she get this? Not from movies and TV. People on screen don't sweat unless they're lying or dying. No girl sidles up to some hunk saying she loves his stink.

I'm hurrying away now to clean up. In fifteen minutes, I'll be the epitome of normal.

'Wait. What do you like for breakfast?'

I stare at her, blinking. Amanda's wearing a dark ribbed top and a very short, very silky skirt. Light from the windows and glass doors surrounds her. I almost forget that I'm shirtless and smelly. I almost step forward to kiss her shimmering head. A residue of common sense stops me.

'Walter, breakfast.'

'Uh, that's okay. I like to eat later.' Up two steps, I turn and thank her for the orange juice. 'It was incredible.'

When she follows Samson, who's nearing the stairs, I say, 'Wait there—ten minutes.'

Upstairs, I'm far too conscious of myself naked in the shower while she plays downstairs with the puppy. For weeks, my dreams have been vague or nonexistent. But last night, the nightmare voices returned as one scold. *You think you're fated to love that girl, to nurture her during her childhood so that when she's a woman, you can love her. What would a judge and jury say?* Familiar with the voice, I woke choking with sorrow.

We walk Samson down Sunnyside Lane. The dog trots along as if he's large and in charge, instead of eight little pounds of fur. He turns his head when we arrive at Broadway, as if to show Amanda and me that he's out and about from now on.

Wayne drives past in a huge bakery truck, different from the meat truck he used to drive. I wave to him and he tugs an imaginary cord. An SUV passes and Amanda recognizes the Baxter twins strapped into contraptions in the back seat. They're fighting for primacy and apparently shouting her name. At the light, we see the nanny turn around, shaking her finger and yelling.

Soon, we stand at the top of Main Street, which is very steep and undulates several blocks down to a sparkling patch of the Hudson River. The view is magical, not of this world. I can't help holding Amanda's shoulder, my palm on her *Real Miranda* jacket.

Samson circles around us, binding us with his leash. We're both lingering, not wanting to separate just yet. Perhaps Amanda also realizes that since spring break has ended, we're beginning our final phase. In any case, Samson's not prepared for her to leave. And we're all stalling. Amanda says that she and her friends work on the newspaper at the diner. 'Otherwise, we would have to attend "home room."'

In December, the head English teacher approved her idea for an advice column called 'Ask Off Line.' Everyone submits semi-disguised smutty questions, assuming the teacher won't notice. Mostly, Amanda says, he doesn't, or pretends he doesn't. 'My answers are snotty. Like, you're boring, or really, you don't know? It's supposed to be funny.'

'Why didn't you tell me? I want to read it.'

'You'll think it's silly.'

'No, I won't.'

She says, okay, she'll bring the next issue home. I ask for back issues, too. She should keep copies for herself, in any case.

'And you'll be there at 4:30?'

'I'm always there. You know that.'

She finds a reason to smile and her voice is breathy. 'Tonight's puppy school.'

'We have to make sure Mike clips Samson's claws.'

Hearing his name, the dog jumps into Amanda's arms. She kisses him goodbye and asks, what do I think? Can she kiss me goodbye?

I smile, because, of course, the question is *not* a question. She puts Samson down and he pulls hard on the leash. She waves and skips down Main Street.

Twenty Eight

I traipse around town for two hours with naughty but friendly Samson. Running to the top of Oak Grove Point, I lead the puppy toward the front porch. He pulls sideways to urinate on the daffodils. He shakes his crooked little leg when Heather Crosby phones. She has Glen Engle on the line.

'Thank you, Heather. I'm just entering the house.' Inside, I unhook the puppy's leash and hear my former boss say 'Hello.' No mention of sending me Leonardo da Vinci quotes. For Glen Engle, saying hello is a concession, but he tosses in another, asking why I haven't sold my soul to the competition.

I deliberately say nothing, so he's not obliged to wonder what I *have* been doing.

'Not long after you left,' he says, 'I decided it was time for me to make a change.' He has now secured proper clients for a new venture and is eager for us to meet.

But before offering him a date and time, I make Glen listen to my gratitude for his interest in me. 'Unfortunately, I'm expected at law school in September.'

'Which law school, teaching what?'

'I'm getting my degree.'

'Why?'

'I always intended to study law but got sidetracked.'

'You'll change your mind after we get together,' Glen says. 'I'm convinced you and I can transform the market.'

He's off the line and Heather's preparing to schedule our meeting. First, however, she mentions Sterling, and rather than listen to more, I propose lunch on Tuesday, the last week of May. 'Unless there's a conflict with Memorial Day.'

There isn't.

Ending the call, I scroll through all my old contacts for the Dean who accepted me into Yale Law School sixteen years ago. Luckily, he answers the old number. Luckier still, he remains Dean.

He says, 'Glad you called, Walter,' as if we speak regularly. I tell him I'm ready to take the LSAT again, as it must have changed several times since I was a prize-winning prodigy.

'No need for that. In your case, Walter, it would be superfluous.'

Assuming the class has been full for months, I clarify that we're talking about next year's enrollment. Should anyone defer, unlikely as that is, I'd like to be considered.

The Dean, who's heard of my work following the financial crisis, says the law school has space for me this year, or any year. My presence will benefit the entire institution. And, if I can find time to visit at the end of May, he would like to introduce me to the faculty.

I thank him and hear myself add that bank regulation in particular interests me.

'Then you'll be in a prime position here,' the Dean says. A famous labor lawyer has agreed to teach an extensive seminar there. He drops a name and reveals that the lawyer 'is currently forming a Wall Street task force.'

I thank him and he thanks me—all of which is far better than I would have ever imagined.

Samson has fallen asleep inside his cage, door open. I arrange to meet with the Dean and the famous lawyer for lunch the day after my proposed meeting with Glen Engle. Which I intend to cancel.

After the phone call, I slide open the glass doors and step into the garden. The backyard flowers sway on tall stems topped by fat green buds tipped with bright color. And, a road map unfurls in my mind. The commute to New Haven, Connecticut takes an hour and a half. Amanda will never miss me.

Except—the realization hits so hard that I fall against a tree trunk, the wind knocked out of me. Amanda *must not* miss me! She'll be in high school!

Her interests will change and keep changing.

Nearly blind with alarm, I wander back inside the house, scarcely aware of the pounding behind my eyes. Samson's awake and out of his crate. He's growling and ripping apart a large throw pillow while my mind mimics shattering glass. Through splintering shards, I glimpse Amanda beside a seventeen-year-old boy driving a BMW. Hopping out, she waves and calls 'Hi Walter!' Dashing from her house, returning to the passenger seat beside the faceless prince, Amanda blows me a kiss. 'Bye, Walter!'

I can endure Olivia's absence. But I refuse to live here as Amanda's kind, dependable neighbor. I'll rent an apartment in New Haven. And if Olivia maintains her rule that I must not visit, Kaye will have to invite me to dinner with Roy Emerson. They can include me in weekend sailing expeditions. In time, Olivia will learn to suffer me the same—really, better—as she now suffers Sterling.

But Amanda must forget me. For if our magical rapport were to continue against all odds, she would miss her adolescence. Happy, sad, hard, confusing, and uncomfortable as it's often portrayed, nobody knows better than I do how skipping this phase can affect the rest of life. She must not spend the next four years in a vacuum, which is what I would be to her—at best. We cannot continue even into summer without stopping time.

So instead of calling Glen and cancelling the meeting, instead of phoning Mike about Samson's claws—the dog is now onto the matching pillow—I phone the man who manages my trust fund. We've only spoken twice that I remember: when I was twelve and my parents folded my deceased sister's portion into mine. And again when I was twenty-one and asked him to name Olivia as the sole beneficiary. Knowing that Sterling would always have more money than she can sensibly use.

On the phone now, I ask him to split the trust, which has grown quite large, between Olivia and Amanda Jonette. I'll send her social security number.

He says, 'Very good, Mr. Mitchell,' and the labyrinthine process of dividing one trust into two is underway.

After this, I lie down for half an hour until my headache dissipates enough for me to run. Before my anxiety can rebound, I locate an alternate path that eventually connects with my usual loop. The exertion relieves my panic.

When Amanda arrives home from school, I'm soaked in sweat again and drinking orange juice. Pillow stuffing litters the floor and Samson's in desperate need of a walk.

Twenty Nine

After puppy school and after Mike trims Samson's claws, we still have time for television. Samson sets us up the same as before. The little black dog swipes at the rug and thumps his tail until Amanda and I get off the couch and down onto the floor. When we start playing with him, though, he growls. I take him to his crate, but he escapes, runs to the couch, settles in his corner, and falls suspiciously fast asleep, snuffling—what Amanda refers to as his 'adorable baby snore.'

She stands in front of the sliding glass doors, luminous against the dark night, and says, 'Take off your shirt.'

When I resist, she reminds me I have promised to let her rub my shoulders—from now on.

She's right, so what's to resist?

A barrage of old and new desires, magnifying every pleasure I've ever known—*that's what!*

Foolishly, I assumed another arousal wouldn't differ much from those I secretly vanquish practically constantly. But these back rubs send a whole new kind of thrilling terror rushing through me.

I take off my shirt, rest my cheek on a pillow, and feel her straddle my lower back. 'Close your eyes,' she says and massages my upper trapezius muscles until they loosen, which makes me loosen. After a few adjustments, Amanda strokes my naked dorsal body with ecstatic reverence. Eventually, she swoons on top of me and my internal alarms blare.

'Stop!' My voice is faint but strident. 'Stop, now!'

She stands up and I lie there, saying, 'Give me a minute, honey.' I need at least that long before I can put my shirt back on and stand up. Amanda waits on the couch. The TV is back on. I sit beside her.

'Fair is fair, Walter. You have to do me.'

I laugh. 'You can't be serious.' My primary rule is that she can touch me but I can never touch her. (Of course, I grant exceptions, probably more than I realize, but for all that, I have not succumbed to a real transgression. As if I should be proud of that! I'm not. Just thankful.)

Amanda's saying, 'I know the rules. Such as, I cannot take off my shirt and you can. Men walk around half-naked in public. Women don't.'

'What men are you talking about? The ones in cologne commercials?'

'No, the fat men at the park, who drink whiskey from thermoses that fool nobody.'

At 10:00, I take Samson's crate to her house and we walk him on the path that leads to the highest elevation of Oak Grove Point. A clearing there presents a large flat boulder. I stand on it and construct a series of arcs proportionate to heaven and earth as I perceive them. Strange and whimsical, I admit. But gazing at the sky, I find an imaginary sphere to support me. It's modeled on Leonardo's *Vitruvian Man*, in three dimensions. I extend my arms and legs within an orb and imagine rolling through universal waves. Like this, I'm weightless. I spin above the ground and yet remain upright, proper, and good.

Amanda appears out of the darkness, talking on the phone and laughing. Samson on his leash sends her flying one way and then the other. I jump from the boulder and she lands close enough so that I can see her expression beckoning me. When I stand near her, she hands me the phone. It's Olivia.

'Hi, sweetheart.'

'Hi, Daddy. Tell me about this puppy. Amanda says he's as much mine as hers.'

'That's right.' (Whatever Amanda wants.) 'You and Amanda can share him.'

'Only in theory, Daddy. If we still lived across a driveway from each other, we would. But we don't.'

A rusty substance trickles inside me like ground water seeping through the crack in a foundation. 'All right,' I say. 'Let's use a looser definition of sharing.'

Olivia giggles. 'I love you, Daddy. "A looser definition." Wait till Karl hears that. Is Amanda still there?'

I hand the phone back to her and take the dog leash. Amanda says, 'After you see him, Liv, if you aren't a hundred percent sure his name is Samson, we can change it. He'll still be a baby and won't know the difference.' Amanda takes the leash from me and Samson pulls so hard that her phone flies in the air. I catch it and put it to my ear. 'Olivia, sweetheart? Did you know the puppy was your mother's idea?'

She laughs. 'No way!' Then she hangs up, but her voice stays with me. I forgot to tell her that when she visits, she can bring Karl.

*

Every school-day morning, we walk Samson together to the top of Main Street and reluctantly part company. I wonder if Amanda also feels our impending final goodbye coming nearer every day. It surprises me whenever she doubts my love for her. I hide what I can out of necessity. But even without the experience of being loved before, she should know: I'm devoted to her for life.

Another reason to linger at the top of Main Street: In the past two weeks, the landscape has become magnificent. I bend toward Amanda while she tells me things she's been meaning to tell me. Standing there, Amanda, I, and even the puppy blend into the morning's breathtaking beauty. We belong to the dazzling fabric spooling beneath our feet.

When Amanda does turn and skip down the hill, Samson whines and barks, vanquishing the suppressed dread within our everyday goodbyes. She's off to the diner until Spanish class at nine. I drag the whimpering puppy on his leash. But once we're past the corner, and Amanda's out of sight, he trots fast along Broadway. If we happen to see anyone, Samson is friendly, his little ears cocked, his tail wagging. If we see another dog walker, he or she and I talk. Samson happily sniffs and snarls at animals ten times his size. Given a chance, he'll intimidate a timid dog. Either way, I've learned to limit the interaction to two or three minutes. Samson races to the Hudson River as if unleashed, despite my strong hold. At first, I had to drag him back uphill to the aqueduct until he discovered he could spare his rump by using his feet. Now, he bounds uphill as eagerly as down.

*

But this morning, the puppy refuses to go outside. It's raining. Really just slightly drizzling. Holding Samson's leash, I push him out the door, onto the porch. He whimpers and claws the painted wood, cowering on the top step. Amanda scolds him for being a baby, swats his nose, and says, 'What's wrong with you?'

He growls. The fur on his back rises in a thin line. Then he jumps under the porch, crouches there, and empties his bladder and bowels before scurrying back to the front door.

So, Samson and I stay put, keeping our paws dry. Instead of waving goodbye, Amanda drops her backpack and cartwheels. Then she stands upright, fetches her books, and disappears. In the kitchen, I shove Samson into his crate and hurry upstairs to watch her dance down the hill.

Thirty

Samson is the smallest and naughtiest dog in obedience training. After our sixth week, and final class, Mike gives each dog owner a final tip. He has asked Amanda and me to bring Samson downstairs to Chester's Paw. He clips Samson's claws for the second time and recommends signing him up for the next training session. He says it's not uncommon for such a young puppy to 'fixate' on a girl like Amanda and be jealous of her father.

I claim not to have noticed this but say, now that he's mentioned it—of course. Gladly then, I pay for another session. Mike won't take money for clipping Samson's claws. The first clipping should have been enough, now that I'm walking him outside. The problem isn't his claws, Mike says. It's that Samson still isn't civilized.

Driving home along the dark, empty parkway, I keep recalling how Amanda called me 'Daddy' in the class. The mixture of annoyance and affection with which she said it sounded so much like my daughter—and not Amanda—that Olivia hovers over my shoulder. Her phantom presence almost absolves me. My love for Amanda began with their friendship.

Before I can recoil from this ludicrous justification, Amanda asks if she's a good liar.

'I wouldn't call the roles you play—to avoid questions you can't answer—lying. It's more like being an actress.'

'No, I've been lying all my life. If I can't answer a question about my mother, why not say so? Instead, I lie. But I feel terrible for lying. Especially because I don't just lie about what I'm doing. I lie about my feelings.'

'Do you lie to me?' I regret these words before they've left my mouth.

She sputters in mild derision and chides Samson to stop squirming. 'If I ever lied to you, Walter, you'd know it. The only time I let down my guard is with you.'

'And the only time I let down my guard—'

'You *never* let your guard down with me! You put up boundaries everywhere.'

'Without some boundaries, I would hurt you, honey.'

'Yeah. In ways that wouldn't show up for ten years, if ever. And that means never. Because even though you obey every rule, you worry. And every time you worry, you add a bunch more rules. Like you're—like you're my *Prude Daddy*.'

'Maybe I am.'

'No, God, I'm sorry I said that.' She shakes her head. 'I get frustrated.'

(*She* gets frustrated?) 'If you want, go ahead and call me "Prude Daddy."'

'Wait, you've never seen the music video, have you? It's been trending all year.'

'You're right, I haven't seen the video. But I can imagine.'

'*Prude Daddy* has this girl taunting a guy into saying she's his "One Sweet Baby."'

'Damn it, Amanda. It's a stupid joke.' But I'm the stupid one. I missed the ring of backward slang; I had thought—naively— that if she called me "Daddy," we'd be safer. Which makes me even stupider.

We may not, as she claims, read each other's mind, but we often feel what the other feels. But to look at her now, an alien from outer space would feel her sadness.

'Walter, I don't know what else to do—I'm sorry.'

'It's okay, hon—When I call you honey, does it sound condescending? I use it as an endearment. But it just occurred to me that it might sound, I don't know, belittling.'

'It does not sound belittling. Nobody else thinks of me like that. I'm either Amanda or Ms. Jonette, or worse.'

'Didn't your mother have a nickname for you when you were a baby?'

If Amanda weren't so unhappy, she'd roll her eyes. But she stares at her hands, petting Samson. 'Jade called me Mandy until Cheryl threatened to fire her. Whatever my mother calls me means "shit" or worse. And, double-shit—I forgot she's coming this weekend. Wanna know why she's been away for four months?'

'Why?'

Amanda readjusts Samson and says, 'Cheryl slaps me. But when she was so awful at Christmas, I slapped her back. Nowhere near as hard as she slaps me. But whenever she calls or texts, she wants to get this straight: Never again!'

'I'm not advocating this, Amanda, not even as a last resort. But you should know that one anonymous phone call—'

'Would land me in foster care. I lie all the time but nobody's fooled. Everybody knows about Cheryl unless they've decided they don't want to know.'

'They know about us, too.'

'They know you do good things for me. They know I'm happy. I went from being "at risk" to being first in the class. You're the only one with doubts.'

243

'Maybe for now. But it wouldn't take much for people to get ugly ideas.'

'So what? We're amazing. So amazing we can live by our own rules.'

'We're going to try. But even if your mother continues doing what she's always done, in four months you start high school. Your whole perspective will change.'

'My feelings won't.'

I pull into the garage and don't move, eyes fixed straight ahead. I'm on guard against condoning false hope—hers or mine. When my pulse slows somewhat, the best I can muster is: 'Everything changes.'

'Walter, shush. If nobody hears you, maybe the world will leave us alone.'

'If we hold our breath, maybe time will forget about us.'

I expect her to laugh. But in the garage, inside the car while Samson whines, Amanda and I sit within a pall of loss. I touch her shoulder. We're fighting the same sensations, eyes stinging.

When I look at her, though, she's mastering the situation. I can see her working her way through a process she's developed over the course of her life. Her lips press together and she blinks very fast, because crying won't help. She straightens her shoulders and—making it look easy—smiles. From somewhere within she's eked out genuine happiness, because her inner light shines at full radiance. Her voice lilts. 'Thing is,' she says, 'you and I will always be great together, no matter where we end up.'

'That's true.'

Usually, we walk Samson just before she and the dog go to her house for the night. But without a word, we agree the puppy has been semi-obedient for hours and deserves an early walk.

Besides, we could use some fresh air. Amanda opens the car door and Samson bounds out, straining the leash, pulling her.

We stroll through the wooded path to the clearing. Face-to-face, we clasp each other's hands and lean back to gaze at the sky. Suddenly, our unique helix feels indestructible. Our combined will spirals above the trees. Hands clasped, we roll through the cold dark night, side by side.

Thirty One

The rhododendrons are still in bloom. The public schools in New York continue through most of June. Today's May 5.

When it's time to tell Amanda I'm going to Yale and will live in New Haven, I don't expect her to understand. But I hope she believes my real motive. Because the painful truth is, unless I make this sacrifice, we'll lose what we've shared. If I stick around, we'll both regret it.

Every time I catch myself worrying about how she'll be without me, I remind myself: Amanda's been taking care of herself since kindergarten. And, what a miracle we've shared!

When I step back and look at how very smart and sensible she is, how generous, strong, and loving, I see that she does not need me. Once she comes into her own, at eighteen, nothing and no one will be able to stop her.

I fill out forms for law school while Samson slobbers against the bay windowpanes. I've already sent Yale my first year's tuition.

Sterling phones. I pick up and she asks what I'm thinking. I really can't say. Samson whines and I tell her, 'I like the dog. Getting him was a good idea.'

'How do you think I'll look as a redhead?' She's at a hair salon.
'How red?'
'Oh, you don't care, do you?'

'It's been a long time, Sterling.'

'Not that long. Have you talked to Olivia recently?'

'Last Wednesday night, briefly.'

'How did she sound?'

'Fine.'

'Even my mother admits she gets keyed-up and acts silly.'

'What's wrong with that?'

'She does this rhyming thing. Mother and Karl say she's pretending she's a rapper, but it sounds compulsive to me.'

'How much time do you spend with her?'

'Not much. She claims I'm toxic.'

'Give her some time, Sterling.' A woman at her end says, 'Let's have a peek.' And then, 'Oh dear, darling! You must have porous hair. We'll need to rinse this out and find something to tone it down.'

*

Cheryl has phoned Amanda to say she will definitely be home for the weekend. It could be a false alarm, but Amanda hides her clothes and stows her bicycle in my garage just in case. She wants Samson to be a secret, too.

'If Mom knows we have a puppy, or even that you have a puppy, she'll make me feel bad.'

'Don't worry. And I won't mention that when we take him to puppy school, everyone thinks I'm your father.'

Amanda imagines her mother's outrage and grins. 'What could she do? Nothing.'

'Not without changing her ways.'

'Promise—no more talks with her. Don't ring the doorbell and say, "Here's my new friend, wanna pet him?"'

'Don't worry, honey.'

We prepare. Come Saturday morning, all of Samson's stuff is at my house, and Amanda is wearing old clothes.

We walk Samson up and down the Point. We tie him to a fence and shoot baskets. I teach her to do a lay-up. After an hour, she's pretty good. We eat lunch and then dinner in my backyard, so we can listen for Cheryl's car.

After dinner, we drink tea. The days are growing longer. Holding Samson on her lap, Amanda stirs honey into a pot of Darjeeling. I add milk to my brew of Earl Grey.

She says, 'You know, this doesn't qualify as a real adventure until we see a pride of lions.'

I remind her we just arrived at this savannah. Unable to suppress my curiosity, though, I say, 'Tell me again, honey, which savannah is this?'

'We're in Tanzania, darling. In fact, we've been here for weeks.' She adjusts an imaginary sunbonnet. I start to ask, what century, when we hear Cheryl's SUV. Amanda gives Samson to me and he jumps from my hands into her vacated seat.

She tells him to be good, and kisses my cheek.

Inside, I put Samson in his cage. He whines and I remind him that he's spent all day with her. I mop the kitchen floor, listening to Rahsaan Roland Kirk's *Bright Moments*.

Upstairs, I'm racked by a sensation of the present moment immediately becoming the past. In Olivia's room, I find her old laptop loaded with videos of the girls through the years. I watch them as preschoolers chasing dragonflies and catching lightning bugs. First grade through fifth—they run through water sprinklers and blast each other with bright-colored, high-powered water guns. I watch them collide on saucer-shaped sleds. They build a snowman that falls apart and throw snowballs at the camera. They're ten and eleven on Halloween. Amanda's wearing a rummage-sale dress of aging lace, the skirt to her feet. She faces a mirror while Olivia plants half a plastic hatchet in her head with hair-glue and wire netting. My curly-haired, mischievous little girl pours fake blood over Amanda's head. It seeps from her hair and drips down her beautiful face and neck, staining the dress.

That evening, without having looked at the Jonette house, I sneak Samson through the backyard and down the hill. For more than an hour, we walk along the aqueduct, in the golden light of nearby houses. The next morning, before my run, I walk him again, going through the backyard and down Sunnyside Lane. He whines and strains at the leash for Amanda. After my run, I listen to him bark, let him out of his cage, and watch him hurl himself against the kitchen door. He's lapping water from his dish when pizza is delivered across the lane. Amanda hates pizza.

I remember I should cancel the meeting with Glen Engle. It occurs to me that a weekend text might reach him before Heather Crosby has a chance to sort through her boss's inbox. Within a minute, Glen replies that he wants to meet as planned. He has time. I reply that I won't change my mind. His response: that's why he wants me on board. I agree to the meeting, having hit upon a further purpose—he should hire Sterling. She's just what he needs and vice versa.

*

At noon on Sunday, I drive Samson to a dog park. He's chasing a brindled beagle-like dog while a heavy white-haired woman sitting in a chair yells, 'Igor! Igor, come here!' My phone pings.

Amanda has sent a text: *Cheryl and Greg are talking about working at a golf resort in Wisconsin. If they do, I'll have to go to high school there!*

She's included an emoticon referencing 'The Scream.'

I reply: *Try not to worry, honey. It hasn't happened yet.*

5. FLIGHT

Thirty Two

May 2015

It's the third week of May. Amanda's eighth-grade graduation ceremony has been scheduled for the last week in June. The seventh-grade girls' choir will sing *Whenever You Remember*. Her mother has promised to attend. Amanda cannot quite believe, however, what else her mother has promised: that shortly afterwards, Cheryl, Greg, and Amanda are moving to the Wisconsin Dells, where Greg owns the Alta Vista Resort. Or to be precise, part of it.

Amanda shows me its website. The resort boasts a first-rate, eighteen-hole golf course, known as Whitewater Canyon. But the main attractions are twenty-six water slides, some indoor and some out. These, as well as water roller coasters and a pool with a wave machine, are surrounded by a vast complex of condominiums.

Greg plans to manage the resort while Cheryl works as head golf pro. Amanda laughs at the idea. And, she laughs at my decision to attend law school. Because right now, the life we share ending like that—is absurd.

Isn't it?

Yes, but...

She maintains her perspective brilliantly. I, however, falter. More often than not, Amanda senses this. That's my impression anyway, when she says, 'We don't know the future, Walter. Nobody does.'

She's so insistent that when I merely start to tell her about the trust fund—that she has money for boarding school if she doesn't like Wisconsin—Amanda hops up and claps her hands over my mouth. 'We agreed,' she says, 'not to admit the future until it's here.'

I nod and tell her that at some point she must allow me to explain a financial arrangement in detail. 'It's a trust fund,' I say. 'Mostly, you just need to sign some forms.'

She nods and smiles and says, 'But not now.'

So far, I've nodded in misty-eyed agreement. When we do say goodbye, the finality will force us to feel rigid, numb, and matter-of-fact.

Last night, thunderstorms rolled in, but this morning the rain stops and starts in spurts. Samson empties his system beneath the porch. No need for a leash. He won't run off. In fact, he's already pawing to get back inside. Amanda refuses to use an umbrella. 'Kids don't, Walter.'

And, she's not interested in a ride.

'Fine, but if there's a sudden downpour, honey, I'm coming after you.'

She dances away from me, off the porch. 'I love walking in the rain, especially when it feels as if I'm walking *between* raindrops.'

She's wearing her faded denim jacket with Miranda on the back, skinny orange jeans, and turquoise high-top sneakers. From upstairs, I watch her round the last mound of shrubbery. Instead of turning promptly onto Sunnyside, as she usually does, she leans down to talk to someone behind the wheel of a silver Volvo.

I recognize the car. That is, I should recognize it but my mind balks. I see myself fleeing. But I haven't moved. I'm still watching Amanda, who straightens and tosses her hair behind her shoulder. I press my hand against the windowpane for the sensory memory of touching those silken, tawny strands. She's turning sideways, pointing to Olivia's bedroom where she knows I always watch her.

She waves and disappears. The Volvo proceeds uphill. My hands and feet freeze. The Volvo is Sterling's.

My nervous system has halted operations, keeping my body alive but inert. I'm still at Olivia's window. My heart pumps out of control as I step blankly downstairs, paste a smile on my face, open the door, and cross the porch.

A woman with screaming orange hair in corkscrews has emerged from the Volvo. She runs, arms open, although her smile wavers at the edges. Sterling shrieks and hurls herself, almost knocking me down.

'Walter! *Why* did you let me go?' She shakes her head. Her orange hair quivers. 'I know, I know: You don't make other people's decisions. I should have been grateful for that. And I was—I am. But I'm home now, my love, and so, so sorry.'

She locks me in an awful embrace. Her hands cover and muffle my ears. We're on the porch but Samson is barking in the kitchen. The Volvo is packed full.

Sterling's not here for a little chat and then toodle-oo. Even if she were, it would still be ghastly.

She pulls me through the front door. I follow Samson's bark and lean against the refrigerator, which does no good. Nothing short of violence will make Sterling pause.

Between a quick kiss and one I fear might never end, she says how much she loves me, and that only I, who am immune to jealousy, would allow her such an idiotic escapade. God help her! Is she ever sorry! She lost control. 'It took me forever to get it back. But never again. I'm sorry, too, for taking Olivia away. But that was for the better. You know that, right?'

'Oh-oh,' she says. 'Look at the puppy! *So* cute!' And, by the way, she's so glad I'm meeting with Glen Engle next week. Heather told her.

Meanwhile, I can't stop blinking. She shakes her peculiar head and pulls me away from the refrigerator to clasp her hands behind my neck. I don't dare push her away—even when it seems she's attempting to suck my face off.

I counter my mental frenzy by forcing my body into near paralysis. Closing my eyes, I re-experience all those life-or-death longings for Amanda. The marvelous girl flickers inside me, lifting me close to the sun. Yet Sterling keeps grasping and plunging me into a cold and bottomless sea. She's drowning me right here in the kitchen.

Eventually, I slip from her clutches and bob to the surface. I let my body relax in a dead-man's float. In fact, my heart has slowed and quieted to normal.

'Is everything all right? Is Olivia okay?'

'Yes,' Sterling says. 'Her moods are extreme, even for a teenager. Even compared—well, to anyone's. She was adamant about staying in Maine.'

'Why?'

'My mother adores her; she adores my mother. She likes her school—and Karl.'

'I can hardly believe you're here, Sterling.'

She smiles coyly and I rub my eyes to stop them from blinking. Also, to buy a moment before returning her smile. The best I can manage is a grimace in her direction. She's too busy talking to notice.

'You bought a new car.'

'Oh, you noticed that. The Mazda always felt like a car to drive to the train station and back. I wanted one to drive upstate if I felt like it.'

'Seems odd,' Sterling says. 'Nobody told me you had a new car.'

I pivot, just irritated enough for my shock to drop a notch. 'With whom do you discuss my driving habits? Nina?'

'Never mind that. You and Olivia would pack all her friends in the Mazda. Then you'd drive them wherever they wanted.'

'They wanted to be at the mall. What's wrong with that?'

'Forget it,' she says, taking my hand. But I need to sit down. I drop into the chair facing the bay window's middle pane. She sits beside me and describes coming home.

'Kevin and I were eating at our favorite restaurant and it started raining like Niagara Falls. A busboy let me out the back door. For some reason, Kevin had his car and I had mine, so I sped to the carriage house, packed my bags, and drove home. If it took all night, I didn't notice.'

'And now you're here.'

Amazing—my idyll with Amanda ends with Sterling acting as if she never left. Outside, the rain continues to drizzle. I stand up and pat my pockets. 'I was just going out for coffee beans. These days I like a strong, hot cup of Ethiopian roast.'

'Don't you want to stay with me? We don't need coffee that bad.'

'Maybe not. But I need to run a quick errand.'

'What kind of errand?'

I stand up and check my pockets for my wallet and keys. When I look at her, my eyelids open and close compulsively as if I could make her vanish. She's still there. She's tapping her foot. Her stand-up twists of hair do not move.

It's like a fit that suddenly stops. 'Sorry, I'm so bossy. Except I'm not, not anymore. You have to believe me, Walter.'

'That's all right, Sterling. Just let me run this small errand.' I'm still blinking and so befuddled that I march past her into the TV room where I stare at the backyard. Seeing the beds of irises that Amanda and I planted as bulbs in October, along with the two Japanese cut-leaf maples, I'm suddenly filled with boundless, unreasonable hope. Sterling leans into me, her chin digging into my shoulder. 'Soon we'll be looking out at a tiered acre.'

I nod and blink, still ridiculously buoyant as she leads me upstairs. She pulls me into the bedroom that was once ours. I remain near the threshold as she flops back on the bed, her arms flung overhead.

Without quite comprehending the plan I've already set in motion, I run downstairs for my cell phone. I make sure the rings and pings are set to the longest, loudest option, and place it on Sterling's nightstand.

Our marriage is over. I will never make love to her again. Sterling will accept this soon, despite her awkward overtures. Because we are no longer lovers. And yet—she *will* save me! She'll field incoming calls, and either cover for me or assert my rights. Sterling will tell Cheryl Jonette that her negligence is— and has always been—criminal.

Most importantly, however, she will protect Amanda! Sterling will do whatever is necessary to prevent any- and everyone from interrogating her, including Amanda's mother! She'll threaten Cheryl against any inclination to intimidate her daughter—or to make even mild insinuations. I have no doubt. As my fledging plan develops, I'm ready and able to pay the consequences. Because Sterling will grasp the situation instantly. And she will know exactly how to stop any official, authority, or procedure from harassing Amanda. She will safeguard her. Beyond question, Sterling will shield Amanda with her life.

Nevertheless, at this moment, Sterling stands naked before me, her arms open.

'Just a minute.' I back away and find a backpack in the closet. Inside a set of drawers there, I find my passport. Turning around, I see that Sterling's between me and the open bedroom door. As I approach, she presses my hands over her soft, loose breasts. 'If you aren't gone long, I'll shower and we can take a nap.'

I almost slip past her, but she grabs my arm. 'Can't your errand wait? Don't you want me?'

I murmur, 'In a minute,' and run downstairs.

In the study, I add a second wallet, with additional I.D. and credit cards, to the backpack. In the garage, I throw the backpack inside the Accord. Before getting behind the wheel, I remember the pre-paid, emergency phone that's in the Mazda's glove compartment. It's parked by the backyard fence. I dash back there and fumble with my keys before remembering I don't lock the Mazda. Seconds later, I'm buckled into the Accord and backing out of the garage in low gear. I turn and glide silently down the spiraling hill. At Oak Grove Point's iron gates, I phone Delta Air Lines and reserve two first-class, round-trip tickets to Orlando, Florida.

By the time I'm cruising down Broadway, the sun has banished the rain clouds. I park opposite Main Street in a parking lot near the entrance to another luxury housing development like Oak Grove Point, except far more extensive with rolling man-made hills. Hands in my pockets, I cross Broadway. Sunlight streams through the leafy trees onto the pavement.

I know exactly what I'm doing. Every morning, Amanda meets her friends at the diner across the street from the middle school's main entrance. Ordinarily, she'd have no reason to walk back up the hill. But today she will. Fate will call her.

Cleansed of every wrong, I know I'm right. My life until this moment has been a prelude to this. This adventure.

While I wait to cross the street, Wayne's wife drives by as she often does when Amanda, Samson, and I stand on the corner. Today, as if nothing's unusual, Wayne's wife gives me a big thumb's up and toots her horn. I check my watch—not yet eight. Time can vanish in a second. And an entire lifetime can blossom within half an hour.

A wall of unearthly brightness affects my vision. When I recover my sight, Amanda and Madison walk inside a splendid aura, directly toward me. The second I see her, Amanda raises her eyes. And Madison seems to say goodbye before turning and walking away.

Amanda runs uphill, her eyes fixed on mine. One minute she's leaping like a gazelle, the next, she's standing in front of me.

'So,' she smiles, linking an arm through mine, 'where are we going?'

'That depends, honey. Do you like surprises?'

Thirty Three

The traffic on I-87 flows along, despite the morning rush hour. Amanda squeezes my thigh. 'Give me a hint so I'm not *too* surprised.'

'I thought we'd go someplace famous for being warm and fun.'

'You mean—on an airplane?' She whoops, rising inside her seatbelt. 'Walter, I'm the only kid I know who's never been on an airplane!'

'If it scares you, we'll think of something else. But I thought we should have an adventure we'll never forget.'

'If I wasn't going with you, I might be scared. But did you know? I've always thought someday I'd travel. See the world.'

'I don't think we can manage that now. Just one adventure.'

She slaps my shoulder in a burst of happiness. 'Don't tell me another thing, not even if I beg.' She turns on the music and out pours a stream of songs from *The Real Miranda*.

The initial song I've always found rather strained. Miranda sings a bluesy ballad but is unfamiliar with the blues. She bends the notes at the wrong intervals.

Amanda asks, 'Is this okay or do you need to think?'

'No, I want to recall the first time we listened to these songs together.'

'Uh-oh, what's wrong? Are we on the lam?'

I laugh. 'Not unless we're in a very old movie. Although, technically, I suppose *I'm* on the lam. You, however, are playing hooky. That's important, Amanda. If anyone asks you about this—but they shouldn't—tell them that I invited you to play hooky. You agreed, because school's easy for you.'

'That's true. It is.'

In the next song, the engineers have altered the actress's voice so it conveys intelligence and feeling. I ask, 'Remember this one? Iris was hovering outside the window. Her bells act as a kind of call-and-response.'

Amanda sings along, her voice sliding down an octave to harmonize with Iris.

This morning, when I saw her leaving the diner with her classmates, I worried that she might be too grown up for Disney World. But her enthusiasm for the Miranda songs encourages me.

Every day, a moment occurs in which I notice a newly compelling aspect to her eyes and lips. The sweep of Amanda's jaw is now proportionate with her cheekbones. Until Sterling arrived, I imagined myself impervious to Amanda's changing figure—high, sprightly breasts as if overnight; her small waist and long limbs newly emphasized by slender but distinct hips, and a round bottom that is neither a child's nor a woman's.

Amanda claims we communicate telepathically about things we share with no one else. I used to laugh at that—*telepathically*. But before Amanda and I were alone together at the top of Oak Grove Point, I was usually silent and often reticent. With her, I can say anything. Although, sometimes, we really don't need to speak. We do think the same thoughts.

The waves of overwhelming joy and their undertow stream from the infinite depth of the love and admiration Amanda and I have for each other. My fear of succumbing to her precocious advances suddenly strikes me as preposterous. She's stroking my leg and I feel no need to stop her.

Traffic slows at the Triborough Bridge. We pass through an automatic toll and I say, 'I hate asking you to lie, Amanda. And I know that you hate pretending I'm your father, because it goes against your feelings. But for this adventure, you will probably need to do that a few times.'

Amanda scoffs. 'The only reason I insist it's a lie is to make sure you understand—I *never* think of you that way, Walter. And, you don't think of me as your daughter. I know you don't. You try to, but you can't.'

'No fooling you, is there?' I wink at her, expecting her to roll her eyes. But she's not joking. So, I say, 'You're probably the most honest person I've ever met. Most people lie to themselves and don't even know it. But you're always honest with yourself. It's a shame that when I take you some place, you have to lie.'

'All I care about is that you never think of you-and-me as make-believe. You and me, Walter and Amanda, are real and true.'

I should simply agree. But I worry about the coming scrutiny. To reassure myself, I say, 'Part of it depends on what people assume. Anyone can see we love each other. If we present ourselves as father and daughter, people understand that. Only someone who knows us both very well could accept how we are together without jumping to the conclusion that I'm a despicable man. You know that, honey, and you have an extraordinary ability to stop people from wondering.'

She smiles her irresistible, wicked smile and whispers, 'I know.'

'You cover up for your mother, and now you'll need to cover up for me. It's wrong because the most important thing is honoring the truth of who you are and how you feel.'

I don't dare to look at her, fearing her pantomime with the lugubrious violin. But she says, 'Walter, you're not forcing me into anything.'

I take this as permission to continue. 'If you accept us briefly escaping together, we need to be devious.'

'Wait a minute. What are we escaping? What's happening?'

'I saw you talk to Sterling in her car. So you know she's home.'

'*That* was Sterling?'

'Who did you think it was?'

'I don't know. I never saw her hair like that.'

'Me neither.'

'So, I'm playing hooky because Sterling has come home to stay.'

'It's true that she's home, Amanda. We won't stay married, but now that's she's here, our time together—yours and mine—is running out.'

Through loud, irregular gasps, she tries to blink away tears, swiping hard at those that pop out. In a gentler voice than I knew I possessed, I say, 'We talked about this, honey, remember? You said maybe if we were quiet, time would forget about us. And I said, let's hold our breath.'

Shaking her head, she says, 'What sad, stupid jokes,' and cries.

I muster businesslike restraint to keep myself from crying. Amanda's entitled to her tears, separate from anyone else's—especially mine.

She stares out the car door window. Before long, she sniffles and asks if I have a handkerchief. Shifting my weight, I dig into my jeans' front pocket and hand her a clean one. In less than a minute, she hands it back. Spine straight, shoulders level, she says, 'You have to promise me, Walter, you won't get in trouble.'

'Honey, every adventure involves risk. I will get in some trouble for this, but I'm prepared for that. Because we need this, Amanda. We really need it.'

She frowns and then she hiccups, which surprises us both. 'Okay,' she says, half smiling. 'We sure need *something.*'

A particular pressure forms behind my eyes—similar to the sensation I get whenever Amanda says I love her more than I realize. Not long ago, maybe even yesterday, I was afraid of my love for her, afraid of its force, and the appalling cravings it aroused in me. But the truth is this: Mostly what Amanda arouses in me is boundless happiness. Also, sublime devotion. If I were capable of denying the attendant cravings, I might be more susceptible to them.

For weeks, I've wanted to say, 'I love you more than you can imagine, Amanda.' Except, I've decided it's better left unsaid.

The feelings we share are a constant, sacred present tense. It will be enough—more than enough—if she realizes that an exceptionally reasonable man loves her beyond all reason.

If she continues to think of our time together, perhaps she'll even consider how much she changed me. All of Amanda's provocations—intentional, innocent, and in-between—tapped emotional powers within me that I would never have discovered otherwise. Because of Amanda, my deep, distant self has grown bold and upfront. My mind and heart are steadfast and immediate.

I must tell her that she has the money to go wherever she chooses. That she can indeed, if she wants, see the world. But right now, for a day or two, we're going where nobody knows us. We deserve a last celebration together.

I park in the airport lot and tap her knee. 'You and I, Amanda, are so far from ordinary, we're going to have to fool all the ordinary people.'

Thirty Four

In the departure area, Amanda steps heel-to-toe in a tight circle, a habit of hers to contain excitement. But her excitement is contagious. And not just to me—everyone waiting to check their luggage smiles at her.

Fingers crossed, I ask if she has a picture I.D. Such a quick girl—she presents a laminated card, *voilà*. The middle-school I.D. includes her name, class year, date of birth, address, and phone number. In a yellowish, watermarked photograph, Amanda rolls her eyes left, her mouth slightly open. It's a funny, fetching pose.

I hand the TSA official our tickets, my passport, and Amanda's I.D., hoping it's sufficient. The woman glances at the card and then asks Amanda, 'Are you going for Disney's Last Minute Getaway?'

She rises in the air. 'Are we, Daddy?'

The security guard apologizes for ruining the surprise. I assure her the timing is perfect and ask if she can advise me on what to do next. 'Her mother let me know weeks ago, but so far I've only bought the air tickets.'

The TSA official doesn't work for Disney or Delta, but she loves Disney World and is especially enthusiastic about the Getaway Program.

The Last Minute Getaway, I learn, offers discounts to parents whose kids attend participating schools. It can be used as an incentive or a reward. Amanda's school would have approved the days off if her mother had said they needed time together. Had I planned better, I would have given Amanda's principal an explanation for her absence today and tomorrow. Now, it's too late.

The sweet-natured guard reassures me that I can buy tickets to the theme parks and make all other necessary arrangements at the Orlando airport. 'Look for the statue of Goofy and his candy store.'

Amanda tells the woman this is her first time flying and beams an all-out smile so that the official halts, briefly suspended. (Amanda's smile always conveys a flicker of stopped time, for me at least, but now I'm witnessing its effect on someone else.)

Unaware, the woman pauses for nearly a full minute. Then, excusing herself, she turns and speaks into a device lifted from her neck. Facing us again, she says, 'You can skip the long line. I'll initial your tickets and you can go directly to that area over there.'

She points to a short security line. Soon, we're putting our backpacks and phones in bins on the conveyor belt. We can keep our shoes on, we're told. I walk through the simple metal detector first. The guard monitoring it says, 'Have fun.'

After we breeze through security, Amanda admires how official everything is.

She pulls me into a corner and reaches for my neck until I bend one knee on the floor. She leans against my leg, her hands holding my face, before she tugs my hair, whispering, 'Disney World, Walter! You knew that's where I've always wanted to go.'

I hug her close and kiss her forehead. Ever since I left Sterling lying naked in our bed, my impulses toward Amanda have lacked all semblance of lust. My love for her is no less thrilling for being pure.

We stand up. 'Where's your phone? I'll text your mother now that she can't stop us. She should at least know where you are.'

Amanda grins and drops her iPhone into a metal trash receptacle.

'Honey! What about your friends? Your music and photos?'

'Oh, yeah.' She gazes inside, then shakes her head. 'I don't care. Just so long as Cheryl doesn't know about this. 'Cause even if you're right and she can't stop us, she'll call up everyone she can think of and scream bloody murder.'

That's true. Cheryl could and would stop us before we reach the Magic Kingdom.

'We have an hour before the flight. Let's wait in the Sky Club.'

I might not have thought of everything, but I did make sure I wasn't stripped of my rarely used membership when Bank of America fired me. She takes my hand, swinging it as we walk. 'You know how when we would cuddle, you'd tell me it was too much?'

'Yes.'

We enter an empty elevator that goes up a short way. 'I figured it out. You and I feel too much for our puny bodies to hold.' When the elevator opens, I'm resting one hand on her head and the other on her shoulder. We step toward the dark glass doors to the lounge and her eyes, lit from within, hold mine in a clarity that seems surreal.

She pulls me closer, reaching up, and I'm drawn right into her otherworldly amber eyes. Then she braces her hands atop my shoulders. 'For me, this is ten times too much, Walter. I love you a million times too much, and I always will.'

'I feel the exact same about you.' I stroke Amanda's head and set her on her feet.

In the lounge, we sit at a table where we can see the jets landing and taking off.

I ask the waiter for sparkling water, much as I'd like a straight Scotch, and say that, 'Disney's undiscovered princess here will have a "Little Flyer's Special."'

When the waiter has retreated, Amanda frowns. 'Really. *Little Flyer's Special?*'

'Silly name, but I think you'll like it.'

When the waiter hands Amanda 7 Up in a frosted martini glass, she accepts it graciously. She extends her pinky, holds the glass stem carefully, and sips slowly. Then, she sets the drink on our small round table and swivels in her chair, giggling. She wobbles her head in a circle counter to her swiveling chair. 'Remember?'

I laugh. 'Bubbles go straight to your head.'

*

We're the only first class passengers, which means we get to board the jet before the hundreds of other people on our flight. I encourage Amanda to take the window seat so she can watch us leaving the ground—and then the earth.

The flight attendant, a woman my age with stiff brown hair in a French twist, smiles at me. I smile back. She wears a uniform of blue and orange, and while Amanda is studying the in-flight magazine, she crouches beside me in the aisle and speaks in a hush. 'Your daughter? She is lovely.'

'Thank you.' (That's the expected response, I'm almost positive, but it sounds peculiar.)

The woman stands and wrings her hands once before bending down again and saying in a rush, 'Forgive me, but you seem young to have a girl her age.'

I glance at Amanda, who pretends not to notice. 'Her mother and I never married.'

Rising quickly to move on, the woman taps her knuckle against my outside armrest. 'But you're married now, I see.'

'Yes, I'm married now.' Halfway to her station, she turns back to smile at me.

Amanda whispers, 'Why was she asking about me?'

'I'll tell you later.'

'But we're okay?'

'We're great.'

While the plane taxis to the runway, third in line, the flight attendant steers a small cart with one hand and carries a towel-wrapped champagne bottle (unopened) in her other hand.

'None for me, thanks.'

She suggests beverages for Amanda, who says, 'We had cocktails in the lounge.'

Again, the flight attendant smiles. 'When you're ready, I have cold salmon with cucumber-dill, roast beef sandwiches, a mélange of melon and berries, and whole-grain chips.' Amanda declines politely, and I do the same.

'It's best to eat something to prevent queasiness. We have strawberry or vanilla-caramel parfait.'

The attendant appears concerned about being pushy, but has a litany she must recite. 'It's important to stay hydrated,' she says, suggesting Perrier water.

'Do you happen to have pomegranate juice we could mix with seltzer?'

'No,' she smiles at Amanda. 'But I've got fresh Cherry Smash.'

'I love Cherry Smash.'

I ask her to bring it later in the flight. The attendant nods and hurries upfront.

The Disney Channel lists a series of interviews with the cast of *The Real Miranda*.

We get our headphones out from our backpacks. 'Don't let me forget to buy you a new iPhone.'

The show starts but then the captain interrupts to describe the flight. After which, the interviews are replaced by a cartoon family demonstrating safety rules and regulations. A voice-over admonishes us to review this important information in the booklet we'll find in the seatback ahead of us. Amanda reaches for it, but I say, 'Look at your screen, honey. It's Sam as a boy.'

In his interview, the young actor who plays Sam on *The Real Miranda* credits wardrobe, make-up, and occasional special camera effects for his miraculous bilocation powers. But to play a super-boy and super-girl simultaneously, he practiced with computerized sensors attached to his arms, legs, neck, and face. Other than clothes, hair, and make-up, the transformation involves using obscure muscles and a subtle variation in gestures. Demonstrating Sam as a super-boy, he narrows his eyes and angles his eyebrows upward. For Sam as a super-girl, his face softens and his mouth puffs slightly. He stands, feet apart, arms crossed, and changes from boy to girl to boy again. 'Of course, I could exaggerate it more, but I think it's more convincing to do less.'

The actress who plays Miranda grew up onscreen as the overeager little sister in an earlier Disney TV show. However, between filming that show and *The Real Miranda,* she attended a regular public high school, instead of being tutored. 'So, I know just how Miranda feels. You enter high school and it really does seem like everyone else has special powers. If only because they all know each other.' The actress enters the set that serves as her bedroom and pauses in front of a teddy bear and canopy bed, to explain why she chose them for the character. The designers have hung a picture of the Manhattan skyline on one of the bedroom walls—something Amanda and I hadn't noticed before. The actress waves like a beauty queen and exits.

Iris appears with an acoustic guitar. She's the songwriter for the show. Her short hair is shaped so that a tiny peak crests on top, emphasizing her pixyish quality.

'Acting means a lot of waiting around, so I sit on the floor and play my guitar.'

The show already had a theme song, but one of the producers overheard Iris singing a song she had written. She plays what is now a well-loved refrain associated with Miranda feeling strange in super-strange Iowa.

'The producer asked me to write an opening and a closing song for each episode. And, you know, some came out better than others, so they hired a co-songwriter. Chris works with me to make sure everything sounds professional.'

She bobbles her head and her eyes turn up—not really like Amanda's but similar enough so that we look at each other and laugh.

Amanda taps my shoulder. We remove our headphones. 'Her songs are so good. I hope she becomes a major pop star. She's so tiny and funny with her pixy ears.'

The flight attendant brings us two icy bottles of Cherry Smash with tall glasses.

'Hey, it's the same Cherry Smash we get at the farmers' market. See? From New Jersey.'

The sour cherry flavor is intense. Amanda says I might want to dilute it with seltzer. But I take a long taste and tell her I love it as is.

*

As the Miranda interviews end, the captain announces we've reached cruising altitude and he expects a smooth flight to Orlando. Amanda suppresses a yawn. We turn off the screens and put away our headphones. She nods and her eyes close.

I tell her that I like Iris best. 'To me, Miranda is just another pretty blonde girl.'

Amanda's eyes fly open and her voice rises. 'Am I?'

'Are you what?'

'I'm sort of blonde, Walter. And sort of pretty. Either way, I'll always look more like Miranda than Iris.'

'You do not look like Miranda or anyone else. Nobody I've ever seen comes close to resembling you. It's impossible to think of you as just another pretty girl. Haven't you noticed how people look at you, Amanda? They try not to stare, but they can't help it. Your beauty is refined, perpetual motion.'

Amanda faces me briefly as she shakes out her hair, and once again I'm arrested by her beauty. After this trip, I won't be allowed to see her again.

'Are you telling me this to boost my self-esteem?' she says at last.

I almost laugh but catch myself; she's not teasing. I reply that, no, I wasn't even thinking of her self-esteem. But she should pay attention to how people respond to her. 'In five years or so, Cheryl will still be your mother, but she won't have as much influence. Chances are that your life will become much easier.'

She rests a thumb on her lower lip.

No reason to hold back anymore, so I say, 'I love everything about you, Amanda, and always have. You opened me up. You made me complete.'

She jumps in her seat. '*Made?* Past tense?'

'Sorry. You make me happy. You always will, whether I'm with you still or only remembering how things used to be. Promise me that you'll keep being funny even if you're alone. And, this is important: Don't let your physical beauty become a mask you hide behind. Normally, even the most interesting people are opaque at first. You're never opaque; it's a rare and wonderful quality.'

She drops her hands in her lap and closes her eyes, but I keep talking.

'If I didn't see you for twenty years, and then we were within a radius of several miles—I'd sense your proximity in a heartbeat.'

'How?'

'Because I feel as if you're with me even when you aren't.'

'If you're near me, will I know?'

'I don't know. When I was growing up, I learned to become unnoticeable. In some circumstances, it was important. But it made me distant even to myself. You changed that.'

She covers a yawn. 'Excuse me. I'm sleepy.' She searches my face for permission and finding it, rests her head against my chest. 'Keep talking, Walter.'

I whisper, 'Your eyelids are heavy, so heavy. You can't keep them open. And now you're asleep. You're in a very deep sleep and when you wake, you'll feel fantastic.'

The flight attendant arrives to collect the Cherry Smash bottles. Seeing Amanda, she fastens our tray tables and allows us to leave the armrest up. 'Let her sleep but keep your seatbelts on. And if you support her head, she won't wake up dizzy.'

I cup her chin and slide a hand under her hair, supporting her long, slender neck. I inhale her scent of exhausted, girlish excitement and marvel that in all our months of fraught intimacy, I never once watched her sleep.

Thirty Five

The jet lands with a gentle bump, waking Amanda without alarming her. While we taxi toward the terminal, she listens to her headphones and I leaf through the in-flight magazine. Seeing a small ad for the Dolphin Hotel, I phone for reservations. A man with a slight southern accent says that most people reserve accommodations months in advance, but I'm in luck. A 'family suite' with two separate bedrooms is available.

Inside the airport, Amanda takes my hand, swinging it to match her subliminal skip. We follow a small crowd into the airport shopping mall and her skip acquires a spinning sensation. We see the statue of Goofy and are immediately inside his candy store. I look past the bins and barrels of candy at an extensive fantasyland that's both overflowing and carefully laid out with a Disney cornucopia of merchandise.

'We need summer clothes, honey. I can already sense how hot we'll be in the—'

'Magic Kingdom. That's my dream.' Amanda picks up a men's dark green Mickey Mouse shirt. 'This would look great on you.' Mickey is wearing a small-brimmed hat. One of his big white feet is high in the air, as if he's dancing to the music coming through his fluorescent yellow earbuds. 'I'm buying it for you,' Amanda says, gesturing for me to turn around so she can match the shirt against my back. 'Walter the hipster,' she says, and I wince.

A cheerful middle-aged saleswoman asks if she can help us.

I start to say we're interested in the Last Minute Getaway package but—saved by hesitation—tell her we'd like two, two-day passes instead. The TSA agent's words resound in my head: the Getaway involves previous correspondence.

Nevertheless, I'm left with a nagging feeling I should offer some kind of justification. 'Her mother is getting remarried,' I blurt out.

Whether this quasi-non-sequitur makes me suspect or not, I don't know. Luckily, the saleswoman nods and says, 'I see. You're here for your own adventure.'

'Exactly,' Amanda says.

The saleswoman escorts us to a long low counter behind the store and its main checkout area. She sits down at a computer equipped with Mickey Mouse ears. I remove my backpack and reach into the outer flap. First to appear are the flimsy printout plane tickets, which I set in front of her. Because even though they're waste paper, they still attest to our having been vetted very recently by the TSA. I then present the woman with my passport and Amanda's school I.D.

By now, of course, I'm acutely aware of how ill-planned this scheme really is. If the woman wonders about us, I'll have to depend on Amanda to rescue us. When she says, 'Daddy,' doubts evaporate. Whereas I cannot explain why my supposed daughter's last name differs from mine. In the bathroom on the plane, I practiced. Trying to look rueful, I sighed into the mirror, saying, 'Well, to expedite the divorce, I agreed to her mother's wish that the second half of Amanda's last name be legally dropped.' It hadn't sounded ridiculous in private. But had I said it where anyone could hear me—even, or maybe especially, Amanda—we would have laughed.

Busy with my wallet, I attempt to gauge the Disney rep's demeanor. If we fail to get into Disney World, our adventure will amount to Amanda watching me led away in handcuffs, while child welfare authorities escort her to a holding facility that will undoubtedly feel just like a jail.

I know the risks we are taking. For as spontaneous as this trip is, I researched kidnapping laws after that time I accidentally drove Amanda across a state line. A man suspected of molesting a child cannot explain it away. If anyone suspects the worst about Amanda and me, I'll be arrested and Amanda will be interrogated by bureaucrats, judicial psychiatrists, and social workers demanding to know where I 'touched her.'

The minute we return home and Amanda is secure, I will confess to kidnapping in the second degree, which is a class B felony. With my guilty plea and Amanda in Wisconsin, no one will need to question her.

Meanwhile, I wink in sympathy at the saleswoman sorting through our haphazard credentials. I try tickling Amanda's neck only to find that her internal dance has jittered into anxiety. She ducks away.

I give the saleswoman my credit card. 'Would you mind swiping that for me? My daughter's upset about something.'

Amanda stands near the entrance and stares hard at a point in space. I slide beside her. 'Everything's fine, honey. Turn around and look. My credit card's going through.'

Seeing this, Amanda bounds back, jumps in front of the saleswoman, and bestows a time-tripping smile on her.

Returning Amanda's smile, the saleswoman recommends that we get the Magic Band magnetic wristbands that allow entry into any of the theme parks.

'I'm sending your particulars to all the Magic Service Centers. You can get your wristbands at any of them.'

On tiptoe, Amanda twirls in a half-circle, thanking the woman. And, she clasps my arm. 'Thank you, Daddy! I can't believe it! Thank you.'

One more thing: The woman says that because neither of us has a Disney profile, she must ask us each 'a security question.'

Amanda places the T-shirt on the counter, and hearing the question, says, 'That's easy. My father's middle name is Galen. Walter Galen Mitchell.'

The woman asks me what Amanda's middle name is. I don't know, but I'm confident that the saleswoman doesn't know it, either. Amanda's school I.D. does not include a middle name or even an initial. So, I say, 'Iris. Amanda Iris Jonette.'

This time, the woman winks at me.

Borrowing my credit card, Amanda buys the hipster Mickey Mouse T-shirt and we leave the store addled by pixy dust and anxiety. The edge and odor of the airport's air-conditioning blast us with intimations of extreme Florida heat. Suddenly, we're both exhausted.

Thirty Six

The airport's shopping mall offers many more shops than just Disney. To our right looms a designer teenage girls' boutique called Rainbows and Unicorns. Inside, a young woman wearing a short lacy skirt and an even lacier top offers to show Amanda the latest attire.

'Some of the trendier styles,' I say without thinking, 'are a little overdone. I mean…risqué.'

'Daddy, please. Go buy yourself some clothes and I'll meet you someplace.'

The salesgirl says we can return anything I decide might be inappropriate. Turning to Amanda, she compliments her denim jacket. 'I haven't seen *The Real Miranda* clothes in those sun-washed colors before.'

I walk away but reappear almost immediately, interrupting a conversation about how short the new shorts are. 'Excuse me. When you're finished, Amanda, meet me at the Sunglass Hut.'

She wobbles her head and rolls her eyes. 'Got it. Sunglass Hut in—' she checks an imaginary watch'—fifteen or twenty minutes.'

Three stores away, I find men's clothing—lightweight, quick-drying jeans in my size and a pair of unbleached canvas sneakers that look like something my father might have worn when he was six. Trying on the shoes, I learn they're a 'special retro edition,' which explains the cost. The jeans, which I don't need to try on, are ninety percent denim and ten percent wick-away microfiber.

At a vast Sunglass Hut, I buy the same Ray-Bans I always wear. But I don't see anything for Amanda. The women's sunglasses are laden with filigree, ornate logos, even rhinestones. I ask the clerk, a short, muscle-bound man with a shaved head, if he has any frames that won't fly off a thirteen-year-old girl.

Perhaps his smirk is all in my mind. Pushing aside a three-way mirror, he opens a drawer and, after digging around, dangles a pair too close to my face. I take them and they're nice—delicate, plastic, honey-colored tortoiseshell frames with rounded brown lenses.

In no time, Amanda appears, carrying two big shiny shopping bags. She's changed into tiny maroon shorts and a little pink T-shirt. Also, sandals of braided orange strips that fasten around her ankles, making the shape and length of her pale smooth legs even more attractive.

'Can you walk around all day in those sandals?'

'Definitely. Guess what brand they are.'

'I don't know—ankle straps.'

'That's the style. Remember Crocs? Those giant rubber elf shoes? These are new Crocs, waterproof, cushy, and created especially for Disney World.'

Now it's my turn to show off. I turn one foot and then the other, displaying my retro kicks. The sales clerk snorts at me and shows Amanda four pairs of sunglasses, arranged on a ledge, backed by a mirror. Reluctant to put down her bags (or something), Amanda asks me to choose a pair and put them on for her. Fitting the frames to her face and adjusting the stems besets me with desire. (My immunity lasted less than three hours.)

I step back and she smiles. The clerk scratches the tattoo on his bicep, saying, 'That brand emphasizes high cheekbones, like yours.' He's at least my age and staring at her. So I'm primed when he takes out his phone and raises it to focus the camera. I grab his wrist and squeeze it until I've wrenched the phone from his fat hand. Holding it well above his reach, I twist his arm behind him. He tries unsuccessfully to stomp on my feet. When he starts to curse, I release him suddenly and he crashes into a stand-up display of Prada sunglasses.

At the store's threshold, I look at his phone and sure enough, the camera's on. I shut it off. Amanda's distress radiates from the back of the store, where she's retreated. Her worry sweeps over me and magnifies my own. Idiot-boy hovers somewhere between us.

While I'm swiping through his latest photos, Amanda invents a diversion. She's put on an exaggerated pair of butterfly sunglasses. Addressing a mirror in a theatrical voice, she says, 'My dear, tell me the truth. Would you mind terribly? I mean, really, truly—terribly?'

'What is *this*?' The picture I expected: his plump, naked torso blurred behind his fat hand squeezing his erect penis.

'Get over here.' And the asshole does.

I glance at Amanda, now wearing sunglasses adorned with strands of pearls. 'Cora, darling, I was, like, to die.'

'That you, big guy?'

'Fuck off. Everyone does it.'

'No, everyone doesn't. Where did you intend to put my daughter's picture?'

Sickened, I drop the phone by the register, ready to walk out. But Amanda is suddenly beside me whispering, 'Please, Walter. I love those sunglasses.'

281

The brute gives me a twenty-five percent discount. Amanda puts on her new Smith Optics, saying loudly as I usher her out of there, 'Thank you, Daddy. I'll wear them forever.'

We wander away and find an exit. Amanda looks sophisticated in her sunglasses and thanks me again for them—for everything. 'But you're scaring me, Walter! So what if he took a picture of me wearing sunglasses?'

'He was going to paste it onto something obscene. But I'm sorry I sunk to his level, honey. I didn't handle that well.'

'It's okay.' We emerge gasping into the heat and wait for a taxi to pull up.

Thirty Seven

In the air-conditioned taxicab, I suggest we order room service for lunch. 'Unless you want a giant turkey leg.'

'What?'

'I'll show you.' But turning on my phone, I find it has limited Internet access. Instead, it flashes a dozen voicemails and fifteen texts from Sterling. I turn it off and describe greasy-faced people chomping on the steroidal turkey legs that Disney World sells. She's appropriately disgusted.

The dolphin motif at the hotel delights her, though. While I check in, she dips her fingers in a big round fountain of pink and blue porcelain dolphins spurting jets of water.

On the third floor, I give her the key card to her bedroom and she gives me the bag with my T-shirt. I open the door to my room and say, 'I'm going to change and if you want, why don't you see if room service has anything we like?'

'*Mais oui! C'est parfait!* Lunch in our suite, *toute de suite.*'

I start to touch her head and stop. Her gaze drops, and then she's inside her room.

My own huge sunny bedroom depresses me. Anxiously, I toss the mobile phone in a drawer, and retreat inside the dim bathroom to put on my new jeans and T-shirt.

When the hotel phone rings, I jump. Amanda, who has never had room service, never even stayed in a hotel before, wants to know if I like club sandwiches and do I think she'd like them. 'Yes,' to both.

'Okay, and do you like half-iced tea, half-lemonade?'

'That sounds great, honey.'

'Do you know how expensive this is?'

'Yes, but it's worth it.'

I collect my things, tie my canvas high-tops, and knock before entering our dining/living room suite. Amanda turns from the window. She was fighting tears but spontaneously breaks into a glorious grin and giggles.

'Walter, you're the coolest daddy ever.'

'Am I?'

'Look at you! Ten times handsomer than any movie star and super-cool—' She leads me to a standing mirror where I'm surprised by my own reflection. The lightweight, slightly stretchy jeans are cut very narrow and hang very low on my hips. A machine-made slash rests near my right knee and a bigger rip rides my left thigh. Meanwhile, Amanda's stuck her whole hand through the pre-fab hole in the back pocket.

'Put your sunglasses on,' she says. 'I didn't get to see them.'

I repress a groan, because I already look like the men who take girls to museums in New York. She gets her sunglasses and holds them up while I unfold mine. In the mirror, she says, 'On three.'

As if we're about to jump through a portal, I count to three—and sunglasses on. In the mirror, we're transformed into a dynamic duo.

We step away and stand back from each other. Amanda could not look more inspiring if she tried. But she takes off her sunglasses to gawk at me, clutches her heart, and mock swoons.

I laugh, shake my head, and take off my sunglasses. 'If I were smart, I'd look like the world's most *scrupulous* daddy.'

'Oh, but Walter—' Her thrilled face grows thoughtful and her eyes enormous. 'Technically,' her voice is husky, 'you're "on the lam."'That means you've broken the law.'

'Technically, yes. But for me, Amanda, this is the best of crimes.'

'*Best of crimes, worst of crimes*—what's that from?'

'*Times*, not crimes, from *A Tale of Two Cities* by Charles Dickens. *It was the best of times, it was the worst of times…*Are you ready for the best of times?'

Knock-knock, and it's room service. Amanda's delighted with the silver domes and Lucite bowls of crushed ice, the fine porcelain plates, and elegant glassware. We eat double-decker sandwiches of Swiss cheese, avocado, and tomato slices on whole-wheat toast, no crusts. The half-iced tea, half-lemonade is served in a Mickey and Minnie Mouse pitcher.

Amanda eats half her lunch. Her eyes fill. Neither of us looks away, but not one tear spills. 'Our adventure is a magical goodbye, isn't it, Walter?'

'We have to say goodbye, sometime. I brought you here because I love you.'

She stares in the middle distance. Her eyes close, flutter twice, and open. She sits up, determined. 'Which do you want to do first? Space Mountain?'

'Your choice, honey.'

'Space Mountain. Definitely.'

We stand up and I'm out the door but she calls me back. We join hands and gaze into the mirror. 'Look at us!' she says.

I embrace her freely. For once, gravity isn't a factor—and neither is fear.

Thirty Eight

In the hot early afternoon, we're waiting our turn for Space Mountain. Amanda tugs my hand. She looks very serious and says, with what sounds like genuine guilt, that she needs to tell me a shameful secret.

'Anything.'

'I've never ridden a roller coaster—not even one for little kids.' She turns away and giggles. 'Oh, my God, it's so embarrassing.'

I laugh so hard that I have to rest my hands on my knees, catching my breath. Amanda shoves my shoulders. To keep my balance, because I'm laughing even more now, I drop to one knee. She circles behind me and slaps my back. I pivot around and see her giggling, hand raised, ready to slap my face. I'm overcome by fresh fits of hilarity. Amanda attempts indignation, which causes her, too, to break into full-throttle laughter. I scoop together her bare legs, drape her over my shoulder, and stand up, dancing side to side, while her fists jab at my backside. We're both laughing uncontrollably and I can't keep her still. She's squirming and clinging and choking back laughter to speak.

'Shut up! Shut up!' she yells, sliding down and around me, her arms clasping my neck, so she's riding me piggyback. 'Everyone's staring at us!'

Indeed, they are. She pulls my hair. 'How dare you laugh at me! Shame on you!'

I try to keep her behind me and she tries to twist around as if to free herself, despite her thighs squeezing even tighter around my waist. Finally, I set her on the ground only to double over, still in the throes of laughing fits.

Back on one knee, I touch her head. She steps so that we're eye to eye. Our impulse is simultaneous. We clap a hand over each other's mouth. This lasts two seconds before we fall back into peals of glee.

The line to Space Mountain has become a semicircle around us. Amanda tries to bite my right hand. I raise it above her reach and wave my left index finger in her face.

'Shame on who? Shame on *you*, little girl! You promised to behave in public! You promised.'

She leaps at me. I fold her over my shoulder again and stand. I spin in a circle, balancing her. She's giggling and shaking. Donald Duck appears and quack-scolds us until I put her down, his huge webbed feet flapping as he stalks off.

We don't entirely recover until the steel car we're strapped into enters the dark of the mountain. The careening ride twists and turns. We cling to each other and scream. By the time the car slows and begins coasting to the end, our hearts are pounding in unison.

Languorous with relief, we wander hand in hand beneath the bright sunshine, our sunglasses on, our legs loose and rubbery. After a while, we're strolling toward the *Pirates of the Caribbean* ride. The line here is especially long, but Amanda's glad we didn't schedule a time using the Fast Magic option. She's happy to wait and I'm perfectly content listening to her history of Captain Jack Sparrow. She prepares me for one steep drop and possibly a ghostly sighting of Blue Beard.

Donald Duck quacks past us again and I ask her for a translation.

'He says …' Amanda puffs out a cheek and offers a good but understandable impression. '*That's* more like it!'

We climb into a boat and watch robotic pirates drinking from flagons and kicking loose planks around. Amanda snuggles beside me and kisses my cheek.

'Oh, no!' She's noticed a little animatronic dog barking on a shipwreck. I assure her that Sterling is taking good care of Samson. 'She always had a dog growing up. Getting Samson was her idea.'

Amanda nods, and in the dim light her finger presses my lips. Now that she knows Samson's being looked after—no more talking.

She absorbs every amusing detail, every entertaining sight and stunt the same way she takes in every moment in real life. But such freedom eludes me. The future is bearing down, wielding a deadly bludgeon.

Except—Amanda throws her arms around me while two pirates drag a captured enemy into a transparent cauldron of boiling oil. My anxiety vanishes. Amanda and I are great together. And her touch—whether her innocent wishes require me to vanquish my sick and dangerous ones or not—fills me with admiration, love, and hope. What on earth is more magical than that?

True, my impulses have tortured me. I have had to maintain my guard against abominable longings. But I've succeeded every time. After my initial revulsion at what lurks inside me, I've learned to recognize my worst urges for what they are. Admitting this to myself and continually squelching selfish lust makes me a better man. A good man. I'm such a good man, in fact, that society will lock me up for a long time. Whereas, if I had ignored her all these months? Impossible, but if I had—if I had turned her away, *that* would have been evil.

After the pirate ride, Amanda decides against Splash Mountain. 'Because Space Mountain was the best.' So, we visit the different castles and interact with Snow White and the Seven Dwarves. Also, the wicked stepmother asking a mirror, 'Who's the fairest in the land?'

A young woman dressed like a newspaper boy a hundred years ago is taking photographs of a little girl and her toddler brother. We watch, and I ask Amanda if she wants a picture of us.

'You mean it?'

'The old precautions are no longer necessary.'

The photographer suggests we sit on a bench but Amanda beckons me down on one knee. I wrap an arm around her and she drapes hers around my neck. The girl photographer says, '*C'est magnifique.*' In an hour, we can pick up the photo at the Main Street studio.

We meander through the shops. She buys a Mickey Mouse nightshirt and a beanie with the famous ears. We enter the old-fashioned photo studio. A young man wearing a green eyeshade says, 'Wait till you see this!'

Amanda's stunning and I'm stunned beside her, inside an aluminum frame. The photograph shows how proud we are of each other, and how thrilled we are to be together. I ask if I can buy a duplicate. Of course, but because the photography shop is about to close, the copy won't be ready until tomorrow.

Amanda asks, 'Can we take this one now?'

Yes, the man tells us; it's film photography and the shop keeps the negative.

We eat hamburgers with French fries in a fanciful restaurant, and when we emerge the air is cooler, the light softer. The Disney parade of characters begins just after dusk. Amanda wraps an arm around my waist. I feel the joy spinning inside her, which sends a scythe of happiness swooping through me. What we've attained seems so rare and wonderful that the rules of ordinary life—with its systems, codes, and languages—don't apply. Amanda and I hold hands, our arms swinging when the fireworks begin.

6. WISCONSIN DELLS

Thirty Nine

May 2019

At daybreak, nobody was awake except Amanda, who wanted to feel the sun's light and warmth spread over the golf course after Wisconsin's bitter winter and a long bleak spring. The fairway glistened with dew. She heard Walter saying, 'After you graduate, honey, fly away. Soar up and go wherever the air currents take you.'

It wasn't a dream. Her mind and body were awake and so attuned to him that everything they shared when she was thirteen whirled inside her, bright and perpetually new.

They had shared a pact, which had started as a secret friendship and became a unique love. Wherever Walter was, he must be thinking of her.

Amanda didn't think of Walter very often. This shamed her. But when she did think of him, she wept until she fell asleep, heartbroken and exhausted. Their time together was so beautiful, and meant so much to her, she almost didn't believe it was real.

But you can only be sad for so long and then, maybe for no reason, you get a little happier. So, in the first light of the year's first warm day, she wanted to recall all that splendor, even if it hurt. How she and Walter had departed from the Magic Kingdom in a boat that took them to the Dolphin Hotel. In their suite, he asked her to excuse him—he needed to answer voicemails. He stopped in the doorway and looked at her. Was she all right?

She was; she was great.

He went into his hotel bedroom and closed the door. He stayed there for hours.

Amanda had refused to worry. They were still at Disney World, still together, and she brushed off her trepidation like dandelion fluff. Although, getting through the evening demanded effort. She couldn't concentrate on the big flat-screen television, and so she had downloaded *A Tale of Two Cities*, grateful that the complicated, old-fashioned sentences absorbed her.

When Walter finally tapped on the door to the suite, Amanda said, '*Entrez, s'il vous plaît,*' and—'You don't need to knock.' Still wearing the hipster Mickey Mouse T-shirt, he sat beside her and peered at her reader.

Had she had enough fantasy?

'The perfect amount.'

'We can stay part of tomorrow if you want.'

She shook her head. 'It wouldn't be the same. Today was perfect.'

Of course, Amanda knew—all those voicemails—that their time was almost over. He looked at her, focusing on her eyes. Amanda recognized the shared impulse to play a staring game, but blinked. She held her reader tight to keep from touching his face.

She stood up and gave Walter her solemn vow that every minute they had spent together, *every minute*, would last as long as she lived. Their time together was different from ordinary time. Not one second that they had shared together would ever change or fade.

Walter's smile didn't hide his sadness, but she could see that he was a little bit pleased. Even though he said she shouldn't promise the impossible.

This was not impossible, she had said. 'It's very possible, just not ordinary.'

Walter had stood and he had hugged her—for maybe half a minute, which was probably their longest hug.

They returned to New York the next morning. Amanda remembered being on the plane and laying two fingers against his lips. She said, 'No second thoughts. We're great. And we're prepared.' She had no idea what she meant. But he took her fingers and then her hand. He told her again that he had known exactly what he was doing, taking her to Disney World. He knew the penalty, which was worth it to him. 'Because you're worth it to me, Amanda. Please—don't forget that.'

The jet landed at LaGuardia and then they drove to the town's library. The plan, which Walter had arranged with Sterling the night before, was that Sterling would drive Amanda to Greg's house in New Jersey, where her mother was waiting. From there, Cheryl, Greg, and Amanda would take a car to Newark Airport and fly to Wisconsin.

The hardest thing Amanda had ever done was to get out of that gray Accord and leave Walter. She felt him watching her, so to prove she was okay, she had skipped—almost danced, really— up the library steps without looking back or even raising a hand for a backward wave, like they do in the movies.

Amanda had pushed on the library door just as Sterling, on the other side, was pulling it. But in her mind, Amanda had followed Walter driving the Accord around the corner, to the police station.

*

Greg, it turned out, was nice, which surprised Amanda. He moved into the condominium with them and gave Amanda his iPad, for keeps. After a few months, though, he and Cheryl broke up. Amanda knew better than to ask her mother about it. But while Greg had lived with them, Cheryl treated Amanda matter-of-factly—no snide remarks, no picking fights.

Amanda had used the iPad to correspond with Madison, who agreed to find out everything she could about Walter. Her father, Gil, said nobody could understand why he went straight to the police and insisted that he had kidnapped her. 'Cause nobody who lived in that town wanted to accuse Walter of anything.

The reason Cheryl had been waiting in New Jersey, though, was *in case* Walter went to the police. Because in New York State, Cheryl could have been charged with child endangerment.

Weeks later, Madison learned that Walter had told Gil and his other friends that he had confessed to the kidnapping because he was guilty of it. But only of kidnapping, nothing else.

Like, what else?

Of course, Amanda and Madison could kind of guess, but when Madison asked her father about it, he got mad.

Later, Madison said she heard her parents talking about Walter's hearing. They said the whole community was upset and confused, and that many had testified on Walter's behalf— Amanda's eighth-grade teachers, the middle-school principal, a social worker, a few volunteer firemen, and even Gil himself. Madison's father had said judges usually didn't allow that, but Walter had a good lawyer who got the judge to make an exception. Still, because of Walter's guilty plea, the best he could hope for was a new hearing in five years. That meant Walter had to spend five years in a federal prison! The situation was so awful, Madison's parents stopped talking about it. No one talked about it.

And after a while, Amanda and Madison had stopped communicating. There wasn't anything more to say.

Now, Amanda was, finally, practically grown up, but—Walter was still in prison! Yet somehow, suspended in a separate sphere, he was also right there. She could hear his voice and almost feel his arms around her.

In two weeks, she would graduate from high school. She would be free of Cheryl. Amanda had won a full scholarship to the University of Chicago. So maybe it had been a blessing that Cheryl had refused to allow her out—to do things with friends, to play sports, or to sing in the school choir. Amanda went to high school and studied. Practically in solitude.

If Walter knew Amanda was first in her class and had gotten that scholarship, he'd be proud of her, but not surprised.

That morning, on the lush, green fairway, Walter spun inside her. Amanda turned cartwheels for him in ecstatic circles.

Walter loved her. And he had allowed her to love him with all her heart. An act of mastery so heroic, only an outlaw would risk it.

Acknowledgements

Thank you, Anna Burtt, Clare Christian, and Heather Boisseau for your skills, quick wits, and insights while publishing this book. RedDoor's support exceeds anything in my experience. My deep appreciation to the whole team.

My husband, Philip Maher, had so much faith in me, and this novel, that he refused to let me quit. For most of our lives, he has edited the pages I write, winnow, and then beg him to read. Having lived with my real-life excesses, he knows when I'm going overboard and accepts that I'm drawn to whatever's contrary. My admiration, gratitude, and love grow greater every day.

Thanks and praise to our son and daughter, who did not disparage my efforts while growing up, and apparently, do not begrudge them now. They, like my husband, saw me write fiction for the love of it, even when frustration and rejection reduced me to tears.

I'm grateful to my late father who challenged me to do better, to my mother who reads fiction as a creative act in itself, and to my siblings for shared experiences.

Finally, let me honor every child who grows up fatherless. Here's hoping someone, male or female, empowers you with the paternal care that reinforces self-worth, honesty, and compassion.

Book Club Questions

At the start of the book, Walter confesses to second-degree kidnapping, but the police chief doesn't want to charge him. Nevertheless, Walter insists, and is sentenced to five years in prison. Has justice been served?

Sterling describes the 'apex of girlhood' as the rare, remarkable time in some girls' lives when they 'acquire a stunning allure and confidence before the arduous trek of adolescence.' Do you agree with this concept?

Walter knows that Amanda has been neglected from an early age and senses that Amanda craves physical contact in the way an infant does. Do you think he's right, or is this is a self-serving rationalisation?

Which scene in the book affects you the most? Why?

When Walter confronts Amanda's mother, Cheryl, he tells her that his feelings toward Amanda are dangerous, and notices 'a glimmer of comprehension' in her eyes before she dismisses him. Do you think he is secretly relieved, and if so, is that wrong?

Does the adoption of a puppy change Walter and Amanda's relationship? If so, in what ways?

Walter worries that he might be harming Amanda in ways he can't foresee. Is giving her the attention and love she craves right or wrong?

About one-third of the way into the book, Walter's narrative changes from past tense to present tense. How does that affect the tone and feeling of the story?

When Walter takes Amanda to Disney World, he is confident that Sterling will manage the situation and protect Amanda from the authorities. Why is he so certain?

Walter's career success was based on his aversion to risk. By the end of the book he risks terrible consequences for both Amanda and himself. Why do you think he changed?

What are some of the ways in which you see Amanda changing from a girl to an adolescent through the course of the story?

Find out more about
RedDoor Publishing and
sign up to our newsletter
to hear about our **latest
releases, author events,**
exciting **competitions**
and more at

reddoorpublishing.com

YOU CAN ALSO FOLLOW US:

 @RedDoorBooks

 RedDoorPublishing

 @RedDoorBooks